Shattered Palms

A Lei Crime Novel

Shattered Palms

A Lei Crime Novel

By Toby Neal

Ebook: 978-0-9891489-7-9

Print: 978-0-9891489-8-6

Photo credit: Mike Neal © Nealstudios.net

Cover Design: © JULIE METZ LTD.

Format Design: Mike Neal © Nealstudios.net

Proverbs 27:8

Like a bird that strays from its nest is a man

or woman who strays from home.

Chapter 1

D etective Leilani Texeira wished she'd come to this enchanted place for some reason other than death. She picked her way down the steps of the raised jungle boardwalk, turning her head to look upward at the canopy of interlaced branches of native koa and ohia trees. Droplets of moisture and golden light fell around her on an understory of massed ferns. She'd heard of the native forest sanctuary accessible from atop Haleakala volcano but had never taken the time to visit. Now she wished she could linger and take in the multitextured beauty of the place instead of hurrying on with their grim errand.

"So many shades of green," Lei murmured, ducking under a lichen-covered branch crossing the walkway. Her curly brown hair caught on it anyway, and she gave it an impatient tug. The ranger who'd found the body, a wiry older Japanese man with the weathered skin of someone who'd lived his life outdoors, glanced back over his shoulder.

"This is what we call a cloud forest, not a rainforest, because it's mostly watered by mist. All the plants you've seen since the helicopter landing area are native Hawaiian species. We've worked hard to keep the invasives out of this area."

"Invasives?" A solitude pierced only by unfamiliar, sweet birdsong brought Lei's heart rate down after the lurching helicopter ride to the remote area.

"Introduced plant species. There are thousands, and they are smothering the native plants and taking away feeding from the indigenous birds. The biggest enemies of this forest are pigs, axis deer, and goats, and the reason this area is so pristine is that we've fenced the entire top of Haleakala to keep them out."

"Interesting." Lei glanced back at her partner, Pono, following her, another ranger bringing up the rear.

"I do my part as a hunter." Pono's smile turned up his mouth behind a trademark bristly mustache. "Plenny game up here, and they're all good eating."

"Well, I don't know what all this has to do with the body you found." Lei wove her way around a giant curling fern frond bisecting the path, her athletic body moving easily even with the elevation.

"I didn't touch the body, of course, but I think he looks like some kind of hunter," Ranger Takama said. "He's in camo gear. I'm no expert, but even I could see what killed him was an arrow, so it was probably a hunter up here that shot him by mistake. If it weren't for the smell, we wouldn't have found him at all."

That smell had been steadily increasing, a sweetish reek that clung to the inside of Lei's throat like mucus.

"We leave the boardwalk here." Takama gestured and stepped down off the boardwalk. Lei jumped down beside him into thick underbrush made up of ferns and bushes. "Normally, no one but authorized personnel are allowed off the path."

The smell of decomp almost made Lei's eyes water. She dug a vial of Vicks out of her pocket and rubbed some under her nose, turning to hand it to Pono, who'd joined her beside the boardwalk. Takama also helped himself, and they followed him, feet sinking into the deep, soft leaf mulch on the forest floor.

Crime scene tape already marked the area around the body. A first responding officer jumped to his feet, holding the scene log on a clipboard.

"Good morning, sir." The young man spoke in the nasal voice of someone whose nose is blocked. Lei spotted white cotton sprouting from his nostrils.

"Hey. Nice up here if it weren't for the smell." She took the clipboard, and each of them signed in.

Passing the tape, Lei spotted the hand first, extended toward them from beneath the ferns, palm up. The tissue was swollen and discolored, masked in a filmy gray gauze of mold that seemed to be drawing the body down into the forest floor. Lei could imagine that in just a few weeks, the body would have been all but gone in the biology of the cloud forest.

The victim lay on his stomach, his head turned away and facing into a fern clump, black hair already looking like just another lichen growing on the forest floor. The body was at the expansion phase, distending camouflage-patterned clothing as if inflated. A black fiberglass arrow fletched in plastic protruded from the man's back.

Lei and Pono stayed well back from the body. Lei unpacked the police department's camera from her backpack, and Pono took out his crime kit. The modest quarter-karat engagement ring on her finger caught a stray sunbeam and reminded her of her upcoming wedding, with all of its accompanying stress. She pushed the thought out of her mind with an effort—she had a job to do.

"How close did you get to the victim?" Pono asked Takama.

Ranger Takama pointed to a scuff mark in the leaves. "Here. I didn't need to touch the body to see he was already beyond help."

"Good," Lei said. "Hopefully, we can backtrack a bit to where he's been and identify the arrow's trajectory."

"I can help with that." The second ranger accompanying them finally spoke up. A tall, ponytailed young man with large brown eyes, he'd been introduced by Takama as Mark Jacobsen. "I've been doing tracking for the Park Service for years."

"All right," Lei said. "Pono does his share of hunting, as you heard, but I'm sure we can use your skills."

Pono and Lei got to work, photographing the area surrounding the body, then the body itself, finally moving in closer to check for marks and trace.

Lei thought the man appeared to have dropped where he stood. There was very little disturbance in the leaf mold around the body, and the ferns were unbroken except for a few near his feet. A deeper boot impression marked the ground behind the body. The man had a canvas bag attached to his belt, and the pockets on his pants bulged.

"About ready to remove some of these pocket items," Lei said. "Ranger Takama, do you know when the medical examiner will be arriving?" The Park Service's helicopter had brought them up the volcano, then been dispatched to fetch the ME and equipment for transporting the body.

"They're on their way."

"I'll go with Ranger Jacobsen to see if we can identify the area where the kill shot came from," Pono said. He and Jacobsen bent over to assess the damage to the plants and moved away into the ferns.

Lei was already intent on the items dangling from the victim's belt. She detached a cloth bag with a metal clip first, shooing a slow-moving blowfly away. Rather than opening the pouch here, she slid the whole thing into an evidence bag. It was light, but she could feel shapes inside. She sealed and labeled it, setting it in her capacious backpack.

Squatting on her heels, Lei reached gloved hands carefully into the man's combat-style pouch pockets, gently tugging out the contents and slipping them into separate bags: a serious-looking bowie knife in matte black and a plastic bottle with a squirt tip of something chemical-smelling, labeled in Chinese characters. Another pocket yielded a metal handle wound with almost-invisible net, fine as human hair. In another pocket was a tiny tape recorder. She pressed the Chinese character on what looked like "play," and a recording of a bird sounded, a single piercing *Tweee! Tweee!* It stirred something in her blood just to hear it. Lei wished she knew what kind of bird it was.

This man appeared to be some sort of bird catcher. She continued on, eventually unearthing a cell phone—a cheap burner. She removed a pistol—a matte black Glock .40—from a holster at the man's hip. That he was armed in a setting like this was alarming. She heard vegetation rustling, heralding the approach of more personnel.

"Try not to crush the plants." Takama, who'd been so quiet that she'd forgotten about him, chided Dr. Gregory as the medical examiner crunched into view, two assistants carrying a gurney behind him.

"Hey, Phil." Lei greeted the ME. She'd worked with him on several cases prior to her departure from the FBI. It was good to be back working with both her first partner on the force, Pono, and the portly doctor with his love of bright aloha shirts. Today's shirt was covered with large graphics of the Road to Hana, the bright red of the Guy Buffet stop signs echoed by red patches on Dr. Gregory's pale cheeks.

"Could have done without the helicopter ride up here,"

Dr. Gregory said.

Lei remembered he hated heights.

"And you gotta love a four-day-old body."

"So that's how long he's been dead, you think?" Lei asked, sliding a sticky loop of wire, the last item from the man's pockets, into an evidence bag.

Gregory leaned over the swollen body and sniffed. "That's my guess, pending further analysis."

Lei gestured to the mold-covered hand. "Do you think maybe the maximum decomp environment up here sped things up? I don't remember seeing mold like that on a body before."

"It's true that this is a totally natural biological environment," Gregory said, taking out small round magnifying glasses and hooking them over his ears, then leaning in for a closer look. He gave no sign that the stench bothered him. "That may have contributed to some exceptional mold and mildew growth. But it's not actually that warm up here. Heat is a greater breakdown accelerator than any other factor."

"From the equipment he was carrying, it seems like he might be some kind of bird catcher."

Gregory's thick blond brows snapped together. "Only scientists with special certification are allowed to capture and handle these birds, and they usually work in teams. If he's a poacher, that sucks. Let me see any bird-related evidence. I'm an avian admirer, and I'd hate to hear that anyone was capturing native birds. They're highly endangered."

"Okay, will do." Lei was already thinking of the lumpy contents of the bag she'd taken off the body and dreading what she might find inside.

Gregory's assistants set the gurney up as best they could, with Takama fussing around the ferns and other undergrowth that they couldn't avoid crushing. Lei withdrew from the body, walking back toward the boardwalk to get some fresher air.

She was labeling the last of the evidence bags when Pono appeared. The big Hawaiian startled her by looming up beside her. Light on his feet, he moved through the forest without breaking a twig or disturbing the leaves.

"Pretty sure we found where the arrow was fired from. Want to take a look?"

"Of course." She got up.

"It's a hunting blind," he said over his shoulder.

"Thought that wasn't allowed up here."

"'Course it isn't."

Lei picked her way carefully after Pono through the dense vegetation, bending to keep from breaking the brittle ferns and foliage as much as possible. He led her to the base of a massive old-growth koa tree.

The native tree, with its sickle-shaped leaves, spread in opulent umbrella-like splendor to shade the forest floor. A few strategically placed knobs of wood were nailed on its silvery trunk, and peering down from the center of the tree, his face almost lost in shadows cast by the sun on the leaves, was Jacobsen. "Up here."

Lei turned to Pono. "Did you find any trace up there?"

Pono shook his head. "No. Went over it with a light and magnifier. No hairs, nothing."

"Damn. Is there room for two?" The area where Jacobsen was sitting looked hemmed in by a circle of branches.

"Sure. Once you get up here, there's plenty of room," Jacobsen said.

Lei reached up and grasped the trunk, setting her foot on the first knob. She hauled herself upward using arms she worked hard to keep strong, hair catching in the branches again. It was only a few minutes until she sat beside Jacobsen on a smooth branch that had been bent over and nailed down as a seat.

"So what do you think this spot is used for?" Lei's voice instinctively lowered to match the soughing of a tiny wind in the branches, punctuated by birdsong. The forest was not a place that invited loud voices, and once again Lei wished she'd taken the time to visit earlier.

"This is an observation station. Probably birds. This area is the habitat of some of the rarest birds in the world. One of them, the Maui Parrotbill or *Kiwikiu*, lives in koa trees and feeds on the bark and insects."

Lei squinted at the knobbed, silvery bark of the koa tree as Pono's buzz-cut head rose to join them. Once again her partner surprised her with the smooth, silent way he moved, settling his muscular bulk easily beside her on the branch seat. He pointed, and she sighted down the brown expanse of his arm.

"See? I think this is where the shot came from. Note the downward angle into the body."

From where they sat, Lei could clearly see the body, the arrow still protruding, as Gregory covered the man's hands and the assistants arranged a black bag beside the corpse so they could roll the body into it.

"Seems like a significant distance to get the arrow so deep into the body." Lei squinted, imitating an imaginary bowshot.

"Compound hunting bow, I imagine. More power and accuracy."

"Glad I have you on this case," Lei said. "This is foreign territory for me."

"Oh yeah? I'll have to take you out hunting some weekend." Pono grinned, a flash of teeth. "You and Stevens can get your first blood."

"Thanks. I'll pass. What I can tell is that there's a lot more going on up here than anyone knew about."

"That's true." Jacobsen's warm brown eyes were concerned, his brows drawn together. "The Park Service certainly wasn't aware of these activities, and I don't think the Hawaiian Bird Conservatory, who manages the preserve area, was aware of this hunting blind either. Takama and I work closely with them, and we'd have heard about it."

Lei frowned as she studied the forest floor, dressed in lush understory vegetation. "Do you think the shooter was hunting the bird catcher? Or was he just sitting up here and the vic passed by? Was it accidental, or intentional?"

Pono glanced at her. "When we answer those questions, we'll solve the case."

Chapter 2

Lei hung the loaded backpack of evidence collected at the scene on the back of her old rolling chair at Kahului Police Department, the big urban-ugly central police station. She and Pono, as higher-ranking detectives, had a slightly larger cubicle in the corner. Other than that and some more personnel monitoring and training, her new rank as lieutenant had yielded little change in the job—to her relief.

She sat down, booted up her computer, and generated a case number for the murder. Pono's bass voice boomed as he made his way across the office, "talking story" and greeting the other officers. He'd been a big part of making Lei's transition back to Maui work, smoothing the ruffled feathers of other detectives as Lei returned to take a plum job in the department after having left to become an FBI agent. Pono's laid-back but determined style got results in a workplace riddled with hidden agendas, and he'd asked to be her partner when she returned.

Captain Omura, the engineer of Lei's return to Maui, stood in the doorway of their cubicle. One manicured hand rested on her tightly clad, uniformed hip. "Report."

"Captain Omura, I'd like to process the evidence and photograph it and have a moment to organize the field notes with Pono." Lei had learned to be as clear, concise, and assertive as possible with the Steel Butterfly, a nickname the captain had earned for her shoe habits and management style.

"Half an hour." Omura turned and tap-tapped away down the hall. Pono arrived just as the captain disappeared into her office.

"We have thirty minutes to get ready to meet with Omura on the case. Let's be brief and amazing."

"We can do that."

"You start the case file and begin our report. I'll take the evidence down and catalog it." Lei lifted her backpack, chock-full of evidence bags, and hoisted it onto her shoulder, hurrying down the hall and thinking about next steps. The twenty-four-hour rule of homicide investigation dictated that they gather as much evidence as possible related to the case within that time to get traction on it.

Once she reached the evidence room, she took out a fresh cardboard box and labeled it with a Sharpie: JOHN DOE MURDER WAIKAMOI, MAUI, adding the case number the computer had spit out. She unpacked the items recovered at the scene, spreading them on the workspace counter with her gloved hands in the presence of Clarice Dagdag, the wizened Filipino evidence clerk. Clarice was really fast with her data entry and inventoried each item as Lei photographed it, including a receipt from the Maui Beach Hotel. Lei mentally filed that as the victim's likely lodging and the next place to follow up. The Park Service had identified a rental car that likely had belonged to the victim due to four days of tickets collecting on its windshield; it was already being towed to the impound yard.

They moved quickly until they got to the cloth bag.

Lei very gently upended the bag, and five tiny bird corpses fell out onto the counter. Clarice gasped, stepping back with her hand to her mouth. "Where these poor babies came from? So shame, this!" The usually stoic clerk was shocked into pidgin English.

"Up the mountain. We think the vic was a bird catcher, maybe a poacher." Lei spread the birds out on the counter to photograph them individually, handling the bodies carefully with her gloved hands.

Each bird was hunched in on itself, eyes closed, tiny claws drawn up as if trying to stay warm. Lei wasn't a birder and didn't know much about them, but she was struck by the vivid coloration of two red birds, bright as the scarlet of a chief's feather cape. One had a long, curved red beak and the other, a short black one. There was a tiny green bird with a black beak and a larger bird that was a mottled black-and-white with a crest, and finally, a medium-sized green bird with a hooked bill and a yellow band across the eyes.

Lei felt sick at the waste, wishing again she knew more about the jewel-like creatures. She was sure that by the end of the case she would. She took several photos of each and then put them into individual paper bags. "Can I store these in the freezer?"

"Of course."

Lei and Clarice stashed the birds, labeled with brief descriptions, in the big Sub-Zero used for evidence that would degrade.

"For shame," Clarice muttered again. She returned to her computer and hit Print on the photos of the items, including the birds.

"Can you forward these photos to Dr. Gregory, the ME? He said he wanted to see any bird evidence, and he might want to speculate on what killed them."

"No problem." Clarice constructed an e-mail and hit Send.

Lei met Pono, each of them holding a stack of paperwork, right outside Omura's office within the thirty minutes they'd been allotted. Lei realized she hadn't had time to pee after the hike and the long drive down the hill. The interview with the captain was sure to make her bladder explode.

"I have to go to the bathroom. Take these in. I'll be right there."

Lei hotfooted it down the hall and barely made it into the unisex stall in time. Sitting on those hard plastic chairs in front of Omura had gotten easier after her trial-by-fire work for the FBI and her former boss, exacting and critical Special Agent in Charge Waxman—but not that much easier.

In the privacy of the bathroom stall, Lei shut her eyes, feeling a little dizzy. She probably needed to eat something, and remembered she hadn't eaten yet that day. She gazed at the ring on her finger and wiggled it to see the sparkle, picturing the ruggedly handsome face of her fiancé, Michael Stevens. He was the commanding officer of Haiku Station here on Maui, and three months ago she'd made the agonizing choice to leave the FBI to be with the only man she'd ever loved.

Lei still missed her FBI partner, Ken Yamada, working with her best friend, Marcella Scott, and certain aspects of her brief career in the FBI—but seeing Stevens every day more than made up for that. She also served as a liaison for the FBI on Maui, a role that kept her in close touch with her friends from the federal agency.

At the sink, Lei used a little water to tame wayward curls away from her face. The sunshine outdoors had brought freckles and color to her olive-skinned face. She washed her hands and hurried out, sliding into a chair next to Pono.

Pono had already submitted the case paperwork to Omura, and his face was tiki-god blank as the captain leafed through and reviewed it, red nails tapping each page as she scanned. Omura's dark brown eyes looked up at Lei over tortoiseshell reading glasses perched on her perfect nose. "You're late."

"Hadn't been to the bathroom since we got the call to check out the body," Lei said.

Omura looked back down at the paperwork. "So the likely scenario is that this man was hunting or capturing native endangered birds. Any guesses as to motive for his killing? Or was this an accident?"

Lei looked at Pono, and he led off. "Doesn't seem accidental to me. It was a perfect kill shot with a bow from a location with excellent visibility. The blind the vic was shot from was unknown and, of course, unsanctioned by the Park Service and the Hawaiian Bird Conservatory, the agency that manages the land where the shooting took place."

"Speculation?" The captain sat back in her chair, taking off her glasses. This was Omura's invitation for them to take their best guess about the case, and this time Pono looked at Lei.

"I think someone was hunting pig and deer in the blind. Someone who's a conservationist at heart," Lei said. "Hunting's allowed to keep the invasive species from wrecking the habitat up there. So this person is up there and sees this guy catching the native birds, putting them in a bag, and shoots him on impulse."

Pono rubbed his lip under his bristling mustache, an old habit. "Another scenario is that someone is hunting and sees a movement out of the corner of his eye. The vic was in full camo gear. He shoots him on accident."

"Or the vic was being hunted intentionally by someone who either didn't like him personally or didn't like what he was doing. He's a John Doe. That doesn't make establishing motive as easy," Lei finished. "Those are the three scenarios we've come up with so far."

Omura looked through the papers again. "I see a lead here. A bar receipt from the Maui Beach Hotel. I also notice the evidence items have Chinese writing on them. Have you notified Interpol?"

"Not yet. Not until we get the prints. Gregory should have that covered." Both of them glanced at the clock—it was 4:45 p.m. "Do you want us to go over to the morgue and get the prints tonight?" Pono asked. "With the state of the body's decomp, I don't know if the doc has been able to process them."

Omura shut the folder and slid it back to Lei. "Tomorrow is soon enough for that. Give the ME time to process the body. Nothing looks too hot on this one but the possible citizenship issue if he's not American—but I want you to nail down the Maui Beach Hotel lead, grab anything he may have left in his room before it disappears, and maybe you'll find identification there. You also have a car being pulled into impound to process."

"We'll check in again tomorrow." Lei picked the folder up.

"Keep me apprised." Omura dismissed them with a flick of her red nails.

Chapter 3

L ei and Pono took separate vehicles to the Maui Beach Hotel since they planned to go home afterward, and on her way Lei put in her Bluetooth and called Stevens. They usually had dinner together after work at either her house or his—but there was no point in that tonight, as she'd be home so late.

"Sweets. I was just thinking about you." Stevens's voice, warm with a smile and a promise, still made her stomach tighten and her body hum into awareness.

"Can't see you tonight. Gonna be really late —we caught a body on Haleakala." Lei sketched him in on the details.

"Well, I'm already at your place with something started for dinner. Don't worry about it. I'll keep it hot and see you when you get home. Keiki and I will just be pining away here. "

"You're the best. I can't believe I'm marrying you in just two weeks," Lei said. "Thanks for understanding."

"Next time it'll be me catching a body and you keeping dinner hot."

"I can keep something hot, but it won't be food." Lei laughed as she hung up.

Her next call was to her guardian and surrogate mother, Aunty Rosario, in San Rafael, California.

"Hey, Aunty." Lei navigated the four lanes of traffic between the police station and the nearby utilitarian hotel with ease. "How's everything at the restaurant?"

"Pretty good. Getting so excited about the big day!" Rosario exclaimed.

"That's what I called about. We have arrangements for a house for you and Dad to stay in, and I wanted to double-check on everything."

"It's all a go. So what's your dress like?"

Lei grimaced. She should have seen this question coming. "It's beautiful. But a surprise, Aunty. I can't tell anyone about the design." She mentally crossed her fingers—she still hadn't even ordered the dress.

"As it should be, Sweets." Aunty Rosario and her father had picked up the misnomer of a nickname given to her by her partner on Kaua`i, Jack Jenkins. "I had a call from Tiare Kaihale, your wedding coordinator. She arranged for my restaurant to do all the food at your reception. Your dad and Aunty Momi are already working on some of it."

"That Tiare. So awesome." Lei felt gratitude washing away the intimidation Pono's efficient wife still elicited. "I can't believe she thought of having you do it. I'm so *lolo*, it never crossed my mind. So how are you getting all the food over here?"

"We're coming in two days before the wedding to have time for food prep. Freezing most of the food and air-shipping it to arrive after we get in. Your dad and I'll pick it up and rent the equipment for prep and heating—you're going to have a real Hawaiian luau with Japanese food, too, down at that beach park. Your grandpa Matsumoto, even he'll find something to eat."

"Great!" Lei said. "Need anything else from me?"

"No, I don't think so." There was a long pause.

"Is everything all right?" Lei asked.

Aunty Rosario's breath hitched, and Lei frowned. Something was wrong. Even navigating the traffic and pulling into the nondescript parking lot of the Maui Beach Hotel, Lei could picture her aunt so clearly: her short, plump body probably wrapped in one of her restaurant's plumeria-print aprons, dark brown eyes with well-marked brows, her hair in a thick salt-and-pepper braid with little curls escaping around an olive-skinned face that was still unlined.

"I'm having some tests done."

"Oh, Aunty! What kind of tests?" Lei felt a familiar band of anxiety tighten around her chest. Aunty Rosario was her mother in all but name, and the thought of anything happening to her was terrifying.

"Oh, I'm sure it's nothing, but I have this stomach pain that won't go away. It's been months now, and my antacids don't do a thing…I almost didn't say anything…"

"No, Aunty. Don't ever hide anything from me."

"Well, like I said, I'm sure it's nothing."

"I will pray it is. And I'm sure Dad is praying too."

Aunty laughed. "You bet he is, and being kind of a pest about it too. He put olive oil on my forehead the other day and had his prayer group over to pray. He's really taking his religion seriously, as you know."

"Well, it can't hurt," Lei said. She'd parked the truck, and Pono was striding toward her from his vehicle. "I gotta go. Can't believe how soon I'll be seeing you. Call me the minute you know anything about your tests."

"Love you, honey," Aunty said.

"Love you too." Lei hung up. Aunty wasn't usually so demonstrative. Must be she was worried about her health. And then there was the wedding. It seemed to make everyone emotional.

Lei and Pono went to the front desk of the modest hotel and showed their badges.

"We're investigating a murder. We have reason to believe the victim may have been staying here or had business here," Pono told the round-faced receptionist. The woman had a gigantic hibiscus blossom arrangement in her hair that Lei couldn't stop looking at.

What had Tiare said about her veil for the wedding?

Oh yeah—no veil. Pikake, those tiny fragrant white flowers, woven into a crown-like *haku* lei. She let her breath out in relief. No giant flower explosions would be coming out of the side of her head.

The receptionist was tap-tapping her keyboard. "When would this person have been here?"

Lei and Pono looked at each other. "Not sure. But he would not have returned to his room, if he had one, for the last four days, at least."

"We charge guests' credit cards when they stay beyond their reservations and their belongings are abandoned in their rooms. We do have someone who was due to check out two days ago and appears not to have returned. I have to check with my manager to see if it's okay to release that information to you, or if I need a warrant." She bustled off.

Lei looked at Pono. "Seems like he was here."

"Hopefully. That receipt was just for the bar."

The errand appeared to be taking a while, so Lei looked around the lobby. The Maui Beach was conveniently located for business and had a decent pool, which looked out across Kahului Harbor to the docking area, where one of the Princess Cruises ships sat like a wedding cake at anchor.

"Wedding cake," Lei muttered. "Tiare said it was handled, but I didn't pay attention to what it was."

"What?" Pono pushed his ever-present Oakleys up, gave a squint. "You saying you don't know what kind of cake Tiare ordered for the wedding?"

Lei felt the blush that had been the bane of her existence heat up her cheeks. "Your wife has things totally under control. I'm sure it's going to be awesome."

"She told me you were the opposite of bridezilla—the bride who can't be bothered," Pono said, the dimple he tried to hide with his mustache very much in evidence. "You're the perfect client. She's having a blast doing everything with no interference."

"I'm just not into it. Thank God Stevens understands. I get really nervous with all the choices and start having escape fantasies. Tiare picked up on that and took over, and I'm so glad."

"Long as you don't leave Stevens at the altar. Don't think any of us can handle another breakup between you guys."

"Thanks a lot." Lei punched him in the shoulder, fairly hard, and ended up shaking out her fingers. "Ow. You must have been lifting."

The receptionist returned with the manager, a dapper Japanese man in the regulation floral print of the hotel. "May I see your identifications?" He had brought a pad and noted them down. "What is this regarding again, please?"

Pono recapped.

"All right. I think it's appropriate to cooperate with the Maui Police Department. We were wondering about the whereabouts of this guest ourselves. We keep abandoned items in our storage facility. Follow me."

The manager led Lei and Pono around behind the counter and down a utilitarian hall to a room marked STORAGE. "We keep things for about six months and then donate them to a charity." He unlocked the door and pushed inward, flicking on a light.

Cardboard boxes lined floor-to-ceiling shelves. They were marked with last name, a room number, and a date in Sharpie. Boxes of paper towels and other supplies took up the rest of the space.

"Wow. Lotta stuff in here." Lei frowned. "How often does this happen?"

"Well, most of it is just an item or two left behind. We keep them as a courtesy. Seldom does a guest do what this one did and disappear entirely."

"So why didn't you notify the police?" Lei asked, as the manager zeroed in on a box marked CHANG, pulling it off the shelf. The sight of the name made her brows snap together, even as she reminded herself Chang was as common a Chinese name as Smith was American. Pono pointed to the name and frowned, glancing at her. She shook her head. This random poacher couldn't be related to her enemies, the Chang crime family on the Big Island. Could he? She dismissed the connection.

"There are a lot of reasons people might abandon their room, and if there's no indication of foul play and they've paid their bill, we don't assume that anything bad has happened. As I said, this doesn't happen often. This client had prepaid his stay in cash, according to my receptionist. He showed an ID for this name." The manager indicated the writing on the box.

Lei pulled a pair of rubber gloves out of her back pocket, snapped them on, and squatted beside the box.

She took the top off. "Was there a suitcase?"

"Yes. We didn't open it because it has a combination." The manager indicated a good-sized hard-sided gray plastic case with his toe.

"You know, Pono, I think we should take all of this down to the station," Lei said as she flipped open the wallet that sat on top of the contents of the box. She held the ID up so Pono could see that the photo matched the distorted face of their victim from the cloud forest.

Chapter 4

Clarice looked at the suitcase Pono had wrestled up onto the table. "It's locked," the taciturn clerk said.

"I know. Got a hammer?" Pono grinned.

Clarice eyeballed him over her rhinestone-studded half-glasses with no sign of amusement. "Find some other way."

Lei had already begun unloading the box of incidentals from the abandoned hotel room and listing them on the inventory sheet. A wallet containing a credit card and ID that looked real, in the name of Xu Chang. One small black men's comb with two hairs stuck in it, which she bagged. A black men's bathroom kit containing an electric razor, travel-sized can of shaving cream, toothbrush, and toothpaste. All the products were American and looked brand-new.

"This guy traveled light. Nothing personal here. I'd bet money that this is a fake ID."

Pono had unfolded a paper clip and was fiddling with the

lock, moving it around inside. "Not sure this is going to work. This is a better-made lock than most."

"You could shoot it open," Lei said, deadpan.

"Yeah." Pono's dimple flashed.

The ribbing was lost on Clarice. "No discharging of firearms in the evidence room," the clerk said.

Lei continued unloading the box. A black satin bathrobe with a dragon machine-embroidered on the back, nothing in the pockets. A pair of black shoes, men's size nine—and the box was empty. She looked at Pono.

"You gotta get that suitcase open. The good stuff must be in there."

Pono was still fiddling with the paper clip, and suddenly the lock on one side popped open. He went to work on the other side and had that open by the time Lei and Clarice had entered all the contents of the box into the evidence log.

Lei moved over beside her partner as he popped the case open. Right in the center of the suitcase, surrounded by clothing used as padding, was a black metal box with a small cylinder attached. A long pause followed as all three of them considered its foreboding appearance.

"That looks like it might be a bomb," Pono finally said. Clarice hurried to her house phone to call for the hazardous devices technician even as Lei held up a hand.

"I think this is for transporting the birds. See this canister? It's got a pressure gauge like you use for scuba. I bet he was going to sedate the birds and carry them back in this suitcase."

"I still want the technician to open that," Clarice said, punching buttons on her phone. "It's my evidence locker that will get destroyed if it's a bomb."

Lei and Pono removed the clothing, careful not to touch the matte black metal case that would probably fool most scanners. The gas in the canister, if it were just compressed air as Lei suspected, wouldn't set off any alarms.

Abe Torufu, wearing a coverall and gloves, arrived with his explosives detection kit. "Where's the fire?" Torufu asked. Lei couldn't resist a quick fist bump with the Tongan giant, whom she'd worked with on several cases.

"We don't actually think it's a bomb." Lei indicated the case with its screwed-on canister. "But Clarice wanted you to check it out."

Torufu opened his kit. "Let me see if it's even something I have to get into gear for. If I do, you all need to clear the room."

"I don't want my evidence room blown up." Clarice fiddled with her glasses.

"And I don't want to get blown up either." Torufu carefully inspected the case. "I don't see any external wiring or trigger mechanism. I'll swab for the usual." He swabbed the flip-top latches of the case, all around the edges, and all over the canister. "Nothing." He held up the swatch of cloth. It didn't look any different. "This detects several chemicals present in explosives. I think we're safe to open it, but I'd prefer if you move outside." He was already wearing a fire-retardant coverall and gloves, but now he pulled a respirator out of his kit. "This is in case of any nonexplosive but otherwise dangerous substances, like biologicals or chemicals."

Torufu put the respirator on with its protective faceplate as Lei, Pono, and Clarice stepped outside and watched through the window in the door. Torufu flipped the latches and opened the interior case, inspecting it on all sides.

He took off the respirator, gestured, and they came back in, clustering around. "Looks like he was getting ready to carry some live contraband," Torufu said.

"I thought as much." Lei wasn't surprised, but she felt dismayed to see the six padded chambers in the case, lined with soft cotton batting, and the plastic air hose running from the canister into each of the chambers. "This looks as if it were made for the birds he'd caught. I wonder how he was going to sedate them. They couldn't have lasted long in this case."

"It's a long flight to China, at least twelve hours from here if you can get a nonstop," Pono said. "Maybe that is why he had six chambers. Preparing for some of them to die in transit."

Lei's chest tightened. She was really coming to care about the sweet-songed, nectar-feeding birds of the Hawaii forest.

"Now I'm curious," Torufu said, sitting on one of the folding chairs, his bulk causing an ominous creak. "What's this case you've got? You guys usually work homicide."

"There is a homicide." Lei filled him in. Clarice displayed no such curiosity. She simply continued filling out her inventory by going through each nondescript piece of clothing, listing the mysterious black case as "illegal wildlife transport apparatus."

Lei drove along the two-lane highway beside the wind-tossed ocean, black and silver under the moon, past the beach town of Paia, toward her home near the small village of Haiku. After the evidence storage, she'd called the Hawaiian Bird Conservatory to schedule a meeting with their biologists the next day, and now it was well past the dinner hour. Turning off the highway onto an even narrower road bordered with plumeria trees, tall red ginger, and banks of palms, Lei smiled, thinking of how much mellower her commute was compared with when she'd been living and working in downtown Honolulu.

She pulled her silver Tacoma inside the chain-link gate of her little plantation cottage, parking it next to Stevens's brown Bronco. She rolled the gate shut and locked it, Keiki, her Rottweiler, doing a happy dance beside her. Lei made a stern face with an effort and snapped her fingers, did the hand signal for "sit." The big Rottweiler parked her cropped behind on the ground, tongue lolling.

Lei rubbed the dog's silky triangle ears and squatted to embrace Keiki's sturdy neck now that the Rottie was sitting and still. She rubbed the sensitive spot between

Keiki's gentle brown eyes, and the big dog shut them in bliss. Lei reminded herself that Keiki was a working dog, and if she didn't maintain discipline, the animal would lose the edge of her police training—but still it was hard these days to keep from loosening up when they were both so much more relaxed.

Lei patted her hip, and Keiki fell into step beside her as she ascended a couple of worn wooden steps. The iron security door they'd added, with its layer of screen for mosquitoes, was unlocked, and she stepped into the dimly lit, white-painted space. She could smell delicious cooking scents coming from the old-fashioned kitchen, and her heart lifted in anticipation.

Coming home to find Stevens in her house, in her kitchen, cooking, still felt like a dream she'd wake up from. They spent most evenings together, and the only thing she didn't like was when he left for his apartment.

Lei bent over and untied her athletic shoes, dirty from their sojourn in the jungle. She set them on the low shoe rack beside the door and padded across the lauhala matting that covered creaky wooden floors.

"Honey, I'm home," she mock sang.

"About time," Stevens called from the kitchen. He sounded good, not too tired or grumpy in spite of her lateness. Lately he'd been irritated with things like their separate dwellings and the seemingly endless wedding preparations.

Lei wondered why she'd felt such a need to have her own

place before they got married, and then, as now, couldn't really explain it. As it stood, Stevens had his apartment in Kuau until after they were married. She walked through the living room, unstrapping her shoulder holster and sniffing the air. Keiki was still plastered to her side.

"Whatcha got cooking?" she called as she headed into the bedroom. Here a king-sized bed, shipped over from Oahu, took up nearly the whole room. She hung her holster over the corner of the headboard and sat down, slipping off her socks. "I'm going to hop into the shower. Had a big day crawling around in the jungle on top Haleakala," she called.

"Sounds like a plan. It's ready when you are." His voice echoed a little within the wooden walls.

Lei walked into the bathroom, stripped off her clothes and utilitarian white bra and panties, throwing everything into the hamper. She stepped into the old-fashioned tiled shower, someone's home-improvement project that was too big for the small bathroom, leaving barely any room for the sink and toilet. It had a giant rain-like showerhead and a small plastic bench left over from other tenants. She lathered up a washcloth to clean the scratches on her arms from climbing the tree.

Stevens opened the pebbled-glass door. Tall, muscled, and naked, there was a hungry light in his crystal-blue eyes as they traveled over her lean runner's body under the fall of water.

"Thought I'd join you."

Lei's stomach hollowed at the sight of him. "Come into my parlor, said the spider to the fly."

The emotion between them felt so intense it had to dissolve at some point—and yet it kept surprising her with its power. He stepped in and reached out a hand to wrap around the nape of her neck, drawing her into his arms. The rain-like water poured over both of them, luxuriously sensual. She delighted in the way she fitted into the spot just under his jaw and wondered if she'd ever get tired of it.

"I love your big, sassy mouth. It's so sexy." He tipped her chin up and kissed her lightly, tracing her lips' outline with his, nibbling. Her body began a hum that felt like being plugged into an electric current.

"We should probably stop seeing each other before the wedding." She broke away, teasing.

He shook his head as water caught the dark strands of his hair. "I'm addicted. I'd be a shaky deprived wreck at the wedding. You wouldn't want that, would you?"

His big hands, calloused from his weapon and a thousand outdoor projects and activities, slid up and down her wet back and over her bottom, raising goose bumps of anticipation. "I know this bench is in here from the old people who were here before us, but I'm thinking we can find some other uses for it."

"Oh." Lei's tongue went thick and her body boneless as he turned her in his arms, his hands never stopping their stroking, bringing tingling hunger in their wake until she whimpered with wanting. He gently directed her to kneel with one hand on the back of her neck and bent her over the bench.

The water fell around them in an endless warm celebration.

On the mat outside the shower, Lei rested a hand on the doorframe, holding on to it for support. "I'm not sure I can walk."

"Me neither. Let's crawl. That might be fun."

"Got to save something for the honeymoon," Lei said. Stevens pulled a big fluffy beach towel off the shelf, wrapping it around her.

"I like you too weak to object to any of my ideas."

"I love your ideas." She reached up and pulled him down for a kiss, feeling a little scared of how happy she was. Growing up, being happy meant something bad was just around the corner. She reminded herself a little forcefully that that was then and this was now. Holding back, trying to protect herself, had only stolen from the present, not saved her from any pain. Stevens had proved his love to her over and over. She had to start trusting that love, and hers for him. Making those vows to him at the wedding was the final proof of that.

"I approve of this too-big shower you were complaining about." Crinkles bracketed Stevens's eyes.

Lei laughed. "I think it's a good thing we decided to move into this house instead of your apartment."

"I'll miss the ocean though." Stevens dried his hair with a towel and led the way down the short hall to the bedroom.

"It's been great listening to the ocean."

She admired the long, graceful line of his spine as he walked ahead of her, the muscular rounds of his buttocks. She never got tired of looking at the intricate tiny curls of hair on his chest, the scars of a life spent in law enforcement tattooing a body kept strong by surfing and lifting.

The house had only one bathroom, as many of the older cottages did, but two bedrooms, one of which Lei used as an office. Keiki lifted her big square head off of her ratty blanket at the end of the bed as they came into the bedroom. Lei slid into a pair of black silk pajamas Marcella had given her. She caught Stevens looking as she buttoned the fabric over her breasts.

She cocked a brow at him. "Thought you'd had enough."

His eyes had that intense focus she'd come to know as he stepped toward her. "I never get enough. I can't figure it out."

"Will it always be this way?" Lei's breath caught, a sensual lassitude softening her knees as he reached out to cup the sensitized round of her breast in the silky fabric.

"I'll enjoy finding out," he said. She watched his hand, deft long fingers contrasting with the black silk and the round shape beneath it. The beauty of the sight hypnotized her as he pinched her nipple gently, rolling it between his thumb and forefinger, watching her watching him.

She found it almost unbearably delicious. Her nipple seemed to swell and elongate, distending the shiny fabric. He bent his head and suckled it through the material.

Lei gasped.

"I think dinner's getting cold," Stevens said, smiling.

"Huh?" She looked up at him through hazy eyes, incapable of coherent thought.

"Dinner."

Lei loved the way the color of his eyes brightened as he looked into hers, the white rays in them intensifying. She was the one who did that to him. It made her feel powerful and more alive than ever. Maybe it was how close they'd come to losing it all that made what they had now so incredible. She didn't know, and maybe it didn't matter.

Chapter 5

They ate the now-cold dinner, a delicious Mexican casserole, and snuggled close in front of the evening news on the couch. Stevens insisted they keep up on the news, as it often pertained to their cases. Sure enough, Wendy Watanabe from KHIN 2, pert in a turquoise suit, reported on the body Lei had been investigating.

"Officials are stumped by a body discovered in the pristine and protected wilderness of Waikamoi Preserve on Haleakala. An as-yet-unidentified man of Asian descent has been discovered, the apparent victim of a bow-hunting accident."

"We aren't stumped. We're at the beginning of an investigation and unable to give her any hard answers yet," Lei grumbled, taking another bite of casserole. She'd finished putting on her pajamas and sat cross-legged, the plate on her knees.

"See, but that's why we need to watch the news. See

what they're saying about us."

"I know Wendy's just doing her job, but I just can't warm up to that woman."

"She's a tough reporter, but you know she's got a heart from how she stepped up for the Smiley Bandit." The previous year, Lei and Watanabe had been in a race to uncover the identity of the same bold young thief—and that chase had led to unexpected consequences.

"I still don't have to like her," Lei insisted, remembering how Watanabe had enjoyed humiliating Lei on that investigation. "She loves implying law enforcement is incompetent."

Stevens shrugged. "Whatever gets ratings. So what's the inside scoop on your Haleakala body?"

"Asian John Doe. Some sort of bird hunter or collector. He had several dead native birds in a bag, which he'd caught by attracting them with recorded calls and a net. He was shot from a blind in a tree with a compound hunting bow. Died instantly." Lei took another bite but found it hard to swallow, thinking of the birds. Even dead, they'd been bright and precious as jewels. "Phil Gregory has his work cut out for himself with a four-day old body, but at least the cause of death is pretty straightforward. Pono's pretty sure he knows what species the birds were, but we're having Hawaiian Bird Conservatory biologists identify them and the equipment the vic had on him tomorrow."

"So what are you thinking? A poacher? Think he was shot by accident or on purpose?"

"Either could be true." Lei summarized their three possible scenarios. "I just really wish I'd gone up to the preserve for some reason other than a crime scene. It's an amazing place—Hawaii before people got to it."

He squeezed her shoulder. "Take me up another time. We'll do it together. Pretty soon we'll have all the time in the world for weekend explorations."

"Yeah, when the wedding is behind us. I can't wait." Lei couldn't think of the wedding without a headache starting.

"Me neither. And don't worry, I haven't used up all my ideas yet, I've got a few I'm saving for the honeymoon." He pulled her into his arms, snuggling her against him.

Lei's phone buzzed. She grimaced, but picked up, mouthing "wedding plans" to Stevens as she got up and headed back toward the bedroom. "Tiare! How's it going?"

Pono's always-industrious wife, Tiare, had opened a wedding-planning business in addition to her nursing practice. She'd insisted on coordinating their wedding at no charge, when excited questions about Lei's plans were met with a blank stare Lei employed for meth addicts— and, it turned out, wedding planners.

"Lei, everything's a go. We have the beach park at Kanaha as the venue with the caterer doing the traditional mixed Hawaiian and Japanese menu you asked for. Fire and hula dancers from Pono's cousin Shannie's *halau*. *Haku* head lei for you and maile lei for Stevens. He already bought an aloha-wear outfit: white patterned shirt and black pants, which will look terrific with the green maile leaves of his lei. Photos by a very competent young photographer who's willing to do more for less. Cake is ordered; booze is ordered. Marcella as maid of honor has purchased a dress in your chosen color, red."

Lei interrupted the flow of words. "This sounds great. I don't know what you need me for."

Tiare gave an annoyed sigh. "The dress. Did you get one?"

Lei felt her stomach drop. "I haven't had time."

A long silence, then: "You had one thing to do, Lei. Just one. Get a dress. You have to get one, and I can't do that for you."

"Okay, I'll find the time. I'll pick something up."

Another long silence. Lei rubbed her temples, imagining Tiare's grimace and eye roll.

"I'm sorry, but it's really hard to just 'pick something up.' Dresses have to be ordered," Tiare said. "Fitted. Adjusted. And I guarantee, you won't like what I pick out if I end up having to get it for you."

"Okay. Got it. Wedding dress. Check," Lei said, writing it in her Notes feature on her phone and setting it as an alarm. "I'll get something going this week."

"And how about the honeymoon?"

Lei had an answer for that, thank God. "Stevens is in charge of that, like I told you. He's been on his phone a lot; won't tell me a thing. I'm sure it's in the works."

"Well, ask him. Make sure. Also, I have a large vacation rental booked with room for your dad, your aunty Rosario, your grandfather, and Stevens's mother and brother. But you should call them too, and make sure they are all set with their travel arrangements."

Lei felt sweat beading on her upper lip as she added that item to her list of to-dos.

"And who do you want to have for your hair and makeup?"

"Oh. I can do that myself."

A deafening silence. Lei rubbed the hammered white-gold pendant that Stevens had given her, which she wore on a chain around her neck, and shut her eyes. She knew Tiare meant well and was probably right. "Who do you think I should call?" Lei asked meekly. "Maybe I will need a little help."

"Lei, it's the pictures. I mean, pictures of your wedding are forever. So you want to look your best, and frankly, sometimes your hair…"

"Yeah, I know." Lei pulled a curl and it extended, springing back into the welter of curls drying after the shower. She'd forgot to put in gel. Stevens came to the door, cocking an eyebrow at her, looking tasty in nothing but his boxers. He gestured to the door.

"Going home," he mouthed. She nodded.

"I'm sure I could use someone to help with my hair at least."

"Okay. Well, call these ladies." Tiare rattled off a couple of numbers. "They really need to get a look at you to appreciate the challenge."

"Okay. Thanks." Lei hung up, feeling hopeless and overwhelmed. She padded back into the living room, where Stevens was shrugging into his shirt. She burrowed into his arms, pressing her face against his neck.

"You love me, right?" she asked, her voice muffled.

"God help me, you know I do."

"Well, I'm incompetent as a woman. I forgot to even look for a wedding dress, and it's only two weeks away."

"You're more than enough woman for me." His hands had begun to wander, waking up her barely dormant nerve endings all over again. "I don't care if you wear a burlap sack or show up naked, as long as you don't leave me standing up there by myself."

Lei was in no mood for joking or being distracted.

"I need a dress. And someone to do my hair, and probably makeup too. Also, Tiare wants us to call the family members who are coming, make sure their arrangements are all good. For you, it's your mom and brother." Lei hadn't met either of them yet. "And she wants to know if the honeymoon is under control."

"You don't need to worry about the honeymoon. I've got that in hand. You know, the wedding isn't really for us. It's for the friends and family who need to witness this miracle." He tugged a curl off her forehead, let go. Did it again. She batted at his hand.

"Really? Because it seems like it should be for us."

"Well, if it were, all I'd need to do is stand with you and promise to have and to hold you." He kissed her, a tender stamp on the lips, looking into her tilted brown eyes, smoothing one of her straight brows with a thumb. "In sickness and in health. For richer, for poorer. Until death do us part." He kissed her firmly after each vow, and she kept her eyes on his, wrapped in his arms, her favorite place in the world.

"Then can we just do that and call ourselves married?" she whispered. "Because I will have you and hold you, in sickness and in health, for richer or poorer, until death do us part."

Blue eyes looked into brown for a long time, and then Stevens sighed. "Not gonna cut it. You still need a wedding dress."

Stevens left for his apartment, always a wrench, and one that Lei knew would end after the wedding. It really was going to be a passage for them, and she was appreciating that more and more. She turned off the exterior lights as the Bronco pulled away, then armed the house and checked all her locks by force of habit. Did her bathroom business and climbed into bed, Keiki ensconced at her feet.

She tossed and turned but couldn't sleep, worries about the mythical dress cluttering her mind. Finally, she picked up her phone beside the bed, still attached to the recharge cord, and called her best friend, probably sound asleep right now on Oahu.

Special Agent Marcella Scott picked up, her voice thick. "This better be good."

"I need a dress for the wedding."

"What?" Marcella was coming fully awake. "Please tell me you're kidding." Marcella, effortlessly stylish, daughter of an Italian fashion-plate mother and a couture shoe importer father, was clearly horrified. "It's in two weeks. I've just had my final fittings for my maid of honor dress."

"I know. I just—well, I hate those boutique places. I get overwhelmed. I went in a couple and walked right back out. Then I sort of blocked it out of my mind. But Tiare says I have to get something. She can't do it for me." Lei put her fingers over her eyes, pressed. She wanted to cry. She'd had just a couple of things to do and she hadn't done them.

Stevens and his love, his vows, and his burlap sack or nakedness didn't help a bit.

"Calm down," Marcella said. "Let me get up, get on my computer. I wish you'd told me this a hell of a lot sooner."

"I'm sorry. This is all you have to do as my maid of honor. I promise."

"Okay. Calm down," Marcella said again, and Lei wasn't sure she was telling it to Lei or to herself. "What we need is a custom place, have them whip something up for you. I've heard of someone who does good custom gowns on Maui. Let me make some calls, and I'll get back to you with the next steps."

"But I don't even know what I want!" Lei wailed. "I don't know what will look good on me!"

"I do," Marcella said. "You have an awesome tight body, but you're a little slim in the hips with small boobs. You should wear something simple in a really good fabric most women couldn't pull off. I have some ideas."

And indeed she sounded like she did, and was excited about it too.

"It can't be too sexy. I'd feel weird," Lei said, thinking of how uncomfortable she'd feel being stared at and photographed in something low-cut. On the other hand, something tight and heavy like a Hawaiian-style holoku gown didn't feel right either. "Thank you, Marcella. I mean really, thank you. If you get this figured out for me, I'll buy you that new weapon you've been wanting—that antique Italian pistol you were telling me about."

Marcella laughed. "You can't afford it, and neither can I, which is why it's a collector's item. If I do this, and I will, I'll have bragging rights forever as the woman who helped Leilani Rosario Texeira be the most gorgeous woman in the world on her wedding day."

Lei felt tears build behind her eyelids. "You're a good friend." She sniffed. "Why is everything about this whole thing so emotional?"

"It's a wedding, girlfriend. They're always cryfests, so just roll with it. Where've you been, under a rock all these years?"

"I guess. I've never even been to one."

"Cultural philistine." Marcella's voice was warm with affection. "You had a deprived childhood and have been a workaholic. But it's time to turn all that around. You and Stevens deserve to be happy. You've had enough heartbreak."

"True. Most of it my fault." Lei got up and went to the bathroom, blew her nose. "Don't know what I'd do without you."

"You can pay me back when it's my turn." Marcella had been seriously dating an HPD detective for close to a year, and Lei wouldn't be surprised if her friend turned up with a ring on her finger.

"Of course, but you'll never do something like forget to order your wedding dress. And shoes! Oh my God!" Lei smacked her own forehead.

"Hey, it's at the beach, right? You can go barefoot. Just bring something for afterward."

"Oh good. Wasn't sure of the protocol on that." Lei got back in bed. "At least Stevens will be with me all the time after the wedding. It's so hard saying goodbye to him. Every time it's hard, these days."

"Why aren't you guys living together? Remind me again." Marcella had been in on their bumpy romance from the beginning.

"I just got to like my space when I was in Honolulu. I thought it would give us something to look forward to, keep things—I don't know—before and after. And besides, Keiki needs a yard, and his place didn't have one." The big Rottie raised her head off the end of the bed at the sound of her name, eyes questioning. Lei patted the bed beside her and Keiki crawled up. She stroked the dog's big broad head.

"So I'll call you tomorrow with where and when you should go for the fitting. Don't worry about a thing."

"Okay, I won't." Marcella would handle it, and was so much more qualified to do so. Lei decided to obey her and put it out of her mind. "So, on another topic, I caught an interesting case today." She filled Marcella in on the John Doe in the national park jungle. "We think he was poaching."

"Holy crap. That's low, poaching endangered birds!"

"Yeah, and who knows. I might need to do an official consult with you because I suspect he's a Chinese national. He had some weird equipment on him, none of it American made."

"That isn't really indicative of anything. Most stuff is made in China these days."

"Well, still. I just have a feeling."

"More will be revealed on your murder, but wait for my call about meeting with the dress designer. I'm making a list as we speak, and hopefully one of them can take you on short notice."

"I'm counting on it—and for you to know what the dress should look like."

"Not a problem. I have just the thing in mind. You called the right Italian FBI agent, baby. I'm on a mission now."

Chapter 6

Lei and Pono stood outside the doors to the morgue. Maui Memorial's morgue wasn't as bad as some, but Lei always needed a moment to gather her fortitude for the smells and sights that lay before them—not so much because they were disgusting (though that was part of it), but because of the association they would always have with one of the most traumatic moments Lei had experienced in her adult life—identifying the body of a close friend.

Pono had been with her.

He reached over and squeezed her arm just above the elbow. "Gregory keeps it pretty clean in there," he said. She nodded and followed him as he hit the pneumatic door with its lever bar. Leslie Tanaka, Dr. Gregory's assistant, was working on a body across the room and hardly looked up, muttering something into a voice recorder. The ME was wearing an aloha shirt done in lurid rainbows. His rubber apron had a smiley face on it, and while Lei could objectively appreciate the attempt to lighten the atmosphere, the blood spatter on the design made her grimace.

"Hey there, detectives," Dr. Gregory said, hosing down a slab with a flexible steel hose attached to a metal arm above the table. "Here about your Haleakala John Doe?"

"Yeah. Wondering if you have anything for us. Feeling no great need to see the body," Pono said.

"Probably wise, as four-day-old decomp doesn't really improve with time. But I do have something for you. Follow me."

He led them to his office corner and punched up a list, ran his finger down the screen and hit another button, opening a file on their most recent murder case, labeled JOHN DOE ASIAN WAIKAMOI.

Lei pointed to the screen. "We found an ID at his hotel. Xu Chang."

"Good." Gregory retitled the case, and Lei checked her phone, dictating the case number to him.

"So I ran his prints," Gregory said. "Not in the system. Given the Chinese writing on some of the implements he was carrying, I sent the prints over to Interpol. I haven't heard anything back yet." He toggled through various gory photos of the body and the autopsy process. "Cause of death was a single arrow. Extraordinarily well aimed. Arrows are often badly placed, and people can take a while to die by this method—but this one hit the vic in the heart from behind and dropped the man like a rock."

"Anything else interesting about the body?"

"Well, the vic appears to be around age forty-five, and dental was consistent with foreign dentistry—in other words, his teeth were in bad shape and they were pulled when they rotted, which tells me he grew up somewhere poor and possibly undeveloped. Could be China; could be somewhere else. I also have an interest in the native birds on Maui and the conservation movement. Thanks for sending me copies of the bird photos. A real shame." Gregory toggled to the series of photos of the birds Lei had forwarded him.

"This isn't the same as a full necropsy, mind you. Just an idea to see how they might have died. What's sad is that these birds died of dehydration in the bag, from what I can tell by looking at the photos. Their eye sockets are sunken, as if the liquid in their tissues was lost."

Lei looked at the photos of the birds, feeling a pang of sorrow at the sight of their bent heads and tiny, curled claws. "This one was the Maui Parrotbill, or *Kiwikiu.*" He tapped his computer screen, pointing to the green one with the hooked bill and the band of yellow. "Critically endangered; only five hundred of them in existence."

Gregory's pink lips worked, and he took his magnifiers off and wiped them vigorously on a towel hanging off a hook on the corner of his desk. "The one with the crest, the *Akohekohe*, is also very rare. In any case, it's a real shame whoever shot this man didn't go check what was in the bag."

"That's so sad." Lei's words felt inadequate to express

the magnitude of loss.

"A man also died, but I have to say, I'm more upset about the birds, because at this point humans are definitely not endangered."

"So do you have any information on the arrow?" Pono asked. "And can we have it?"

"Sure. I extracted it and cleaned it for you. No other interesting trace on the body."

"Were you able to identify the birds? We have a meeting scheduled with the Hawaiian Bird Conservatory people who manage the Waikamoi Preserve, but this would give us a little advance notice," Lei said.

Gregory rattled off the names of the birds in Hawaiian and Latin. Lei took notes but knew she wouldn't remember the names without repetition—and it was unknown whether the type of bird they were had played a part in the crime. Still, the fact that the man was up there, on private conservation land, hunting them meant that, dead or alive, the birds were important.

"Thanks, Phil." Lei jotted the names as best she could in her notebook.

"Happy to help. And happy to do anything I can to catch someone preying on our wildlife. So little of it, and so precious."

"Well, I'll take you hunting next time," Pono said. "Can you handle a compound bow? We hunt for pig, axis deer, and goat. All of them good eating, and all of them ruining the native forest."

"I'm not much of a shot, but I'd love to try," Gregory said. "Let me make copies of some of this stuff for you." With his usual attention to detail, the ME gave them individual photos of the bird bodies Lei had sent over with their names noted at the bottom, the man's fingerprints, and the autopsy report. "Don't forget to check with Interpol tomorrow on this."

Back at the station, Lei sat at her desk and booted up her computer. She logged the arrow and autopsy report into the case and did some work on their other cases. One was a domestic violence murder and another a meth-production-related murder, both more common Maui crimes than the new bow hunter case. Before she knew it, the front desk clerk paged them that the biologists from the Hawaiian Bird Conservatory were in the conference room. Lei scooped up the case folder. "Do you have the video recorder?"

"Got it." Pono waggled the small camera they used to video interviews. They found the two scientists in the conference room with its smoked-glass windows and whiteboards all around the walls. Both stood as Lei and Pono entered.

"Dr. Jud Snelling," a tall, thin man said, shaking Lei's hand. "I'm head of Hawaiian Bird Conservatory here on Maui."

"Dr. Cam Rinker." The other biologist, sandy-blond, also

shook hands. "I'm head of the land management project at Waikamoi."

Lei and her partner introduced themselves, and they all sat. "Mind if we tape this? Helps us if we need to go back for clarification about anything," Pono said.

"No problem." Snelling seemed to be in charge, by his posture and eye contact. "We were shocked to hear a man had been accidentally shot in the preserve."

"We don't know how accidental it was," Lei said. "We think he might have been a poacher, catching native birds. He had a number of dead birds on his body, and we'd like your help verifying their species."

She opened the folder, spread the photos that Gregory had identified out in front of the biologists. "Can you confirm that these are the species of birds that our medical examiner identified?"

Snelling and Rinker leaned forward, and Snelling jerked back, picking up the photo of the green bird with the yellow banding. "Oh my God. This is a Maui Parrotbill!"

"All of these are rare, but these two are the most critically endangered." Rinker tapped the mottled black-and-white bird with the crest and the hook-billed one Snelling still held.

"Can you confirm Latin and Hawaiian names of the birds noted on the bottom of these photos?" Lei asked. The biologist took the Sharpie she handed him. In a moment Rinker looked up. "These are identified correctly."

"What can you tell us about what this man might have

been doing and how he was doing it?" Lei took out the photos of the equipment the man had been carrying. The conservationists took their time, and finally, Snelling tapped the photo of the net wrapped around a stick and the recorder.

"This is probably how he caught the birds. The Parrotbill, in particular, is very territorial—part of why it's so endangered. Only one pair can live in any given area, and our most common way to trap the birds for banding is to play the song of another Parrotbill. If there's one in the area, it will be curious and come to investigate. Then we can catch it in these nets we string. They're called mist nets because they're almost invisible."

"What about these other things?" Lei tapped the sticky wire, the needle-nosed bottle.

"These are other ways to capture birds. Except for the Parrotbill, the birds you have displayed here are nectar feeders and do what we call trapline feeding, where they work their way over the outside of an ohia tree—you know, the one with the fluffy red flowers called lehua," Snelling said. Lei thought of the red flowers, each a round burst of fine filaments. She nodded, and Snelling went on. "If a birder observes their nectar-gathering pathway, he can be pretty sure the bird will be coming back by within a few hours and working the same trapline after the flowers have regenerated their nectar. So he could string a sticky wire or put the glue on branches where the bird is likely to land and catch them that way."

"Dr. Gregory said the birds were alive in the bag but eventually died of dehydration after the hunter was shot." Snelling and Rinker both winced at this, and she felt echoes of that pain within herself. "What could be a reason to capture live birds of these types?"

"Perhaps—and it's a best-case scenario, —for a private citizen to captive breed them. Or they could just be part of a collection, alive or dead. The ranger said there were some indications that the man responsible might not be a US citizen?"

Lei pinched her lips together. Takama and Jacobsen shouldn't have been talking. "All we know for sure is that he had a Chinese passport."

"Well, something you should know is how very passionate birders can be. Many birders come from all over the world, wanting to just spot a Parrotbill in order to check it off their list of rare avians. It's not too far of a stretch to imagine that some people might collect rare birds."

"So this isn't something you've come across before?"

"Well, the habitat and dietary needs of these birds are part of what makes them so rare. It makes breeding them in captivity, one of the ways one protects species, a tall order. The nectar feeders have to have these few types of flowers they will feed on, and the Parrotbill, while an insect and bark feeder, has a preference for the koa tree, and as I mentioned earlier, it's territorial with other birds. So keeping the birds alive would take considerable commitment. That makes stuffing them for a collection more likely."

"It should be a crime," Rinker said.

"You mean it's not?" Pono's eyebrows rose.

"Well, there are fines. But jail time? I'd be really surprised to see anything like that." Snelling shook his head. "But you folks are law enforcement, so maybe you can tell me more about that."

"Actually, we were hoping you could tell us more about the blind in the tree the man was shot from," Lei said, turning the question back to him. "Were you aware of it? Are there any more blinds in the preserve area?"

Snelling cleared his throat. "Actually, yes. There are. We have noticed several of these hunting blinds throughout the conservation area. We've questioned our staff and volunteers; they all deny knowing who made them. What's noteworthy is how cleverly they're disguised to blend into the forest, how subtly the handholds and supports are done with found materials. We've also discovered evidence that someone may be living in the conservation area, but until now it didn't seem urgent."

Lei perked up at this. "What evidence?"

"Well. Whoever it is knows how to live rough. Just small signs, some singed plants showing a heat source was used, crushed bedding areas, a hand-dug latrine. Whoever it is just uses a bedroll, probably a camouflage tarp for rain, and a small gas cooker. Which means, at some point he or she has to go down the hill and resupply. There's virtually nothing up there to eat but a few berries and fern tips."

Lei and Pono both made notes. "Can we track him?"

Pono asked.

"I don't know," Snelling said, frowning. "We've been thinking this person might be some sort of birder, as the blinds are for bird-watching rather than hunting. Maybe it doesn't have anything to do with the case."

"That's for us to determine," Lei said, with a smile to take the sting out of the words. "Let's see if we can find this mysterious camper."

"Well, we'd appreciate your help getting that person down out of the area in any case," Snelling conceded.

"Sounds like a win-win. Let's get this guy." Pono's eyes were wide and nostrils flared, his muscles bunched with excitement.

"One of our staff can guide you, or you can contact the rangers," Snelling said.

"I think the Park Service is more appropriate for potential confrontation," Lei said, standing and offering her hand to dismiss the biologists. "We'll call you as soon as we know something or if we need more information."

Pono had turned away, already working his phone to make the arrangements.

"We're going up the mountain to hunt the camper tomorrow morning, four a.m., with Takama and Jacobsen." Pono's eyes gleamed, and he rubbed his hands together in anticipation as they reentered their cubicle. "I think once we get this guy, we'll have some answers."

"I'd like it better if you phrased it like, 'looking for the person of interest in this case.'" They grinned at each other and Lei went on. "I think the bird hunter's murder was a crime of opportunity. Someone was sitting in that blind when he or she saw the poacher and shot him, probably pissed anyone was stealing those birds. The camper might have nothing at all to do with this murder. We don't have any trace tying the camper to the body, or even to the blind."

"That illegal camper up in the forest made the blind and did the poacher," Pono retorted. "We just have to prove it." He took a sip of the coffee, scowled, and rubbed his mustache. "These bird people. You don't know them like I do from hunting. They're crazy for those birds; will do anything to protect them."

"Maybe so, and I'm beginning to understand the birding craze a little more." Lei had been doing some searches on bird watching and other avian interest activities. "People seem to really get into it. There are these lists of birds, regionally and around the world, and birders try to spot them and check them off. It's like hunting, but without the killing. I just don't know that catching the camper up there is going to do anything for our case one way or the other."

"I think it will."

Lei shrugged. "Okay. Any excuse to go back up there to the cloud forest is fine with me. It's a beautiful place and outside the office."

They walked down to the impound lot and began processing the vehicle that had been towed down, starting with Pono jimmying the door.

Lei was just snapping on her flashlight to look around inside when her holstered phone rang. She checked the little window on the phone and answered for Marcella, turning to walk a few steps away from the vehicle.

"I hope you have good news about the dress."

"I do! You got lucky, and one of the designers I called had a reschedule and can take on the project. I have a measurement and discussion session scheduled for four thirty today."

"Oh, thank God. Did she have a lot of questions? Because I told you I don't really have any idea what I want or what will look good…" Lei's eyes wandered over the corrugated green folds of Iao Valley directly in front of her, registering the beauty without seeing it.

"Yes. I told her you are the clueless bride type, and we've already had a lengthy Skype session. I forwarded her some pictures of you so she could see your coloring and body type. The dress is mostly designed, and all the fabric choices are picked out. She just needs to measure you and get a load of what she's dealing with."

"Funny. That was exactly the phrase Tiare used when talking about getting my hair done. Is it very expensive?" Lei asked. setting the box on the well-lit steel counter outside the evidence room. They needed to inventory the contents before going any further.

"Not too bad because it's a simple design without much embellishment, but we chose a really good fabric, so that's a little pricey. No worries, though. This is from Marcus and me and my parents as a gift."

"Oh my God, really? That's too much." Lei and Stevens had some savings, but the wedding and whatever mysterious honeymoon Stevens had planned was sure to wipe them out.

"No arguing. It's done. Just cooperate, okay? And try to enjoy yourself. So what's happening with your case?"

"We found the victim's belongings abandoned at the Maui Beach Hotel. Checking his car left on top of the mountain now. I should go."

"Well, call me when you meet with the designer, I want to hear about everything. And keep me posted on this case. We're noticing some funny activity around the Chinese consulate."

"Like what?"

"Can't say right now, and it may be nothing or completely unrelated. What's the guy's name?"

"Chang. Small world, right?"

A long pause as Lei listened to the silence of the FBI agent's mind working.

"I don't think he could be one of your Changs," Marcella finally said. "It's a common name."

"That's what I've been telling myself." Lei punched Off.

Pono looked back at her over his shoulder. "I thought of that when I saw the guy's name."

"The Changs are over now that Healani died," Lei said.

"That's not what the 'coconut wireless' is saying from

the Big Island," Pono said. "Seems the grandson Terence Chang has stepped up now that Grandma's gone."

"Too bad." Lei leaned into the backseat, shining her light around and suppressing an inward shudder at the memory of the young man's narrowed eyes shooting hate at her on her last FBI bust. "Looks clean back here."

"Yeah, I'm not finding anything up here either." Pono withdrew. "Not sure what we're looking for, anyway."

"Maybe just some more idea of who this man was, what he was doing up there." Lei straightened up and slammed the door. "Let's have them move this vehicle into the garage area in case we need to do a trace search on it. Right now I don't think it has anything to tell us about who shot its driver with a bow." They headed back to the guard's kiosk, and after putting in the order to have the car moved, headed back toward the main building.

"Good news. I have a dress fitting today. Marcella set it up," Lei said.

Pono looked over at her. "Good girl. I'll report to Tiare that you aren't going to show up naked after all."

Lei smiled, but it felt more like a grimace. She still

wished it was just her and Stevens going to the courthouse.

Chapter 7

After a full afternoon processing evidence, Lei arrived at a modest storefront location in old town Wailuku marked *Ohana Wedding Design* in curlicue script on the mirrored front door. She pressed down on the brass handle and stepped hesitantly inside as a door alarm chimed.

The showroom lighting was dim. Spotlights were aimed at fully dressed bridal mannequins standing on silvery gray carpet in various poses. A scent of vanilla pervaded the room, and Lei sniffed appreciatively, glancing around. A satin curtain parted, and a woman stepped through it. She was petite and blonde, and she clapped her hands at the sight of Lei, lively brown eyes alight.

"You're even prettier than your friend told me you would be! Like my vanilla aromatherapy? Supposed to help brides feel calmer. I'm Estelle. Come on back to my workroom."

Encouraged by Estelle's friendly greeting, Lei followed the designer through a connecting door into a bright workshop on the other side. Sewing machines, drafting tables, and bolts of fabric in stacks lined the walls. Estelle walked around Lei, looking her over.

"Your friend Marcella faxed over a design sketch, and I can see she was right with what she's suggesting. You have a wonderful athletic figure, and this dress will really set it off."

"Thank you," Lei said. "Can I see the sketch?"

"Not yet. I have to measure you first," Estelle said. "We may need to make some modifications. Step behind that curtain and remove your clothing down to underwear."

Lei obeyed and came out to stand on a carpet-covered dais at Estelle's direction, wearing nothing but her plain white bra and panties. The woman used a flexible measuring tape to measure Lei's neck, arms, bust, waist, hips, and upper thighs, muttering all the while.

"I feel like one of your mannequins," Lei said, lifting her arms as the designer measured around Lei's flat abdomen.

"Almost done," Estelle said, tightening the tape around Lei's hipbones. The woman straightened and wound the tape up. "Okay. Come over here and check out the sketches your friend sent. I'm going to modify them a little for your proportions, but I think this will be a great design for your body, and since you're Japanese, Hawaiian, and Portuguese, according to Marcella, a nod to your heritage as well."

Lei followed Estelle to the drafting table, and Estelle fanned the simple drawings out. Lei gazed at the sketches, and her hand came up to cover her mouth. Her eyes filled.

"I can't wait to see it," she whispered.

"The silhouette is like a calla lily, and with your figure, that's just what you'll look like. So you like it?"

"Oh yes."

"Requires you to have your hair up. I have someone excellent if you need someone to do your hair for the big day."

"I think my planner has someone for me to call. I love it. Marcella knows me so well."

"I've got my team starting on this today. We'll just need you to come back for a final fitting the day before the wedding."

"Sounds like a plan."

Lei left for home, feeling the gratitude she'd begun to experience so often in the last few years. Life was rich now that she'd been letting friends and family get close to her—so much that sometimes she felt overwhelmed. She even wished, thinking of the details of the dress that hinted at her Japanese ancestry, that her mother had been alive to see this day.

If she'd lived, surely Maylene Matsumoto Texeira would have been clean and sober, and surely they would have healed the wounds of abuse and neglect by now. Lei knew it was progress that she could think of her mother with a different kind of grief—a bittersweet sense of what they might have shared if Maylene had lived, instead of angry, conflicted sorrow.

Once home, Lei called the numbers Tiare had given her and lined up the hairdresser and a makeup person. After that, she reported in to Tiare and enjoyed the other woman's rare praise.

"I know you think this is a lot of silly fuss, but someday you'll be turning the pages of your wedding album with your child and you want to look your best for memories that will be with your family forever," Tiare said. "I can't wait to see you in that dress on your big day. It sounds amazing."

"The design is beautiful," Lei said. She still wasn't comfortable imagining a family with Stevens; the thought of a child looking at her album made her nervous. She got up to fill Keiki's food bowl. "I'm supposed to have my hair up because of the dress, so I'm glad I'll have someone to do it for me."

They revisited a few more details. Lei hung up and discovered that, for the first time, she was looking forward to the wedding. Knowing she'd be wearing the perfect dress had a lot to do with that.

She spent the evening alone, reviewing her notes. She'd called Stevens to tell him she had a very early manhunt on top of Haleakala to get to in the morning, and they both knew if Stevens came over, sleep would be the last thing on their minds.

Chapter 8

Lei was a little carsick from the long drive up to the top of Haleakala in Pono's raised purple truck. It was almost enough to make her wish for the stomach-dropping ride to the summit in the helicopter, which at least had been over in a mere twenty minutes. She kept her eyes off the swaying pair of fuzzy dice and mock Hawaiian war helmet dangling from the mirror and on the view passing by as they climbed higher and higher.

Broad, grassy meadows, dim velvet blue in the predawn light, rolled away down the volcano's slope into the expanse of ocean. The biggest town on Maui, Kahului, nestled in the waist of the island below, its lights sparkling like a belt of stars in the purple shadow of morning.

Dawn broke and cast a net of hot pink, lacy clouds over the vast bowl of sky as they pulled past the national park entry booth and turned left, following Takama's pickup truck, to park in a small pullout lot at the head of a trail. Head-high yellow *mamane* bushes bloomed all around them, and Lei spotted a few of the bright native birds, out feeding on the flowers. She shut her eyes against the memory of the tiny, jewel-bright bodies in the evidence freezer.

"No wonder you wanted to leave so early," Lei said, hopping down to the ground and slamming the door of the truck. "The helicopter was faster."

"I asked to get flown up here. Captain said too expensive," Pono replied. "Hope you wore your hiking boots."

Lei looked down at her feet, clad in running shoes. "All I got. It'll have to do."

Takama and Jacobsen met them at a padlocked gate leading into the preserve, and Jacobsen handed them a plastic scrub brush. "Brush off your shoes. You might be carrying seeds into the preserve."

Pono snorted but complied, bending over to scrub at the rugged soles of hiking boots as Takama went on. "We pack in and out anything we bring. No seeds or fruit pits, nothing that could grow in this environment."

Takama unlocked the gate, and once all their soles had been scrubbed, they climbed over a barrier into the conservation area. Conifers of various types towered around them. The air was chill, and rosy gray morning light misted through the leaves. Lei could hear the birds singing in the distance, high, sweet notes like drifting petals.

"These don't look indigenous," Lei said, gesturing to

the trees as they started down a rugged red-dirt road into a dense, diverse forest.

"No, they're not. These are an experimental grove of trees planted by Ralph Hosmer, a territorial forester, around the turn of the century. He was trying to find types of trees that could be harvested for lumber in Hawaii," Takama said. The two rangers strode rapidly, and Lei jogged a bit to keep up, turning her head to take everything in.

"Seems like he found some lumber that liked it here." Lei pointed to a towering tree she kept noticing, shedding bark in colored ribbons.

"Eucalyptus. They grow well here and were used to create erosion breaks all over Haleakala. But they also have spread out of control and they have highly acidic footing that keeps other vegetation from growing. Also, the lumber is too splintery to use."

"What a waste."

"A lot of our early attempts to figure out land use and crops in Hawaii were."

They walked on. Lei's running shoes raised little puffs of fine red dirt. The trees rustled and squeaked in a cool morning wind high above them. Far off, she could hear the native birds. Her heart rate settled and her mind stilled as she breathed the pine-scented air.

"Tell us more about what you know about the camper," Pono said.

"I didn't know about him," Takama said.

"Some of us who patrol through the forest began spotting things that looked like more than just a hunter passing through. Evidence of fire covered up. A forest latrine. Things like that," Jacobsen said. "I mentioned it to the Hawaii Bird Conservatory people."

"Why didn't you tell us this before?" Lei asked.

"I'm sorry. I was so distracted I didn't think of it."

"Do you think a hunter built the blinds?"

Takama shrugged. "The one we found already seems more like a bird observation post than a hunting blind."

"Yes," Jacobsen agreed. "I've found a couple of others. They are usually located in good bird observation areas rather than the areas ungulates typically go once they get inside the fence."

Lei glanced at Jacobsen. "Ungulates?"

"Hoofed invasive animals. Goat, pig, axis deer. Easier to say than have to list the types every time." Jacobsen held a branch aside for her. "They typically forage along paths because it's easier access for them. They also have stream areas where they like to drink. These places would make more sense for a hunter to build a blind." He paused, then blew out a breath. "I have a theory. This camper is someone who has worked with one of the conservation agencies and come back to the forest for his or her own reasons. Seems to have a degree of forest survival skills and to know where to observe birds, not something a total stranger to the forest would know."

"That's a good lead," Lei said. "I'll contact the agencies for a list of people who've worked with them when we get back."

They'd continued descending gently toward the cloud forest area and now were leaving the varied pines of Hosmer's forestry experiment behind. "Not long until we get to the helicopter landing area," Jacobsen said. "I thought we could start at the crime scene and backtrack to some of the sites we think the hunter has visited. See if we can pick up any evidence of him."

"I like your theory as much as Lei does," Pono said to Jacobsen. "If we can get a fingerprint, something from the camper, we might be able to identify this guy."

"I don't know," Lei said, pulling Pono aside to whisper so the rangers wouldn't hear. "Just because we identify the camper doesn't mean he killed the bird hunter. And have you thought that the bird hunter might be the camper?"

They each considered this quietly while they walked on. "No," Pono finally whispered back. "The guy was staying at the Maui Beach Hotel, short term, paying cash. He wasn't camping out here longer than it took to catch the birds he was after."

They exited the trees and walked into the wide-open clearing above the path leading into the cloud forest.

"Anyone feel nature calling? We do all human elimination in this area before we go into the sanctuary area," Takama said.

Pono headed into the underbrush along with Jacobsen, leaving Lei with Takama. She eyed the leathery, fit ranger. "You seem to love your job."

"It's important work. It suits me."

"I like it out here, in the forest," Lei said. "I didn't expect to like it so much. I haven't spent much time out in the wild."

"The forest really hits some people," Takama said. "And when it does, you want to protect it."

Lei tipped her head back, looking at the trees and sky, listening to the wind and the birds. "I guess so."

Pono and Jacobsen reappeared. "Lead on," Pono said.

They turned down the path into the cloud forest, winding along a switchback trail through graceful ferns. Birdsong rose around Lei like auditory fragrance as they made their way through lush, flowering ohia trees. Takama led them back to the first blind, from which the poacher had been shot, and Lei gazed over to where the body had been found.

The ferns had recovered, the leaf mold settled. The spot looked as wild and untouched as the rest of their surroundings. Jacobsen checked a compass reading.

"I have headings for the blinds we've found. Follow me, and try not to break or trample the understory."

He led them through waist-high ferns, delicate *olapa* plants, and *akala* berry bushes heavy with large native raspberries. Lei followed Pono, letting the big Hawaiian forge a careful way behind the ranger for both of them. Progress was slow, and they didn't talk in case they alerted the camper to their presence.

The next blind was in an old-growth ohia tree, split by lightning and bowed into two separate arches that had continued growing, branches coming up from the downed halves in a mini-grove effect. Without speaking, Takama pointed out the handholds leading to a perch in the middle of one of the arches.

"You go. You're smaller. Look for trace," Pono whispered. Lei nodded, pulling on rubber gloves and beginning her climb. She was glad she wore relatively flexible shoes as she shimmied up into the tree, easily locating the blind's sweet spot about fifteen feet up off the forest floor.

It was ideal for bird watching, with the crown of a nearby ohia flowering within twenty-five feet. Even as she settled onto the bench made of a nailed branch, she spotted one of the bright red, curved-billed birds on the nearby tree. "I'iwi," she murmured, having taken some time to memorize the birds' Hawaiian names.

The showy scarlet nectar feeder hopped from one bright red blossom to the next. Its coloration made sense in its habitat, as it virtually disappeared among identically colored flowers.

"See anything?" Pono hissed from below. Lei was startled into activity, taking out her high-wattage penlight and shining it over the bench, the bark of the tree, and the branches that surrounded her.

She descended, shook her head. Jacobsen took a reading and struck off in another direction. This time he led them to a small clearing. He gestured to the ground, artificially swept clean. "I think he was here."

Lei and Pono both went to work, scanning the earth. Lei spotted something white under a fern. She dug gently with her hands and uncovered a white cardboard Starbucks cup, holding it up triumphantly.

"Prints," she mouthed to Takama and Jacobsen, bagging the discarded cup. She dug some more and unearthed more discarded trash, packaging up each of the items.

"What's your most recent camp site?" Pono whispered to Jacobsen. "Now that we have something with trace on it, let's go right there and maybe we can pick up his trail."

Jacobsen nodded, brown eyes gleaming, and set off, his compass out in front.

"Dogs would really speed this up," Pono said.

"No dogs allowed in the preserve," Takama said from behind.

"This is a murder suspect," Pono hissed.

"Never mind. Let's just go. If we don't find anything more today, we can try to borrow the K-9 unit," Lei whispered.

They filed after Jacobsen, hiking for a good length of time through increasingly dense underbrush. A light, misting rain began cooling Lei's hot cheeks, and she could feel her hair corkscrewing even tighter in the moisture. They reached an open spot in the brush, and this time Lei could see a crushed pattern where the camper had slept and a scorch mark where he'd had some sort of camp stove in use.

Jacobsen left them checking for trace and began casting about, carefully bending and searching, and he gestured. They followed him as silently as they could.

An eruption of movement ahead of them was so startling Lei found herself whipping out her weapon and dropping into a shooting stance—only to see an axis buck leaping through the ferns. Originally from Indonesia and smaller than Mainland deer, the buck was the red of Hawaii earth and dappled with white. Lei jumped as Pono, just ahead of her, took a shot with his pistol. The buck leaped in response and disappeared into the brush.

"Not what we were after, but some venison stew can't be a bad thing," Pono said, his eyes alight. They ran through the ferns, but the deer was gone.

"You not only alerted the camper to our presence; now you have to file a report because you discharged your weapon," Lei said. "Oh my God, my partner fires his weapon on the job and takes down a deer." They all laughed except Takama, a discharge of nervous energy, and continued tracking the animal through the ferns.

Jacobsen bent a fern to show Pono a smear of blood. "You got him." A few yards farther, Jacobsen bent over. "There's a faint trail here."

A camouflage-clothed man burst out of the brush in front of them—and Lei was so startled she had to restrain herself from pulling her weapon to fire at him.

"Halt! Police!" Pono bellowed, leaping after the fleeing man. Between the surprise of flushing the camper and the deer they were tracking and prepared to shoot, both she and Pono were a little trigger-happy. Pono was mowing down ferns and underbrush like a linebacker, Lei in his wake. Their progress was slowed by the dense growth, but Lei was smaller and faster. She managed to edge past Pono to charge after the camper as he bolted along some memorized pathway she couldn't see.

"Stop! Police!" she yelled. The suspect poured on more speed, if anything, running like his life depended on it and pulling ahead. Lei could hear Pono swearing as he fell behind, tangled in a clump of low-growing maile vine.

Lei tried to register as many details as possible even as she ran—approximately six feet tall, male, camo gear clothing, a satchel, a compound bow and arrows slung across his back, a field hat in camouflage. He disappeared suddenly, and Lei, running full tilt, realized why as the ground, concealed by ferns, dropped out from beneath her.

Lei cried out as she fell through space and hit the ground, rolling down the steep side of a canyon to fetch up with a bone-jarring crunch against a boulder. She lifted her head to see the camper, leaping gracefully and rock hopping down the stream, then disappearing from view through overhanging trees and underbrush.

"Damm it," Lei said when she had enough oxygen back in her lungs to verbalize. The suspect was probably young and certainly physically fit, and appeared to know the forest like the back of his hand. Pono peered down at her from about fifteen feet above, his brows drawn down in a thunderous scowl.

"You okay?"

"I think so. A few bruises is all." Lei sat up, feeling her ribs. Taking a deep breath made her gasp. "Maybe a cracked rib."

"Tiare is going to kill me if I let you get injured before the wedding," Pono said.

Takama was already climbing down. "Don't get up. Let me check you over." Jacobsen and Takama helped her climb out of the steep gulch after giving her a quick once-over.

"You okay to walk?" Pono picked a leaf out of her hair as she was boosted over the lip of the cliff.

"Just a little short of breath. Maybe I should get my ribs checked out," Lei said, holding a hand against her side and breathing shallowly.

"We should go back, have you get that looked at," Takama said, his angled brows knit.

"Another reason we try not to move too quickly out here," Jacobsen said. "All kinds of invisible hazards."

"The unsub really knows his way around," Lei said, as Pono hoisted her to her feet. "I mean, the suspect."

"Yeah, that Fed lingo's still sneaking in now and again," Pono said, referring to her stint in the FBI. "Tracking is over for the day. At least we know a little more about the guy and we've got some possible trace."

Jacobsen spotted another fresh blood mark. "We should still get the deer," he told Pono.

Lei waved a hand. "Ranger Takama can take me back to the truck."

Jacobsen and Pono peeled off to find the deer, and Takama walked with Lei back toward the parking area.

Lei was in pain, hunched over with a hand pressing her ribs, by the time they'd hiked the two miles back to the vehicles. She lay down on the soft grass beside the parking area to wait for Pono.

Takama elevated her feet, gave her water, and, after feeling her ribs, said, "Probably just a bad bruise. Just take it easy."

"Guess I don't have much of a choice," Lei said, sipping

from her water bottle. "I'd like to be able to bring some tracking dogs up here, try to get this guy. We know he's a real pro in the forest now, and that's going to make it challenging."

"We'll keep an eye out, stay in touch about it." Takama sat beside her, looping arms around his knees in a comfortable, active pose that revealed a man who was used to living without furniture.

"Not sure if I'm going to be the one to make it back up here, but I can tell Pono will want to."

Just then Jacobsen and Pono appeared, walking through the trees. Pono wore the field-dressed, bloody deer carcass over his shoulders, his face split in a ferocious grin.

"Gross," Lei said, gesturing to the stains on Pono's shirt. The big Hawaiian gave a heave and tossed the buck into his truck bed.

"Worth the report I have to write." He pulled an impressive-looking bowie knife from a holster on his belt. "You guys want some venison?"

A few minutes later they pulled out. The buck lay in the back, minus the hind leg Pono had whacked off to leave with the rangers.

"To the doctor with you," Pono said, glancing at Lei's pale face.

Her nose wrinkled. "Phew. I've never liked the smell of blood."

"At least it's not human this time."

Halfway down the mountain, Lei had to have Pono pull over so she could vomit.

"You don't look good," Pono said, as she got back in the cab. "You pregnant?"

"God no. That would be terrible," Lei said. "No. It's carsickness and the fall making me queasy. They don't tell you how windy this road is in the travel brochures."

"What's so terrible about you getting pregnant? You guys are finally acting like adults and getting married. And don't start with that 'I had a bad mother so I'll be a bad mother' crap. I've seen how you are with dogs. Best indicator of parenting abilities is how people treat their dogs."

"I don't want to talk about it." Lei leaned her forehead on the cool glass of the window and watched the road, breathing slow to calm her roiling stomach. As they drove down the volcano and headed toward the hospital, Lei considered what he'd said. She couldn't remember exactly when she'd last had her period, not that she'd ever paid much attention to it. Could she be pregnant? She was on the pill, but lately she'd been distracted and had missed a couple of doses. They'd stopped using condoms once they were exclusive, and somehow, Lei had never imagined the world's oldest relationship complication could happen to her.

The weird way she'd been feeling lately was probably

just stress with the case and planning the wedding.

At the emergency room, she called Stevens. "Sorry, honey. I fell down a cliff. I'm at the ER."

"Good God, woman. Can't you get through the week without ending up in the hospital?"

"Don't know. Never tried it," she said, going for humor. "Nothing serious. I'll be done by the time you come pick me up, I'm sure. They're just x-raying my ribs."

At the radiology lab, the technician handed her a questionnaire, and Lei paused at the question *Are you pregnant*?

Her heart sped up, and the print of the letters danced in front of her eyes, turning to hieroglyphics. A wave of nausea swept over her, and she dropped the clipboard to reach for a nearby trash can. There wasn't anything left in her belly, but when the technician came back, she said, "I could be pregnant. I better find out before I get the X-ray."

"No problem. We have some pregnancy tests if you'd like one. You really shouldn't have an X-ray unless you know."

Oh God. She wasn't even going to be able to procrastinate.

Lei wasn't sure she could even pee on the little stick, but finally she was able to go. She set the plastic wand on a paper towel and wrapped it up so she didn't have to look at it before she washed her hands.

She'd be a terrible mother. Lei felt sick at the thought of

the responsibility, at the possibility of hurting a child as her mother had abused her.

Lei also couldn't ignore the leap of something like joy at the thought of a baby with Stevens's eyes, with her curls. She splashed water on her face and hands, wondering if she had the courage to unwrap the plastic wand and look at it. She decided she didn't. She put the wand, still wrapped in the paper towel, back in its original box and stuck it in her purse.

"I need to wait on an X-ray," she told the technician. "Can the doctor check me out some other way?"

Chapter 9

Lei was feeling better the next morning. Her ribs, examined by the ER doc by visual and touch exam, were "probably just bruised"—but that didn't stop them from hurting every time she took a deep breath.

"No more chasing perps on foot until after the wedding," Stevens had said when he picked her up, folding her into his arms and kissing the top of her head. "I don't want you on crutches or something on the big day."

The pregnancy test felt like a lead weight in her purse. She still didn't want to look at it—she'd open it with Stevens on the honeymoon if her period hadn't started by then. That way, no matter what the test told them, she wasn't dealing with it alone.

Lei booted up her work computer. She had extra lieutenant duties to fit in, including reviewing a patrol's scheduling, making sure trainees' ongoing logs were looking good, and other departmental minutiae Captain Omura had lobbed her way. She slurped down a couple of Advil with her coffee, paused to wonder if that was okay if she was pregnant and decided it had to be; she wasn't going to cut into more lifestyle choices until she knew for sure. Besides, she was in survival mode with her bruised ribs.

Lei called down to the lab that was processing some of the trash she and Pono had picked up yesterday on the 'Bow Hunter' case, as they'd nicknamed the Waikamoi murder.

"Get anything off that cup and those wrappers we submitted yesterday?" Lei asked Roger Ciman, the island's top trace analysis expert. She'd pulled him off other work to get something off the trash on the camper before she left on the honeymoon.

"Yeah. Got a fingerprint. It was a little degraded, but enough. Ran it already. No matches in the standard databases."

"Damn," Lei said. The case had just gotten even more challenging. "Thanks for the quick work. Send it to me, will you?"

"No problem, sir." Lei opened her mouth to protest the unfamiliar salutation but remembered that she was a lieutenant now, and the MPD called all officers "sir" regardless of gender.

She checked her e-mail. E-mail lists of names of volunteers and grad students who'd worked with the different environmental agencies had arrived in her inbox. She printed them out just as her e-mail dinged with the arrival of a blown-up, enhanced copy of the camper's fingerprint.

Lei printed the reference photo and put it in the case file, staring at the black-and-white whorls on the paper.

Now what? How to match the unknown print with an unknown name? She was certain that the camper was someone who'd been involved in conservation work. But if he wasn't in the system, how did they find out who he was? Calling in that many people for fingerprinting, from potentially all over the country, just wasn't practical or even justifiable—at this point the camper was technically just a person of interest.

Lei sipped coffee, considering as she leafed through the file. Finally, she made a list of all the agency heads and their contact numbers. Maybe someone from one of the agencies would have a suspicion about one of their students or volunteers that could lead to something.

Pono arrived, setting a plastic-wrapped musubi next to her elbow. "Tiare forbids you from getting injured before the wedding and sends you something to eat."

"Thanks!" Lei unwrapped the compacted rice topped with fried Spam wrapped in thin, pounded nori seaweed, making a tidy snack. She took a bite, chewed. "Delicious, as always."

"How're the ribs?" Pono asked, booting up his computer.

"Not so good. I'm thinking a day working the phones isn't a bad idea. What do you think of this?" She told Pono her plan to call the various conservation nonprofits on Maui, including the Park Service, to fish for leads on the camper.

"Sounds like a plan. I'm going to call Interpol about our vic's prints. I'm off to get some coffee." Pono left.

Pono's mention of coffee reminded her of how she'd started the pot that morning and then returned to the bedroom. Stevens had spent the night at her place to "keep an eye on her" after her fall into the gulch. Lei smiled at the memory of his long muscled body in her bed, his shadowed, sleeping eyes, the way he looked waking up— and reaching for her.

"Daydreaming of the honeymoon?" Captain Omura's dry voice at the doorway of her cubicle made Lei start, spilling coffee on herself. Lei felt a blush burn her cheekbones— even now that she knew Omura valued her on the Maui team, the captain's almost unnatural ability to read her mind made Lei edgy.

"As a matter of fact, I've got some things to catch you up on," Lei said, dabbing her shirt with a napkin. She filled the captain in on the chase yesterday, the camper's fingerprint, and her plan for today as Pono returned with a chipped mug of black brew.

"Glad I stopped in, then. You might have updated me sooner," Omura said, with a glance shared between Lei and

Pono.

Lei shut her mouth on protests that they hadn't had time as Pono ducked his head. "I've got something to check on in the lab," he said, and disappeared again.

Omura stepped inside the cubicle and sat on Pono's chair. "I also wanted to give you something." The captain crossed her legs, sleek in a tailored blue pencil skirt and black sling-backs. She handed Lei a box. "I bought you a gift. Thought I'd give it to you personally."

"Oh." Lei held the precisely wrapped package, tied with gold cord and trimmed with two origami cranes. "Thanks. It's too pretty to open!"

"I like to do a little *tsutsumi* now and again." Lei was aware of the Japanese art of present wrapping, where the presentation was as important as the gift. "Go ahead and open it. It's just a little something."

Lei tugged on the cord and carefully unwrapped the gift, preserving the paper and decorative cranes. She opened the box, and took out a gold-painted dowel about three inches long with fishing line tied to it. Pierced through their white parchment bodies, a series of folded origami cranes fluttered from the line. Lei stood up to be able to hold the fragile mobile above the ground, and the ivory paper birds lifted and spun.

"A little good luck for you both," Omura said, referring to the Japanese custom of giving origami cranes at weddings.

"I couldn't do a thousand, but there are a hundred to get you started."

"Captain, I don't know what to say." Lei watched the graceful little birds move in the draft coming down the hall. She set the mobile carefully on her desk and embraced Omura, smelling a hint of the other woman's delicate perfume, feeling a tightness in her throat as she thought of the captain folding each tiny bird. "We'll treasure it."

"That's more than enough. So glad you came to join my team."

"I've decided Maui's home. Thank you for bringing me home."

"Well, then, since you're home"—Omura gave Lei's shoulder a pat—"keep me updated on the case more closely next time."

It didn't take long for Lei to work her way through calls to the five agencies that did conservation work on Maui—but she didn't get anything of interest until talking to Jud Snelling at Hawaiian Bird Conservatory.

"Our team had already been discussing who the camper could be and whether we had any ideas about volunteers and interns. We had a Canadian grad student, Edward Kingston, about three months ago who was kind of paranoid—was working on his own side research project, which he had trouble letting go of. He had some behaviors that concerned his field supervisor," Dr. Snelling said.

"Can I get the supervisor's name?" Lei hastily jotted down the name "Edward Kingston."

"Dr. Lana Biswandi. She's with University of Hawaii, but we coordinate our location with some of their biology programs. She was concerned about his outlook, but he completed his internship successfully, as far as I know." He rattled off the professor's phone number.

"Did Kingston go back to Canada?"

"We assumed so, but maybe Dr. Biswandi will know."

Lei dialed the professor's number.

"Dr. Biswandi here." The professor had a low alto voice and an Indian accent.

Lei identified herself and described what they were looking for and why.

"Yes, Kingston was under my supervision on a field project involving habit patterns of the native birds—do you need to know what we were studying?"

"No, just the behaviors that concerned you about Kingston."

"Well, then. He was secretive. Always making notes in a little journal, hiding samples from the field, et cetera. I confronted him, and he admitted he had his own research project going. I forbade him to work on it at the same time as our formal project, and he seemed to comply—at least, I never caught him working on it again."

"What was he like personality wise?" Lei leaned back in her office chair, forgetting about her ribs and almost groaning aloud as pain lanced across her sternum.

"He was a loner. Quiet."

"Okay. And where did he go after his internship ended? Back to Canada?"

"I don't know."

Lei's pen stopped as she waited. She blew a curl out of her eye. "What do you mean, you don't know?"

"I mean, I assumed he went back to Canada. We had a goodbye lunch with all the interns. But it's possible he stayed on Maui in violation of his visa. He did say he had his own project he was working on. It makes sense that he might be your unknown camper because he was good at survival camping. We learned from him in the field—to make fire, other skills."

"That sounds like the man we're looking for. This person knows how to live out in the wilderness and leave little trace."

"What are you investigating him for, exactly?"

Lei considered her options, decided that Dr. Biswandi might be helpful in this too. "We want to question him regarding the murder of an unidentified Asian man who was capturing native birds."

A long pause.

"Interesting," was all Dr. Biswandi said. Lei was disappointed. "I'll call our other interns and ask if anyone knows where he is."

"It would be great if they didn't know why we're looking for him."

"Of course." Dr. Biswandi cut the connection with crisp decisiveness.

Lei put the phone handset down slowly. It looked like she'd found a strong candidate for the mysterious camper—but catching him was another thing entirely.

Chapter 10

Dawn crested Haleakala in a blaze of salmon-pink glory, filling the chilly, shadowed eucalyptus grove they'd parked in with powdery golden light reflected off nearby clouds. Lei and Pono got out of the purple truck as the SUV with the K-9 unit pulled up and parked next to them for the manhunt. Takama, his lips a line and hands on his hips, frowned at them in front of the gate into the preserve. Jacobsen, beside him, looked no less worried about what the search would do to the delicate forest.

"You sure this is necessary?" Takama said, indicating the dog, a flop-eared hound called Blue, with a flick of his fingers. Blue's handler, a young, fit officer named Freddie Lee, was still unloading and prepping the dog.

"Yes. We need to capture and interview this man," Lei said. "Our captain spoke to Dr. Snelling; everyone's on board. We'll try not to damage the plants."

"The understory," Takama corrected.

"Right."

Lei had spent the rest of yesterday tracking Kingston. She discovered that he'd never used his passport to leave the island, and his classmates from the research project hadn't seen or heard from him since the goodbye luncheon. Dr. Snelling had been able to bring an abandoned ball cap Kingston had worn down to the station.

Lei restrained herself from going over to pet Blue's sleek head—the dog was in "work mode," but it was hard for her to resist any dog. Pono handed Lei her Kevlar vest. "Mandatory."

"I can't handle the Velcro with my ribs the way they are."

"Guess I have to leave you here, then." Pono put his hands on his hips and eyed her until she put the vest on, leaving it loose.

"I've always hated these things," she muttered.

"I know. You've also seen what a compound bow and arrow can do—and the perp might be otherwise armed."

They set off at a good clip down the dirt track into the forest. Lei breathed shallowly to ease her ribs. The dog was silent, trotting beside his handler. They made good time all the way to the boardwalk. Finally, under the cathedral of arching koa and ohia branches, with birdsong sweet in the air, Lee gave Kingston's hat to Blue to sniff.

Almost immediately, the dog began casting about in the

ferns. Takama's lips were tight as the animal nosed the ground, making tiny whining sounds. Suddenly, the hound lifted its head and charged into the understory. Freddie Lee followed at a run, Lei and Pono bringing up the rear. The ferns took a beating as the dog bolted through the brush, the rest of them close behind.

Lei, slowed by her injury, jogged up just as the dog leaped on a bundled shape in a camouflage sleeping bag. The man gave a cry of surprise. Lee restrained the dog, and Kingston sat up, the sleeping bag still around his waist.

Lei recognized him from his passport photo, though he was bearded, with the bushy hair of months outdoors.

"I hope you've come to get the poacher," Kingston said, dark eyes worried as he looked around at the ring of faces gazing down at him. "He has a gun."

"Someone got him, all right," Pono said, hauling the biologist up by the arm. "And we want to talk with you about it."

"I know about the man who was shot with a bow. There's another Asian guy out here," Kingston said. Kingston asked to call his lawyer on a satellite cell phone the biologist produced from his waterproof backpack.

"Doesn't look good, you calling him when we haven't asked a single question." Lei gave Kingston her best intimidating stare. The biologist pushed his hair out of his eyes and stared back calmly.

"I know my rights in the United States," he said.

"Getting deported is one of them," she said, but Kingston just pushed a speed-dial number and held the phone to his ear.

Back at the station, Lei swallowed an Advil with coffee. She and Pono had left Kingston in the interview room while they waited for his lawyer to arrive, and they'd just come from informing the captain that they had their person of interest in custody. Lei was weary from the early morning, the vigorous hike both ways, and the hour-long drive up and down Haleakala.

"Do you think Kingston was bullshitting us about another poacher?" Lei felt the tightness of anxiety drawing her brows together.

"Don't know. But without finding a bow in his camping gear, it doesn't look good for us to hold him any length of time."

"I want to wait to call Immigration and Naturalization Service about his visa violation until after we question him. It might give us a carrot to get him to talk if we offer to let him stay long enough to finish his research project."

"Good idea," Pono said. The partners gazed at Edward Kingston through the mirrored wall of the interview room. The biologist had settled down in a corner, folded his legs into lotus position, set hands with finger and thumb together on his knees, and shut his eyes. He looked utterly peaceful. "So much for leaving him to sweat—he seems pretty mellow."

Kingston's lawyer arrived, a man with the bullet head and the thick neck of a pugilist.

"Shawn Shimoda," he said, handing Lei a card. He and Pono had already exchanged a chin lift of acknowledgment. "What are you holding my man on?"

"We're not 'holding' him on anything. We just want to question him as a possible witness on the homicide of an unknown man up in Waikamoi Preserve," Lei said. "Don't know why he needed you called before we even got started."

"And I'd like to know how a Canadian national who ditched his research group and violated his visa has ended up having one of the best lawyers on Maui already on retainer," Pono said, with narrowed eyes. "Makes me wonder if he didn't know he was going to need one."

"Where's my client?" Shimoda's face was carefully blank.

Lei led them to the interrogation room.

"I'd like a moment alone with him," Shimoda said. Lei and Pono exited and watched through the safety glass of the door as Kingston scrambled up from his yoga pose and shook hands with Shimoda. Their heads were close as they whispered, but there was a constraint between them that spoke of unfamiliarity.

"I don't think Shimoda's met him before," Lei said. "Wish I could read lips."

"Shimoda's not cheap. Kingston must have called him some time ago and put him on retainer—he only works with a down payment against services before they're needed." Pono always seemed to know the backstory on people they interacted with.

Shimoda looked up and gestured for them to come in. Both of the men sat down on molded plastic chairs across the table from Lei and Pono. Lei turned on the recording equipment with a switch on the wall and addressed Kingston, who, in spite of his meditation and counsel present, looked pale.

"We aren't charging you with anything at this time. We just want to interview you, to see if you know anything about the death of a man shot in Waikamoi Preserve."

"I know there was a dead man. I smelled something bad, and the odor led me to check it out. I thought it was a deer or something. I was surprised to see it was a human body."

"So you didn't think it was appropriate to report an obvious murder?" Pono asked, frowning.

"I didn't want to get involved." Kingston looked down at his hands. "I thought this might happen—this right here. I didn't need the interruption to my research project."

"Research you were conducting illegally," Lei said. "Were you aware the murdered man had native birds on his body in a canvas bag? Birds that ended up dying of dehydration?"

Kingston winced visibly and kept his eyes down. "No, I was not aware."

They let a pause go by to see if Kingston would volunteer anything more. He didn't.

"So, when we picked you up in Waikamoi this morning, you said you hoped we were there for the poacher. What did you mean by that?"

Kingston looked up, and this time there was some animation in his pale, bewhiskered face. "I want to help with this investigation. I just don't want you suspecting me. There's another poacher up there now, catching birds like the first one was."

"Tell us more," Pono said.

"I was watching the birds, you know—for my project." Kingston swallowed. "I'm up there for a research project— an important one."

"We know you're trespassing illegally in violation of your visa," Lei said.

"That is not for you to determine," Shimoda snapped. "If you want my client's cooperation, I suggest you refrain from prejudicial comments." Shimoda's first contribution was a heavy one.

Lei folded her lips together, and Kingston continued. "I have some places where I watch the birds, and I saw this other man in camouflage gear using a mist net to catch them."

"Where and when?" Pono asked.

"I can't tell you exactly where. I have GPS coordinates of my watch stations, though, and I could retrieve that information for you. Anyway, I use binoculars to watch the birds' behaviors, and I could see this man had a handgun in a holster on his belt."

"What did he look like?" Lei asked.

"Asian. Not sure of age. Sturdy build, medium height. Knew how to handle birds and equipment. At the time I spotted him, I was most worried he'd realize I was there and either turn me in or shoot me."

"These observation spots, are they the blinds the rangers and Hawaiian Bird Conservatory staff showed us?"

Red spots appeared on Kingston's cheeks above the luxuriant growth of beard masking his face. He opened his mouth to answer, but Shimoda cut him off.

"Please confine your questions to the information that's useful in apprehending someone you suspect for the murder or in catching this poacher," he said. Shimoda was good— he was protecting his client from admitting to anything that could be later used to support criminal charges, Lei realized.

"All right. How many times did you observe the bird hunter?" Pono asked.

"Just once, yesterday. It appears that with the other hunter gone, they've sent someone else."

"They?" Lei pounced. "Who are *they*?"

"I don't know. Whoever is wanting to catch the birds," Kingston said. His eyes had begun blinking rapidly.

"Well, thank you for your concern about that, and we will alert the Park Service and Hawaiian Bird Conservatory staff that there's someone up there catching birds, but for all you know, this guy could have been a biologist on a legitimate project," Lei said.

Kingston shook his head. "No. When I was trained, I learned protocols that protect the birds, and biologists up there work in teams. Besides, why would a biologist be carrying a handgun?"

"This is all speculation," Shimoda said. "If you have no further questions, I insist you release my client."

"We do. Tell us more about how and when you saw the body and your rationale for not reporting it," Lei said. Kingston provided a time two days before they'd gone to the boardwalk as when he'd seen the body. Lei felt sick at the waste—the birds on the poacher's belt might have been saved if the body had been found sooner.

They eventually let Kingston go, in the company of his lawyer, with the understanding that they wouldn't report his visa violation in the next week in case they needed him for more questioning. "But Hawaiian Bird Conservatory may want to bring charges against you for trespassing and destruction of property," Lei said. "And we may want to charge you at another date."

"Don't bother my client with idle threats," Shimoda said, following Kingston out of the interview room. "You have no physical evidence linking Mr. Kingston to the murder. Let me know if you find any."

"Where is an address where we can reach you?" Pono asked Kingston.

"I'm staying at a vacation rental cottage in Haiku," Kingston said. "I've been coming down from the mountain every so often to resupply and work on the computer." He gave them the address and left with Shimoda.

Lei watched them leave, then got up and snapped off the recording equipment. "Now what?"

"We have to go over the trace again and see what we've come up with from Kingston's campsite. We need to find a link to the body if we're going to charge Kingston with anything. For now he's just a witness to another poacher being in the preserve."

Lei worked the phones while Pono went back down to the evidence room to process the items they'd confiscated from Kingston's campsite.

She called Takama first. "Just wanted to let you and Jacobsen know that Kingston confirmed there's another bird catcher up there. Could it be anyone legitimately up there, capturing birds for a project?"

"Working alone? No. We always work in teams." A long silence. Finally Takama said, "I'd be in favor of taking the dog back up and looking for the other poacher."

Lei knew how much it cost the taciturn Park Service veteran to concede that, and she sighed. "I can ask the captain, but the time and expense of using the K-9 unit to hunt a trespasser who has no connection to our current murder investigation is not likely to get approved."

"I didn't think much of bringing the dog to track, but compared to us randomly trampling through the preserve, it was effective," Takama said. "Please let me know if you do get that approved. And you said the man is armed. That can't be good for public safety in a place like the cloud forest."

Lei laughed. "You should have been a lawyer! I'll see what I can do. Hey, I do have some bad news. The victim had birds in a bag on his belt. They were alive when he was shot, but they eventually died of dehydration because it took so long for us to find the body. Sad, huh?"

A long pause, and when Takama replied, his voice was slow and heavy. "I'm so sorry to hear that—what a shame.

I'll get in touch with some trackers, see if we can chase this poacher out of the preserve ourselves."

"Be careful. Remember he's armed," Lei cautioned.

"We'll be armed too," Takama said, and hung up with a decisive click.

Chapter 11

A week went by. Sitting at her desk one morning, a list of to-dos and a cooling cup of coffee at her elbow, Lei found herself rubbing the white-gold medallion on a chain around her neck. Her ribs were better, but she'd traded that ache for a roiling in her belly that never really went away. She was getting increasingly stressed as the wedding approached and there were no new breaks. She'd wanted to have this case wrapped up before they left on the honeymoon.

Kingston's gear had yielded no clues, Omura had nixed using the K-9 unit in Waikamoi to hunt the alleged new poacher, and her period still hadn't come.

Last night after work, Lei had felt tense, her skin too tight, ever since she'd taken the pregnancy test out of her purse and hidden it in the bathroom cabinet. That small, brown-paper-wrapped package seemed to be sending out sonar pings, unnerving her. What if Stevens found it? What would it tell them? She felt claustrophobic.

She'd met him on the porch outside her house when he arrived for their usual dinner together. "I think we should take a break before the wedding," she said.

"Relax. It's just me." He reached out to hug her. She'd wriggled out of his arms. He'd taken her face in his hands, kissing her soft and full. His mouth on hers was gentle and persuasive. Lei's lashes fluttered shut. She tried to get into the kiss.

Her childhood rapist, Charlie Kwon, had possessed eyes so deep a brown, the pupils barely showed. Those eyes swam up from hell, filling her mind, haunting her.

Those eyes turned her love to fear, her hunger for Stevens to sickness, her confidence to ash. She was "Damaged Goods," his special name for her—and always would be. A fraud, a fake, a whore in disguise. Not a victim of abuse, a *participant*.

"I'll make you like it," Kwon had said.

Lei had never liked it. But she'd endured it, because there was no choice and because he said she was special to him. At nine years old, she'd been so starved for attention that even his abuse had been better than nothing.

She was sick, beyond saving.

She'd be a horrible mother.

Even as these thoughts flickered through her mind, she knew they were old beliefs, old dysfunction. She'd combatted so much with the help of her therapist, Dr. Wilson—but right now it was all too much. Revulsion rose up her throat like bile, and she broke the kiss and stepped back. "I just need a break. Nothing's wrong. I just need a little space."

Stevens stayed where he was, one foot on the top step, the other below, hands resting on a black leather belt loaded with sidearm and badge. He wore broken-in jeans, old boots, and a short-sleeved polo shirt she'd given him that brought out his sky-blue eyes.

Those eyes had gone flat and metallic. His dark brows drew down as his mouth thinned out into a hard line. "I'm sick of this, Lei. Really? We're going to do this again?"

Lei crossed her arms over her thundering heart. "Nothing's wrong. I want to really look forward to the honeymoon and to being with you. That's all."

"I don't believe you."

"You don't have to. You just have to respect what I'm asking."

He removed his foot from the step. "Prove it to me. Come here. Kiss me and show me you still love me—that this isn't about Kwon, some last-minute psycho freak-out. I think I deserve that much before I leave."

Lei wanted to kiss him, but her feet were rooted to the boards of the old porch. She gulped and tasted bile. "I shouldn't have to prove I love you like that. This is no big deal."

"I think it is. Now I'm worried you're going to cut and run."

"I won't. I promise." The feeling in her legs unlocked enough for her to lean forward and give him a peck on the lips. "But even if it is about Kwon, I'm marrying *you*. I just need a little space before the big day."

"I'll leave if you call Dr. Wilson. Call her right now."

"You're treating me like a child. Calling this a psycho freak-out. Telling me to get ahold of my shrink." Lei tried to sound angry. The best defense was a good offense, her mother had always said.

"This is all those things—a childish, psycho freak-out— for which you need professional help. You've left me twice, and I'm not at all sure three times won't be the charm."

Lei felt the precipice of another breakup yawning before them, a severing more terrible than all her conflicted feelings. Losing Stevens was even scarier than Kwon's eyes, than the little wand of the pregnancy test.

Lei sat down right where she was, folding up her legs on the porch, and Stevens turned away and sat on the top step. She took her phone out and called Dr. Wilson's personal cell—she no longer saw the police psychologist regularly, just for "tune-ups" when needed, and she didn't know if she was relieved or terrified when the psychologist's phone went to voice mail.

"Hi, Dr. Wilson. It's Lei on Maui. Listen, our wedding's going to be in a few days, and I'm wanting some personal space. Stevens thinks something is wrong and wanted me to call you. Please get back to me when you can." She pressed Off. "There. You satisfied?"

She spoke to the back of his head. His broad shoulders had sagged, and he'd threaded his fingers into coffee-brown hair, ruffling it as he did when upset. Her heart squeezed, and she set her hand on his back.

"I'm sorry. I hate being like this."

"I hate it too. Makes me wonder what being married to you is going to be like, if we make it that far." He stood and walked away without looking back at her, leaving Keiki whining, forlorn as he shut the gate behind himself with a bang.

His words had made her run back through the house to throw up. She wasn't at all sure she was up to either the wedding or being pregnant. Stevens had picked up on that in spite of her excuses.

Lei refocused her eyes on her to-do list, rubbing a dry Bic pen in circles on the paper to get the ink flowing— so vigorously she hit her mug with an elbow. The coffee sloshed, dangerously close to spilling on her workspace, and she caught it, blowing out a breath.

The thought of Stevens leaving her made her belly clench—but she'd basically sent him packing. He was probably as nervous as she was about what would happen on their actual wedding day. Tonight she was supposed to pick up Aunty Rosario and her father, Wayne Texeira, from the airport. There were only three days left until the wedding.

She hated to leave right now. Maybe there was just a little more she could do on the bow hunter case before she left for ten days of honeymoon. She held down a speed-dial button on her phone.

"Did you get the wedding dress?" Marcella asked by way of greeting.

"One last fitting. It's going to be gorgeous, Marcella. I can't believe you know me so well. I love what the designer came up with."

"I knew you would." They confirmed a few more details, including what time Lei would pick her up from the airport the following day.

"Can you have Ang put a watch or alert out on the Internet for someone looking for native Hawaiian birds? I think we might have a poaching order out for them, possibly originated in China." She filled Marcella in on the little they knew about the poachers.

"Sure," her friend said. Just then Lei's desk phone rang.

"I gotta go. See you when I pick you up tomorrow." Lei clicked off her cell phone and picked up the handset of the desk unit. "Lieutenant Texeira here."

"This is Sally Shu at nine-one-one operations. I had an anonymous tip that someone's dead in Waikamoi Preserve. The caller left your name to contact."

Lei's heart lurched and went into overdrive. Another body up there? That couldn't be good. "Did you send officers to respond?"

"No. Thought it could be a hoax, and since you're on the murder case up there, I called to see if you could go directly instead."

"Any other information? Like where the body is located, general description?"

"If I had any more information, I'd certainly give it to you, Lieutenant," Shu said.

"We're on our way," Lei said, already looking around for Pono.

Lei took her own truck up Haleakala toward the preserve since, whatever the outcome of this errand, she needed to go to the airport at four p.m. to pick up her aunt and father. Weaving up the winding curves of the familiar two-lane road to the summit, Lei found her mind returning to the confrontation with Stevens in spite of the dreamy vista of green fields and majestic cumulous clouds. Even the grim errand she was on couldn't keep her thoughts from returning to the painful words they'd exchanged yesterday evening.

She hoped Dr. Wilson called her back soon.

Lei slowed the silver Tacoma and pulled alongside the kiosk at the entrance of Haleakala National Park. She held her ID up to the ranger in olive drab at the window.

"Official business. We have a report of a death in the Waikamoi area." The K-9 unit was also en route, since they had no idea where to look for the body.

The ranger waved her through, Pono following in his vehicle. They turned in to the Hosmer's Grove trailhead area. Lei's heart rate picked up as she pushed thoughts of Stevens and the wedding out of her mind to focus on the job.

The job. It was always there, life and death, when all else failed.

Chapter 12

Lei and Pono bent over the Asian man in camouflage gear lying just off the boardwalk, close to where they'd found the other body. The dog hadn't had a scent to follow, but when they reached the reserve area, Blue had let out a howl and towed his handler straight to the downed man.

The victim wasn't dead after all. Lei called for a helicopter ambulance as Pono tried to assess the man's injuries. He appeared to be conscious, his eyelids fluttering, but did not respond to their questions. Protruding from his back was another arrow, this one striped with yellow banding.

"Same MO, though the arrows are different." Lei squatted beside the man, patting down his pockets. She took a sleek Smith and Wesson 9 mm pistol out of a molded holster on the man's belt. Like the other poacher, he was wearing cargo pants with loaded pockets. She whipped an evidence bag out of her back pocket and dropped the weapon into it.

"I'd like to elevate his feet," Pono said. "He's not

bleeding too badly, but there's no telling what that arrow has punctured."

The arrow had pierced the victim's backpack too, penetrating through tough nylon layers before lodging itself in the man's upper back. The backpack might well have saved his life. Remembering the birds on the other poacher's belt, Lei carefully unzipped the netted top of the backpack—and sure enough, inside in a delicate mesh bag, were several brightly colored birds.

The birds were still alive, Lei saw with relief, as she removed the bag from the backpack. She photographed them both in the bag and with Pono holding them before they released all three—two red ones with curved bills and a green one. "*I`iwi* is the red one and *`amakihi* is green," Pono said, as the birds fluttered weakly into the trees.

"Think they'll be all right?" Lei asked, frowning. She could hear the percussive thrum of the helicopter arriving in the open landing area.

"Can't have been in the bag too long. As long as they get water soon, they should be okay." Even as they watched, the birds began to hop around on the branches, then sip nectar from the red lehua blossoms of the tree they'd fluttered onto. Pono crunched off into the ferns to try to determine where the arrow had been fired from, the dog and his handler assisting by looking for scents.

Lei helped stabilize the victim after emptying his pockets into evidence bags—she couldn't wait to sort through the items she'd recovered, spotting a Chinese passport.

The man moaned and writhed in agony, still not responding to questions, as the medical technicians lifted him facedown onto a pallet for transport. The arrow still protruded from his back, blood welling sluggishly around the entry site to soak his clothing and the backpack. The victim's sturdy build required all five of them to assist in carrying him back up the trail to the helicopter. Lei handed the med techs a pair of handcuffs.

"When he's been treated, cuff him to the bed until we can get there. He's under arrest."

"What for?" the tech asked, frowning as she took the cuffs.

"Trespassing and poaching, to start with." Lei wasn't sure what else they could throw at him, but keeping the victim from escaping was an important first step.

Lei and Pono hiked back toward the trucks, discussing what next. "Why don't you check on Kingston's whereabouts?" Lei asked her partner. "I'll call Marcella about running this guy's passport through Interpol."

They worked their phones, and by the time they got to her house, they were able to verify that Kingston was at his vacation rental (his landlady verified his whereabouts), and Marcella tracked the name Lei gave her to a Chinese national wanted for smuggling tiger parts and elephant tusks. She had no record on Xu Chang, murder victim.

"Chang is probably an alias. I'll help with processing for this guy Xiaoping, if he recovers from his wounds," the FBI agent said. "How bad is he?"

"We don't know. The arrow wound wasn't bleeding too badly, but he was pretty incoherent. On the other hand, I don't think he spoke English." Lei reached her truck and beeped it unlocked. "Did you hear anything from Ang about finding a 'contract' for native Hawaiian birds on the Internet?"

"Not yet."

"Well, let me know of anything else that comes up on this guy. See you tomorrow. I can't believe it's so soon!" Lei clicked off.

"Can you go check on our victim at the hospital? I'm just in time to pick up Aunty if I hurry," she told Pono.

"No problem. I'll make sure he's secure. Good to know we caught a bad guy, at least."

"Yeah. I just hope he makes it, so we can question him."

Chapter 13

As she drove down the mountain, Lei's phone vibrated with a call from Dr. Wilson. Lei put her Bluetooth in and picked up for the petite blond psychologist.

"Dr. Wilson! So glad you called me back!"

"Lei. Always good to hear from you. Sounds like you and Stevens are having some last-minute jitters."

"Maybe that's what it is. Did you get my invitation?"

"I did, and I'm flying over with Bruce Ohale." A pause. "Lei, are you trying to provoke something? Push Stevens away?"

"Maybe. I don't know." Lei kept her eyes on the road, but one hand crept up to rub her medallion. "I just need some space because—I'm worried I'm pregnant." She told the psychologist about the test and how she was handling it.

"Okay. I need you to stay in adult mode now. Rely on

the decisions that brought you this far—the happiness you two have made. Don't listen to your emotions right now—they aren't a reliable guide. You don't have to have all the answers about being a parent and whether or not you are going to be a good wife. Heck, if any of us knew what life might hold, we'd all be too scared to leave our houses in the morning! Just stick to the course you've chosen. Remember the choices that brought you to this point and that the times you veered off that course out of fear didn't end well."

"I wish you were right here," Lei said, her voice small.

"I wish I were, too. Consider yourself hugged," Dr. Wilson said. "You can do it. Just put one foot in front of the other and say 'I do.'"

Lei laughed. "I will. Or, I do."

"There. See? Whatever happens, I'll be there to support you. Also, I want to know what that pregnancy test says."

"Thanks, Dr. Wilson."

Lei hung up, heartened. She wasn't to trust her emotions. This time, she liked that advice.

Her tall, curly-haired father, Wayne Texeira, and his short, round sister, Rosario, were already waiting at the curb of the airport when Lei pulled up. A mountain of bungee-corded coolers, assorted boxes, and bags were mounded beside them. Lei leaped out, not sure who to grab first, and ending up in a three-cornered hug with both of them.

"It's so good to see you!" Lei exclaimed, kissing her father's craggy cheek and hugging her aunt again. "I can't believe you folks are really here and we're really doing this!"

"You stole the words right out of my mouth." Aunty Rosario smiled, laugh lines bracketing brown eyes framed by mobile black brows. She was wearing her "traveling muumuu," a denim garment embroidered with plumeria at the neckline, her thick hair escaping the braid she'd captured it in.

Lei opened the back door of the extended cab for Aunty Rosario as Wayne began loading the mountain of foodstuffs and luggage into the back of the truck. Lei noticed more gray in Rosario's hair and that her aunt had lost weight—the muumuu was loose, and Rosario's shiny brown complexion was ashy. Lei remembered her aunt had said she was having medical tests, and her chest tightened with worry.

"Tiare has done some trading and found you guys a vacation rental for the week with two refrigerators and a big freezer, so let's go straight there and get the food put away," Lei said as they settled into the truck. Lei twisted to look at her aunt in the backseat, and winced, putting a hand to her injured ribs.

"What's happened to you now?" Wayne asked, a furrow

between his deep-set eyes.

"Took a tumble into a gulch. Just a few bruises," Lei said. "It's much better already."

"So do you know where you're going on the honeymoon?" Rosario asked as Lei pulled away from the curb and merged into traffic.

"No. That maddening man is keeping it a surprise. And you know how I like surprises."

"Not at all," Wayne said. "Even when you were a little girl, you always wanted to know what was coming."

"Good survival instinct," Lei said. The brief phrase summarized a world of hurt.

Wayne reached over and squeezed her shoulder. "It's time you learned surprises can be fun."

Lei just smiled, afraid the telltale prickling in her eyes would turn to tears. The wedding was making her way too emotional. They chatted, eventually pulling up at a sprawling Asian-style estate in Haiku on a bluff overlooking the ocean. Lei got out of the truck first, turning to survey the lush vista, the ocean sparkling cobalt off the end of the velvety bluff. "How did Tiare swing this?"

"You didn't see it before?" Aunty asked, getting out of the truck, carrying her capacious purse.

"No. She just told me she'd worked something out with the caretaker."

"What a great place. You've obviously got friends who've got friends." Wayne went around to the back of the truck to get the food and supplies. They each took a load and carried the items into the gorgeous teak-floored mansion. Once the truck was unloaded, Wayne surveyed the huge steel refrigerators, a gleam in his eye. "Rosario, take Lei for a walk. I want to unpack this."

Lei and her aunty walked through the modern house, all shining wood and open beams, out a sliding glass door, and across smooth grass toward the ocean beyond. Rosario took Lei's hand, an unusually affectionate gesture, and they walked all the way to the edge of the cliff. Lei looked out at the vista of ocean, West Maui Mountains dressed in green, bowl of sky. Far out on the sea, she could see the spume of a passing humpback whale.

"I can't believe this is happening." Lei leaned her head against her aunt's. Rosario circled an arm around Lei's waist, and Lei flinched.

"Oh, honey," Aunty said.

"It's okay. The ribs are really much better," Lei said. "I was chasing a suspect on Haleakala and couldn't see a gulch through all the ferns and fell in. Lucky it's not a broken leg. That would have been great on my wedding day."

"You have to take better care of yourself. I've been telling you that for years," Aunty said, shaking a scolding finger at Lei.

"You should talk, Aunty. What did those tests say?"

"It's not important. What's important is that you have a wonderful wedding."

"Oh, Aunty." Lei turned, put her hands on the shorter woman's shoulders, gazing into her dark brown eyes. "It's bad news?"

Aunty just gave a single nod of her head. Both their eyes filled, and Lei folded her aunt into a tight embrace.

"Tell me," she whispered into her aunt's ear.

Rosario shook her head and pulled away. "There's a time and a place for everything. This is your time." Her aunt turned and walked with her usual energetic stride back toward the magnificent edifice of the house.

Lei took a moment to pull herself together. Her aunt had always been stoic and wouldn't tell her anything before she was ready. Lei would just have to wait, and she'd never been good at waiting.

Wayne had got the food unpacked, and they helped put it away in the big silver refrigerators. Lei exclaimed over the deep aluminum dishes of laulau, teriyaki chicken, and kalua pig, the bags of Aunty's purple poi rolls. "We're making the poke, noodle salad, regular salad, rice, and appetizers tomorrow so they're ready for your big day Saturday," Aunty said.

"Oh my God. It's the day after tomorrow," Lei said, feeling the blood drain out of her face. She put a hand on the counter to steady herself. Lei thought of all the officers they worked with who'd be off duty and attending with their families, her grandfather, her colleagues from the FBI.

And she'd be standing up in front, making promises she'd always been afraid of.

"You can take down hundreds of perps and kill a man with your bare hands, and you're scared to wear a dress, stand in front of a crowd, and say a few words," Wayne said, reading her mind. "Good thing I'm going to be up there doing the service. I got my minister's license finalized just in time."

"Dad! Really?" Lei embraced her father. "Congratulations. That's such good news!"

"I'm not sure. That guarantees everyone at the wedding will need tissues," Rosario said. She opened a covered dish, serving up plates she put into the microwave. "Thought we could try some samples."

"When did you decide you wanted to become a minister?" Lei asked her father.

"God was showing me the rest of my life belonged to him back in prison," Wayne said. "I just needed a few years on the outside to confirm it. Did an online course in Bible and ministry and applied for my license. I already lead services at the homeless shelter in San Rafael."

"You should hear him speak. He does good," Rosario said, serving up plates loaded with laulau, kalua pork, and sweet potato. She set a roll on each plate. "Missing the vegetable, but this will give you an idea of what we'll be eating."

Lei hugged her aunt and kissed her cheek. "You're too good to me."

They took their plates outside to the wide deck looking out at the ocean and sat around a round teak outdoor table. The sunset gilded the outline of the West Maui Mountains to the east, and palm trees swayed at the corners of the lush lawn. Wayne took Lei and Aunty's hands for grace, bowed his head, and prayed over the meal.

"Thanks, Lord, for bringing our family together to welcome a new member, Lei's soon-to-be husband, Michael. Bless this food, and let it make our bodies strong. Amen."

Lei sneaked a glance at her father's silvered head, feeling love and worry as she did so, similar to how she felt about Aunty Rosario but for different reasons. She still wondered who'd hired the hit man who killed her childhood molester, Kwon, last year—and she suspected her father, in spite of his repeated denials and his seemingly selfless lifestyle. She shook her head to clear it of those negative thoughts and stood up.

"We forgot drinks." She got up and went back into the kitchen, pulled cold beers out for each of them—but when it came to popping the top on her own, she paused.

They said not to drink when pregnant. Until she was sure, it might be better to pass. She poured water for herself and brought the beers back out with glasses on a tray she found.

"None for you?" Aunty's eyes were sharp, assessing.

"Counting calories," Lei said.

Wayne snorted. "You need a few pounds, if anything."

"You haven't seen the wedding dress," Lei said, thinking of the design being created that capitalized on her slender build. "You'll look graceful," the designer had said. "Not everyone has your figure." Lei was supposed to try on the dress for a final fitting tomorrow.

They ate and chatted about the wedding, discussing the plans for the next days.

"It's not a big deal," Lei said, for about the third time. "I only have Tiare and Marcella as attendants. Stevens has his brother and Pono standing up for him. Tomorrow Stevens's family and my grandfather get in, and I've got a final dress fitting. I don't know how I'm going to fit it all in with work—I can't leave this case just when it's heating up. It's about conservation of these amazing endangered birds on Haleakala." She sketched a few details about the unusual case.

"Doesn't matter what's going on with your case," Wayne said. "Day after tomorrow, it'll be time to let Pono handle it."

Lei knew he was right, but she couldn't imagine being

able to just walk away.

On the way home, she called her partner, navigating the winding, two-lane road along the picturesque coast with her Bluetooth in. "What did you find out from the latest victim?"

"They wouldn't let me talk to him. Took two hours to extract the arrow and stabilize him. He's still heavily sedated, but I did get a cuff put on him in the hospital bed. The staff thought it was ridiculous. He's in no shape to talk, let alone get out of the bed, but I insisted."

"Good. Did you find anything in the stuff we took off of him? Like where he's staying?"

"Haven't had time. Dropped it all off into evidence. We'll have to go through that tomorrow. Speaking of, Tiare tells me you're picking up Sophie and Marcella and having a fitting tomorrow. Why don't you let me take the case from here? Your family's in town. It's time to switch gears, get into wedding mode."

"No. I can still work tomorrow."

Her partner was silent. She pictured him rubbing his lips beneath the bristling mustache, his forehead knit. He sighed. "Lei, seriously. You gotta let go. The world will go on without you for a couple of weeks."

"I feel bad leaving the case when it's just heating up again, leaving you to deal with everything." Lei couldn't help noticing the shining golden light of sunset gilding the galleons of cumulous cloud scudding over the ocean. Even in the most ordinary moments, Maui was an ever-changing visual feast.

"What, you don't trust me to handle the case?" Pono had injected hardness into his bass voice.

"I do trust you. You know I do. It's not that." Lei squeezed the medallion at her throat.

"What is it, then?"

"I'm—nervous. Working helps me."

"Well, tough. Take a Xanax."

"I'll be in to the hospital to interview the poacher with you before I pick up Sophie and Marcella at the airport."

"Would you just pick up your girlfriends in the morning, and let me handle things for once?"

He clicked off abruptly, but Lei knew behind the gruffness he was just trying to help her. Too bad. She was going to talk to that victim, and Pono could be pissy about it all he wanted.

Lei pulled into her driveway and rolled the gate shut behind her. The little cottage was dark and cool under its shading trees, empty and silent but for her dog's ecstatic greeting. She missed Stevens with a sudden and terrible longing, but she resisted calling him.

She'd made her bed, and now she'd lie in it—alone.

Chapter 14

Lei sat down on one of the molded plastic chairs next to the hospital bed with Pono standing behind her. The victim from Haleakala was propped against pillows, his face bleached-looking in the overhead fluorescent lights, eyes closed. The nurse, checking his pulse, frowned at them. "I don't think he speaks English."

"Have you been able to determine what language he does speak?" Lei asked.

"No, but I don't think he understands our questions." The woman tweaked the handcuff on the man's wrist. "He's weak from loss of blood and he's on a ton of medication. Are you sure this is necessary?"

"We need to make sure he doesn't escape."

"Well, he's not going anywhere." She eyed them once more, gave an audible sniff, and left. Lei took out a small handheld voice recorder and turned it on. She stated the location and names of all present, including the name on the man's passport.

She shook the wounded man's arm. "Wake up."

Several shakes later, the man opened his eyes. Focusing on them, he burst into a spate of foreign language that Lei was pretty sure was Chinese.

"Do you speak English? We need to find out who shot you," Lei said, slowing her words down.

"I never see," the man said, his words heavily accented. "Why I am...?" He seemed to grope for words and shook the handcuff.

"We need to find out more about your situation. Do you speak Mandarin?"

The man nodded.

"What is your name?"

"Chen Xiaoping," the man said. Lei thought that sounded dimly like the name on his passport. She had him repeat it, and she spelled the words out phonetically in her notebook.

"I will be back with a translator to interview you further," Pono said. "What were you doing in Waikamoi? On the mountain?"

The man looked down, folded his lips, and shook his head.

"Who were you catching the birds for?" Lei caught his eye, made a fluttering gesture with her hands. "Who? The birds?"

Now the man lay back and shut his eyes—and though Lei shook his arm, he was done talking.

She handed Pono her notes out in the hall. "Hope you can find out more with a translator. Seems like a Chinese national to me. Wonder what you'll find in his room."

"Probably a pile of fake IDs," Pono said, disgustedly. "I hope he's the last poacher we find on the mountain."

Lei pulled the Tacoma up to the curb outside the Kahului Airport for the second time in two days. Marcella Scott and Sophie Ang stood on the sidewalk, each so striking they caused heads to turn. Marcella wore a clingy wrap dress splashed with scarlet poppies and little heeled gold sandals. She waved, large brown eyes brightening at the sight of Lei, long chocolate hair tossing in the Maui wind.

Sophie Ang was a tall, toned foil to Marcella's feminine glory. Sophie's regal cropped head and sculpted shoulders were set off by a crisp white tank the tech agent wore with a pair of slim black pants and ballet flats. The only feminine touch Sophie wore were baroque pearls the size of cherries dangling from her ears, drawing the eye to lustrous golden-brown skin.

Lei felt frizzy and plain in comparison, but she shoved

those feelings aside, excited to see her friends. She jumped out of the truck. "Welcome to Maui! Can't believe you both made it over."

"Ken will be here tomorrow for the wedding," Marcella said, referring to Lei's former partner in the FBI, as they hugged. "Said he wouldn't miss it."

"Good. Throw your stuff in the back of the truck. I want to take you for a drive to see where my latest case is. Marcella, you're going to have to change."

"That's what I told her," Sophie said.

"Well, hell." Marcella looked around the busy airport, hands on her hips. "Should I change here?"

"No. We've got to go to my fitting next. You can change there."

They drove to Ohana Wedding Design in Wailuku. Estelle, the designer, and Marcella greeted each other with cries and cheek kisses like long-lost friends, while Lei and Sophie exchanged a nervous glance—but both of her friends exclaimed when Lei stood on the little dais in the dress. Estelle buzzed around tweaking, but the gown needed very little adjusting, and Marcella assured Estelle they'd pick it up tomorrow morning.

It wasn't long before they were headed up the mountain. "You aren't taking us up here to pick our brains for your investigation, are you?" Marcella asked, having changed into jeans and running shoes. "Because I'm pretty sure you should be on vacation as of now, and I'm in no mood to tromp around looking for clues for your case. I'd rather have a mimosa on that deck at Stevens's apartment and look at the ocean."

"I have no ulterior motives," Lei said. "I just want to show my two friends the beauty of a place I wish I'd seen before it became a crime scene. We can't go into the preserve, but I can show you Hosmer's Grove and the birds we're fighting for, at least." She described the birds and their habitat, how beautiful it was.

Sophie chimed in from the backseat, "Yes, until you called and asked me to put an alert out for someone poaching these birds, I wasn't even aware of them. Why don't we see them at lower elevations?"

"Avian malaria was brought in by nonnative birds, and it's carried by mosquitoes. When these native birds are bit by mosquitoes, they die. They haven't had time to develop immunity to the malaria before they're being wiped out. They can only survive at the elevations where there are no mosquitoes."

"So birds like cardinals, mynahs, and doves that we see all the time are immune to malaria?" Sophie asked.

"That's right." The women drove on in silence. Marcella and Sophie craned to look down the sweeping grandeur of the flank of Haleakala to the narrow waist of the island, where the ocean gleamed visible on both sides of the figure-eight shape of two volcanic ranges.

"This island is really something," Marcella said. "I thought Oahu was pretty, but wow."

"Maui has these vistas," Lei said. "Having lived on the Big Island, Kaua`i, Oahu, and now here, I can tell you each island has unique features to fall in love with."

"I'd like to try some of my run hiking here," Sophie said. "I've gotten into long distance outdoor running this last year, and I found a club that focuses on using the hiking trails. I bet there are some great places to run here."

"Absolutely." Lei glanced back at Sophie's face—her friend's features reminded Lei of the famous head of Nefertiti sculpture. She and Sophie had been beginning a friendship when Lei decided to leave the FBI to come back to Maui, and Lei felt like they'd never had time to really get to know each other. "Maybe you could come spend a weekend with us, and I'll take you on some long runs. Keiki would love it. She hasn't been getting enough exercise lately."

"After the wedding," Marcella said. "And the honeymoon. And after all of your cases wrap up…"

"Yeah, those just keep coming." Lei halted the truck at the entry booth and showed her park pass, and they drove in, turning left onto the short drive to Hosmer's Grove. "I'm not sure how I'm going to be able to be gone a whole ten days."

Marcella leered. "I'm pretty sure Stevens has plans to

keep your mind off dead bodies."

Lei grinned back. "I know he wants to try."

"When am I going to see him? Gotta give him my condolences."

Lei pulled the truck into a parking stall. A short path wound through eucalyptus trees and tall yellow-blossomed *mamane* bushes directly ahead of them. "At the wedding."

Something in her voice must have made Marcella suspicious, because she frowned, turning to Lei. "Something wrong? You've got the runaway bride reputation now. I'm sure he's nervous."

"Not as nervous as I am." Lei jumped out of the truck and slammed the door. "Trail's through here." She didn't give Marcella time to quiz her any further, instead forging out into the underbrush.

Sophie didn't let her get away. The woman's long legs easily kept stride with Lei.

"So where are these famous birds?" Sophie asked. The hike was short, ending in a gulch overlook filled with ferns, sandalwood, and blossoming ohia trees. Lei held a finger to her lips as Marcella crashed through branches behind them, muttering.

"See?" Lei whispered, pointing to the showy *i`iwi* hopping its feeding pattern over a nearby ohia tree. They stayed a half hour or so and spotted a green `*amakihi* and two bright red, short-beaked `*apapane*. Sitting on the bench, observing the peaceful beauty of the birds in their native habitat, Lei could see the magic of the place casting its spell on her friends. They walked back to her truck in silence, and in the parking lot, Lei frowned, spotting Takama's navy-blue Ford with its distinctive pipe racks.

"Hey. Ranger Takama's here. He's been helping with the case. Maybe he'll be able to let us into the preserve." Lei walked briskly to the ranger's truck, looking around. Takama was nowhere in sight. Lei leaned on the truck and dug her phone out of her pocket. She'd inputted Takama's number at the beginning of the case, and as she scrolled through her contacts, she spotted something out of the corner of her eye—a curved shape in the space behind Takama's seat. Pressing his number and hoping there was cell service, she swiveled to cup her hand, cutting the glare so she could see into the truck's window—and what she saw made her tighten her grip on the phone.

"Hello?" Takama's voice sounded tinny.

"Ranger Takama? This is Lieutenant Texeira. Happened to be up here at Hosmer's Grove and your truck is here—are you nearby?"

"I'm about five minutes away. Would love an update on the case."

"Of course," Lei said smoothly. "I'll be waiting by your truck."

She hit Off and turned to Marcella and Ang. "What do

you see behind his seat?"

Marcella leaned in, looked. "A bow. One of those fancy ones."

"Yeah. That's what we think was used to shoot our poachers."

The three law enforcement officers were lined up against Takama's truck when he appeared, carrying a bag of litter, a backpack, and some tools. He unlocked the gate and came toward them. "What brings you up here, Lieutenant Texeira?"

"Recreation, actually," Lei said, gesturing to her casual jeans. "These are my friends, Agents Scott and Ang of the FBI."

"Are you working the case as well?" Takama asked them, slinging his bag of trash into the back of the truck.

"Informal consult," Marcella said.

"The victim of yesterday's shooting is in stable condition in the hospital," Lei said. "Speaking of, I notice you have a compound bow in your vehicle."

Takama carried himself with the straight back of a much younger man, and his strength was evident as he unloaded the shovel, machete, and backpack he'd been carrying into the back of the truck. He turned to her, his dark eyes affronted. "Yes. What of it? We all use these weapons to bring down ungulates when we can."

"You know a bow is the murder weapon. I'd like your

permission to check this one, rule it out."

Takama appeared to be struggling with his temper. His lips were tight, brows furrowed, but he inclined his head. "Arrows, too?"

"Please."

She took the weapon, holding it with a napkin Takama gave her. Marcella took the arrows in their plastic case. "Thank you. I just want to rule you out as a suspect. Who else of the Park Service staff has a compound bow?"

"Pretty much everyone."

Lei shook her head. "We really missed the boat on this. I wish you'd said something." Takama just glared, and she realized it was probably a stretch that he would offer up his Park Service colleagues for investigation. "What about the Hawaiian Bird Conservatory people?"

"I think that's your job to figure out," Takama said, getting into his truck and slamming the door. He pulled out abruptly, leaving her holding the bow.

The bow was bulky, weighing only about three pounds as she hefted it, made of black carbon fiber with an architectural look. A broad spread of pulleys, molded grip, and flexible cords gave the bow its power. She had to resist the urge to cock it, just to experience how it would feel to aim.

Lei read the logo on the bow: "BowTech. I wonder how much these run."

"I think that brand's between four and six hundred dollars," Sophie said. "Nice rig."

"You ever do any shooting with these?" Lei asked her as they walked back to her truck.

"Yes. I like to be as familiar as possible with a variety of weapons," Sophie said, with the precise understatement that was such a part of her personality.

"You'd better call Pono," Marcella said as they got into Lei's truck. "Looks like you guys missed a major lead here, and you're off the case as of now—we have girl time planned this evening. The three of us are going to the Grand Wailea Spa in lieu of a bachelorette party."

"Dammit on missing this lead," Lei said, speed-dialing Pono after stowing the bow behind the seats. She got ahold of her partner, explaining about obtaining Takama's bow as she drove.

"I'll drop it by the lab for analysis," she told him. "But you'll have to subpoena all the bows and arrows from the Hawaiian Bird Conservatory staff and volunteers. I don't know why we didn't realize so many of them might have these weapons."

Pono cursed. "I'll get things rolling, but the guys and I are taking Stevens bowling for his bachelor party. I won't be hanging out in the lab for the next few days."

"Okay. Well, we need time to get the names and subpoenas anyway."

"We nothing! You have bride duties now! Get to it!" Her partner hung up on her, the second time in two days.

"I'm forbidden to do anything more on the case," Lei told the agents.

"I told you that," Marcella said. "We're spa bound. The only person I know who needs a massage more than you is Sophie."

Lei swung by the station and submitted the bow and arrows to the evidence clerk. Waiting for Clarice to fill out the inventory slip, Lei looked down at her phone, thinking of Stevens, worried he hadn't called by now. She wondered if he was waiting for her to do something, decided that was probably it—after all, she'd been the one to ask for "space." She texted: *I love you. Can't wait to marry you tomorrow.*

Waited a long moment. No response.

"All set," Clarice said, and hit Enter on her computer, peering at Lei over her glasses. "Here's a little something for you and Stevens." She slid a square card envelope over to Lei. "I'm sorry I can't make it to the wedding; I'm working, as usual."

"Wow, Clarice," Lei said, feeling her cheeks warm as she took the card. "That's really sweet. Thank you. I'll see you in a couple of weeks."

"Have fun," the clerk said, and winked broadly. "I mean, have a *lot* of fun."

Lei's face was still hot when they got on the road to Wailea for a night of feminine debauchery. Stevens still hadn't texted back.

Chapter 15

L ei woke up the next morning by unwilling degrees, glad the wedding didn't begin until four p.m.

Last day as a single woman.

She was glad she'd resisted Marcella and Aunty Rosario's pleadings to join them overnight at the mansion—she wanted a little time alone.

Keiki, alert for any stirrings, came up to whine in Lei's face, threatening to lick her if she wasn't let out. Lei swung her legs to the side of the bed, getting out and sliding her arms into the coral silk robe Stevens had given her a few months ago, saying, "I love the way this color makes your skin look." Remembering that moment made her smile, but when she checked her phone, plugged in by the bed, he still hadn't texted her. She frowned, picked it up, and called, needing to hear his voice. It went straight to voice mail.

"Hi, Michael. I just wondered if you got my text.

Because—I love you. And I can't wait to marry you today. Call me when you get this, please. I'm nervous." Lei hung up, setting the phone down, feeling anxiety rise up, strangling her. She thumped her chest to knock it loose.

She needed a run.

Lei bundled her hair into a rubber band and pulled on her running clothes. Keiki, seeing these signs, whimpered with eagerness, hind end gyrating and toenails clicking. Lei slid the phone into the pocket of her shorts.

Running down the narrow, jungle-choked road a few minutes later, Keiki galloping beside her, Lei's mind wandered around like worrying a sore tooth.

Her aunty and father were working hard at the vacation rental house. She'd dropped Marcella and Sophie off there late last night. Their plan was to help prep during the day. Her own job was to pick up the finished dress and get ready. The hair and makeup people were arriving at the mansion timed for when Lei got there after picking up the dress. They were all supposed to take a limo from the mansion to Kanaha Park.

Lei and her friends had enjoyed a lovely evening soaking in the baths, getting massages, and having drinks and dinner in the fancy restaurant the hotel sported, built over a tide pool with schools of fish swimming beneath. Lei had only one drink, but in spite of all the activity of the day, she'd had a hard time falling asleep.

Her mind ticked over the details of the wedding. They hadn't had a rehearsal, as Tiare said the format was so simple and casual, so it seemed like the next time she'd be seeing Stevens was at the ceremony.

She really needed to hear his voice.

She took her phone out, frowned at the blank screen. He still hadn't called. Just then the phone rang, and she answered it quickly, seeing Pono's number. She stepped off the narrow road onto the shoulder, stretching her hamstrings. Keiki flopped in the damp grass, panting.

"Hey, partner," she said.

"You sound out of breath. Running?"

"Yeah. I'm nervous. I told you. What's up? You didn't keep my groom out too late partying, did you?"

"No, got him home at a decent hour. We won't even have any embarrassing YouTube videos from the night," Pono said. "Just wanted to let you know I'm going into the station this morning to get started on the bow you brought in and the other subpoenas. So don't worry about it. Captain already gave me Gerry Bunuelos to help out while you're gone."

"Oh good," Lei said, blowing out a breath of relief. She'd worked with the energetic detective on several cases. "Gerry's going to be a big help."

"I thought you'd like that. I hope it will let you relax a little more. So, see you at four o'clock at Kanaha Beach

Park."

"So Stevens—he's okay?" Lei found herself rubbing the medallion around her neck and let go of it deliberately.

"Sure. Seemed fine. Why?"

"Nothing. Just excited to be getting married today!" Lei said with false cheer.

"Just show up, Lei. Seriously. It's going to be okay. He's a good man, and he loves you. Let him."

"Sound advice from my oldest friend," Lei said, feeling tears prickle her eyes as a car whisked by. She looked out at the dense, multilayered jungle. "See you soon."

"Oh yeah, Tiare wants a few words." He handed the phone off to his wife.

"Lei, you must be so excited!" Tiare exclaimed.

"Actually, I'm terrified. I'm taking a run to calm down before I go pick up the dress."

"Don't worry about a thing. I've been on the phone with your dad and aunt; the food, the setup, the music, the photographer—it's all a go and should be smooth as silk. You just relax and think about all the sex you're going to be having later on tonight."

"Ha-ha," Lei said hollowly. Everybody seemed more in the mood for that than she was. Half the items Tiare had just mentioned hadn't even crossed her mind, and once again she felt inadequate—but that's why she had Tiare handling things, she told herself. "I gotta get going, Tiare. I'm on a schedule for the day."

"You sure are. Marcella and I will be backing you up at the ceremony, and like I said, it's all in hand. Don't worry about a thing but having fun."

"I can't thank you enough," Lei said. "See you soon." She slid the phone into her pocket, and this time ran as hard as she could, until the thoughts banging around in her head were silenced by the drumbeat of her heart.

Lei came out of Ohana Wedding Design in Wailuku, carrying the dress. She draped it in its plastic wrap, like a ghost on a hanger, over the seat beside her. Firing up the truck to drive to the oceanfront estate to get ready, Lei thought of one last thing she could do for the investigation, and doing it would help calm her down, keep her distracted for a little longer. Ranger Jacobsen had said he lived in Wailuku; she could swing by his place and pick up his bow for Pono and rule him out as a suspect.

She pulled down the Toughbook computer in its glovebox holder and typed Mark Jacobsen's name into the DMV database. Sure enough, his name and address popped up in a subdivision nearby.

He was probably at work. She should call first to see if he was home. If he wasn't, she'd save a trip, but if he was, he could have the weapon ready for her to pick up. He'd been so helpful with the investigation, she didn't imagine he'd insist on a subpoena. But when she checked, he hadn't listed a phone number on his license information.

Lei used her navigation system to find Jacobsen's house. The young ranger lived in a duplex in a quiet neighborhood in Wailuku Heights. Lei enjoyed the view down into the valley as she drove carefully over the speed tables in the pleasant suburban neighborhood landscaped in palm trees and well-groomed grass.

Jacobsen's truck, a black Tacoma, was parked in the driveway of his address. She pulled up behind his vehicle and got out, straightening folds in the creamy silk of the wedding dress draped over the passenger seat.

Jacobsen had left a single pair of rubber slippers resting on the rubber mat beside the door of the modest apartment. The door's wood finish was peeling from the sun. Lei knocked.

Nothing.

Her phone buzzed with a text. She slid it out of the pocket of her jeans, hoping it was Stevens. It was Marcella.

So excited for your big day! See you at one p.m.

Lei wished she felt the same way. Instead her stomach was roiling. It was only eleven thirty; there was still plenty of time until one, when she had to meet everyone at the house to primp for the ceremony. She slid the phone back into her pocket and knocked, louder this time.

Still nothing.

His truck was there. Perhaps there was a workshop or something in back, or perhaps he was just sleeping in. It was worth a look.

She walked around the front of the apartment and through the tidy front yard, bare of any ornamental plantings.

"Ranger Jacobsen?" she called. "Anybody home?"

Her phone buzzed again as she approached a wooden gate on the side of the house, and she looked down to pull it out of her pocket again.

Lei felt a sharp tug on her hair and heard a *thunk* across the yard; turning, she saw a black arrow quivering in the ornamental palm across the yard.

Instinct took over and she dove for the ground, face-planting into the cool, damp grass as the next arrow barely missed her, whizzing by in a silent blur of dark motion. The arrow shattered the spine of a palm frond, breaking it with a swish and crack.

She had to identify herself—maybe the ranger felt threatened, hadn't recognized her. "Jacobsen!" she yelled. "This is Lieutenant Texeira! Police, stop!"

In answer, another arrow buried itself in the ground.

Lei didn't have body armor on. She didn't have her weapon; her ID was in the truck. She'd been distracted, gotten sloppy, and dismissed pleasant-faced young Jacobsen as just a helpful ranger. Now she was pinned to the ground in the open, a proverbial sitting duck, with no real idea where he was shooting from.

Lei tucked her arms tight against her body and rolled as fast as she could across the lawn until she fetched up against the house. Looking back, she saw two arrows quivering in the earth where she'd been.

She dug her phone out of her pocket and called 911. "Officer needs assistance!" She identified herself and her badge number, flattening herself against the side of the house and slowly sliding to stand upright.

"Stay where you are, Lieutenant," the 911 operator said. "Do not try to follow the suspect. Help is on the way."

"Roger that," Lei said, and slid the phone back into her pocket. She was pretty sure that the angle of the house prevented him from getting a bead on her, but the thought of one of those hardened-steel, razor-edged arrows burying itself in her body didn't appeal. She'd seen the damage they could do.

From where she was, she heard thumps inside the house. He was escaping! She stayed as flat as she could, sidling along the building until she got to the gate. Reaching out a hand, she pressed down on the metal latch. It wouldn't budge—locked. She turned to look up just above her—a simple slider window was open, and only a screen separated her from access into the house.

She grabbed the top of the wooden fence, hoisted herself up, and swung a jeans-covered leg up to kick at the screen. It flew inward with a disturbing clatter.

Her arms were trembling. She didn't have strength to climb in yet, so she dropped back to the ground—but now she'd alerted Jacobsen to her whereabouts and provided a nice open window for him to shoot her from. How she wished she'd brought her Glock—but she hadn't planned on the stop going deadly. The smart course was to run back to her truck, get in, and lock the doors—she at least had a can of pepper spray in the glove box.

She jumped up to grasp the window frame—and heard the front door slam. He was going for his vehicle—but she'd blocked him in. He wouldn't be able to get away. He'd have to return to the house—unless he left on foot.

Lei hoisted herself up into the window frame, kicking her legs to propel herself over the ledge and into the room. The metal edge of the frame caught on the button of her jeans, digging into her hips and suddenly reminding her she might not be alone in her body—she might be putting someone else at risk too.

"Dammit," she muttered, thinking this kind of activity was another good reason she shouldn't be a mother. She landed gracelessly on the wood laminate floor of what appeared to be Jacobsen's bedroom, if the untidy twin bed and piles of clothes on the floor were any indication. She scrambled to her feet, looking for a weapon, anything she could use if Jacobsen came back in—and spotted an aluminum bat propped behind the door.

Lei grabbed it and hefted it, walking on the balls of her feet to the doorway, peering down the hall.

She heard the roar of Jacobsen's truck starting. What was the point of that, when she had him blocked in? Then she heard the rumble of his garage door going up. She trotted through the house to the front door in time to see Jacobsen pull deep into the garage, trying to get enough space to reverse out past her vehicle.

Armed with just a bat, Lei had no hope of stopping the truck, and she didn't want to step out of the doorway and expose herself in case he had a weapon. Looking around frantically, she spotted several of the bows she'd been after hanging on a rack on the wall—and beside them, a quiver of arrows. She ran over and grabbed one of the lightweight, bulky contraptions off the wall along with a handful of arrows and dashed back to the door.

The black Tacoma was already reversing past her truck, and it slammed into the side, tearing off her mirror and scraping down the paint.

"Shit!" Lei exclaimed as she loaded an arrow into the channel above the grip. She cocked the string back, a surprising effort that, once cocked, was easy to hold. She aligned it with her ear and, sighting down the channel, shot the arrow at the truck's tire.

It hit the ground and bounced, spinning. Clearly her archery skills needed work.

She cocked another arrow as the Tacoma reversed into the road and, burning rubber, roared away. She shot, but the arrow just pinged harmlessly off the back bumper.

"Gotta work on my aim," Lei muttered, lowering the bow. She reengaged the 911 operator and described the fleeing truck and its make and model. "Get an APB out on it right away."

Next she called Pono. "Got a lot of bows here in Jacobsen's living room. Happy to report I'm also still alive."

"What! What the hell are you up to now?"

"Need a warrant to search Jacobsen's house and subpoenas for all his bows and equipment for hunting. He seems to have a lot." She swiveled, glancing around. "He took several very close shots at me and fled. I think we just had a major break in the case. I'm calling Tiare to put the wedding off."

"No way! You have too many people coming, too many people who have spent money to get here for your special day. Listen to your oldest friend—you're replaceable on the job. Gerry Bunuelos will be filling in for you, and I think now is a great time to break him in."

"No." Lei sucked a breath, blew it out. Squeezed the pendant at her throat so hard it dug painfully into her hand. "I'm the bride. I'm making this call. And I need another twenty-four to forty-eight hours to solve this case."

"Are you in the house?"

"Yes. I had to get out of firing range and try to get him, but he tore up my truck pulling out instead."

"I'm on my way. I've got the subpoenas, but anything you find in there without a warrant will be fruit of the poisoned tree, so get out of there now. I'll talk sense into you when I get there." Pono hung up just as the wail of sirens announced backup.

Lei set the bow she'd used down on the top step and sighed. There was no point in rehanging it on the wall; she already had to explain how she was inside and had come to be using it. Explaining the situation and completing all the reports was definitely going to make her late, anyway.

Lei trotted down the steps to her truck, moaning over the mangled paint job and dangling side mirror. Her door was dented in, but she was able to open it to verify that the dress still draped in lovely splendor over the seat. She sat in the front seat and made several very difficult phone calls, postponing the wedding. Tiare, her aunt and father, and Marcella all started out outraged and ended resigned when she wouldn't be swayed. When she was done with that and still sweating from the conflict, she called Stevens.

He still didn't pick up. "Listen. We've had a major break in the case. I am postponing the wedding until tomorrow. It's a drag, I know, but I can't leave until we wrap it up further. Hope you understand. This is nothing about you and me. But please call—I need to hear your voice." She turned the phone off completely and opened the door to go deal with the aftermath.

Chapter 16

Pono handed Lei a Styrofoam cup of coffee swimming with little white creamer chunks as they sat in the conference room of Kahului Police Department, waiting for Captain Omura to join them for their case update.

"I can't believe you." Pono narrowed his eyes and shook his head. "You've got me in serious trouble at home, Lei. Tiare's pissed, and when Mama's not happy, ain't no one happy."

"Can't be helped," Lei said, and set her jaw. She glanced at the clock on the wall. Four p.m. She should be walking down an aisle of flowers right about now, but she wasn't, and that was just the way it was. The job came first. Always would.

To her credit, Captain Omura, when she joined them, said nothing about the change in wedding plans. Gerry Bunuelos, a short, wiry Filipino, followed her.

"Gerry's joining the case. Jacobsen still hasn't been located, but we had a call from Haleakala Ranch. They found the truck abandoned on ranch land near some bird habitat. Not only that. The ranch employee who found the vehicle reports blood in the back of the truck."

"So he was injured while fleeing?" Lei frowned. She hadn't actually seen the young man shoot at her, but he'd certainly been moving fast—not moving like someone who was injured.

"Did you see anything in the truck bed when the vehicle was leaving the scene?" Pono asked her.

"I—dammit. I don't think so. That's weird about the blood. Did he nick his hand and smear it on the back or something?"

"No. The ranch employee reports the amount of blood in the truck bed is significant, more like a puddle. Could be he was injured and went to lie down in the truck bed. We don't know. Either way, I already called for the K-9 unit to meet you where the truck is so you can track Jacobsen in the forest. ETA is sixty minutes from now."

Pono's thick brows had drawn together as he looked at Lei. "Can you remember anything about the truck, anything in the back?"

Lei closed her eyes, trying to remember. She'd pulled up behind Jacobsen's black Tacoma. The garage door had been down. She'd been distracted, fussing with her dress lying on the seat. She tried to remember the back of the truck. "There might have been a tarp or something in the back. I'm sorry. I just wasn't paying attention. I never should have stopped by."

"No argument there," Omura said, inspecting her manicure. "But since you did, it knocked some interesting things loose. We might as well make the best of it. Gerry, stay here and study the file. I want you to be prepared to take over for Texeira. I'm only allowing her twenty-four more hours before mandatory leave for her wedding."

"Yes, sir," Gerry said, taking the file she pushed over to him. Lei opened her mouth, and Omura narrowed her eyes and leveled a shiny red nail at Lei.

"Twenty-four hours. Tomorrow at four we are all going to a wedding, and Gerry can carry on your duties. Period."

"Yes, sir," Lei said. No other response was possible. She followed Pono's stiff back to the weapons locker for Kevlar vests and extra weapons.

As they got on the road for the Haleakala Ranch entrance outside of Makawao in Pono's truck, Lei broke the tense silence. "I wonder if Sophie Ang ever tracked down anything on the Internet looking for the birds."

"Haven't heard from her," Pono said. "You were the one who spent the evening with her last night."

"Didn't come up in conversation. And I don't want to call her right now." Lei's phone was still off in her pocket.

For just a little while, she could shut out all the clamoring voices, even those closest to her, and stay focused on the objective. "What's going on with Kingston? Does anyone know where he's at?"

"Deported to Canada. His visa was canceled. Just heard the news on my way over to Jacobsen's."

"You sure he got on the plane?"

"Heard an officer accompanied him to the airport."

"Hmm." Lei frowned. "Kingston seemed so fanatical. I'm actually having a hard time seeing Jacobsen as someone so bird crazy he'd commit murder, but not Kingston."

"We have to follow the evidence, and right now the evidence is pointing to Jacobsen."

Lei and Pono bounced along the rutted dirt road, following an employee from Haleakala Ranch, who drove ahead, unlocking the gates for them. The fields were rich and lush, dotted with volcanic rocks and a few clusters of runaway prickly gorse and stands of eucalyptus. The SUV carrying the tracking dog, Blue, his handler, Freddie Lee, and a partner, followed them. Lei's heart rate was up, excitement to catch Jacobsen finally banishing the angst brought on by postponing her wedding.

They reached a clearing with a final fence and pulled up beside Jacobsen's black Tacoma. Wild green forest beyond beckoned Lei as she jumped down from Pono's truck. She pulled on a pair of rubber gloves and looked into the bed of the truck. Sure enough, there was a significant bloodstain pooled in the metal channels.

"That could be deer or pig blood," Pono said. "That's kind of how my truck looks after hunting."

"We have to test it." Lei got out her crime kit and took several swabs. She turned on her high-powered light and shone it over the truck. Smears and blots lit up here and there. "We might have some prints here."

Blue barked, a deep, eager sound, as Freddie Lee unloaded him from the SUV they'd pulled up in.

"We'll have to come back and work the truck over. Let's mark it and leave it for later." She and Pono draped crime scene tape over the black Tacoma, and as she did so, Lei couldn't help remembering another black Tacoma and the part it had played in her life.

"This brings up the question—with this restricted access, how would Jacobsen have got through these locked gates?" Lei took her Kevlar vest out from behind her seat and slipped it on over her head.

"I thought of that. The rangers are issued keys, in case they need to go retrieve something or respond to a park-related emergency on shared land. Jacobsen had apparently checked the keys out two weeks ago, and they hadn't been returned."

Lei bundled her hair into a ponytail and pulled a dark green-billed hat down over her curls.

"I called and spoke to Takama about Jacobsen," Pono said. "He was pretty shocked Jacobsen was being looked at as a suspect. Said the guy was hardworking and dedicated, but didn't show a lot of—what did he call it—'outside the box thinking.' He also, according to Takama, was fairly new to Maui and had gained his tracking experience working in other parks."

"Hmm," Lei said, frowning as she checked her Glock, expelling the clip to check it was full, ramming it home inside the cool pebbled grip. She patted the cargo pants pockets, checking that she'd brought a spare clip and had packed Taser, pepper spray, and handcuffs. She slung on a light backpack loaded with crime kit and water bottle.

Lee and his partner, Kahakauwila, also checked their gear. Blue was already questing about on the ground after being given Jacobsen's hat to sniff. Lei lifted her feet to look at the soles of her shoes for trapped seeds—she didn't want to bring anything new into the forest.

Blue flung up his head and gave a single bark, tugging on his leash to go through the gate in front of a trail that led into the forest. "Dog's ready to work," Lee said.

Chapter 17

They all moved at a fast walk, single file behind the dog. Blue trotted confidently up the path.

The Haleakala Ranch employee who'd unlocked the gates brought up the rear.

"Sure seems to know where he's going," the young man said. He'd introduced himself as Henry Ferreira, and they'd brought him along to answer any questions about the ranch or flora and fauna they encountered.

"This dog helped us catch our last perp within an hour," Pono said. "So tell us more about this forest while we're going through here. Pretty big path here. Where does it go?"

"This is a shared sanctuary area called the Maile Trail," Ferreira said. They'd begun to climb, and the trail had gotten narrower. Blue showed no signs of slowing down. Lei spotted the shiny, dark green leaves of the sacred maile vine twining around the trunks of guava, ohia, and old-growth koa trees, interspersed with thick clumps of kahili ginger, whose stems grew long, glossy sword-shaped leaves forming fernlike patterns. Tall spires of sweet-smelling blossoms thickened the air with scent.

"We try to manage the invasives, like all this kahili ginger, which really came from India." Ferreira made an arm gesture encompassing the vast stand of six-foot-tall, showy plants. "Ginger's really hard to kill because it spreads via rhizome. If even one little root is left in after you dig it out, it'll come back."

"Why is it important to get rid of?" Lei asked, her heart pumping as the trail narrowed and the incline increased. Hundreds of the gingers had been hacked down beside the trail, but new sprouts were already growing.

"Well, it chokes everything else out. It's pretty, though," Ferreira said. Lei thought the air had a velvety texture to it from the acres of rich orange, yellow, and white ginger blossoms.

Suddenly, Blue bayed again and turned off the path into a hacked-down stand of ginger plants, dragging Lee over to a patch of turned-over soil.

"Uh-oh," Lei said.

"Seems like a pretty good spot for a body dump. If we hadn't used the dog, we'd never have found this," Pono said.

Lei took her backpack off, removing her crime kit and putting on gloves. Blue continued to circle the mound of disturbed earth, whining.

Lei and Pono used their hands to dig, and it wasn't long before the coppery tang of blood rose through the earth, causing Blue to put his head back and howl. The dog was still agitated when Lei uncovered a portion of torso clad in a camouflage T-shirt. They had enough confirmation for Pono to call for the medical examiner.

"I wonder who it is," Lei said, hanging her soil-covered, gloved hands off the ends of her bent knees.

"Seems that there must be more than one perp involved in this situation," Pono said, frowning. "Dr. Gregory said he's about forty-five minutes out. Henry, can you drive back and open the gates for him?"

"Sure." The young man, looking green, trotted off quickly.

Blue had begun casting around on the ground again, and he gave an assertive bark. "He's picked up a scent," his handler said. "Do you want to follow it?"

"Can you tell if it's Jacobsen or someone else he's wanting to follow?" Lei asked, straightening up and stripping off her gloves.

"Can't tell, but the scent will be related to Jacobsen in some way," the dog's handler said.

"Then we should follow it. If we have anything to follow,

we should get it while we can," Lei said to Pono. "But someone needs to stay and secure the body."

"We should go," Freddie said, gesturing to his partner. "We can run down whoever it is."

"It's our case," Pono said. "One of us should go. Lei, you stay with the body. It's my turn to fall into a gulch."

"No. You know I'm faster," Lei said. "Besides, I outrank you. Stay with the body, Pono." She winked at her glowering partner. "Put up the tape around it. Probably won't get the perp, since whoever buried the body has had several hours' head start—but I need a workout."

Pono folded his arms and scowled as she and the K-9 unit set off up the trail.

Blue really seemed to have the scent, towing his handler up the path, which grew increasingly narrow and steep. The trail finally dead-ended at a tall fence with a built-in step to climb over it. The hound, stopped by this obstacle, trotted back and forth.

"This must be the edge of the fenced conservation lands," Lei said. "The fence is to keep the goats, deer, and pigs out."

"Seems pretty effective," Kahakauwila said. "The scent seems to continue on the other side."

The two helped the dog over the barrier, and Lei followed them.

The trail, hardly more than a track now, wound back

and forth through a thick jungle of maile vine and ohia and koa trees. Ferns and *olapa* plants, their slender leaves shimmering, moved in an almost imperceptible breeze. As before, Lei felt her jangled nerves settling in the forest, even with the deadly discovery they'd just made and the possibility of danger ever-present. Sounds reduced to the clink of the dog's chain, the panting of their breath as they wound their way through the overgrown jungle, the padding of their feet, the sweet calls of the native birds as coins of golden light fell through the canopy around them.

Lei wondered who was in that shallow grave. If it was Jacobsen, it meant he had an unknown partner, or had somehow been involved with the shootings. If it wasn't, then Jacobsen was the one Blue was so earnestly seeking. She'd been so wrong in her estimation of the young ranger as to be embarrassing.

Blue suddenly tugged off the trail, and now the going was really rough. Lei clambered over rotting fallen logs covered with moss and lichen, through tight clumps of ferns, around trees leaning in all directions, until they came to the steep edge of another gulch.

Blue sat back on his haunches, panting, as Kahakauwila and Lee looked around. "What do you think?" Lee whispered to Lei.

Lei could hear the tinkle of a stream, hidden by ferns, at the bottom of the gulch. "If he's camping out here, he's going to be by water. If he comes this way, or came this way in the past, there must be a way down." She kept her voice low.

"I think there would be more signs that he's climbed down," Lee said. "I don't see a trail, any broken growth, nothing."

"What is Blue telling you?" They all looked at the dog, who was lying down, tongue hanging out in apparent exhaustion.

"He's lost the scent here," Lee whispered.

"Well, I think there's some reason he led us here. I'll find a way down, look around." Lei took off her backpack, chugged down half a bottle of water. She then scouted along the edge, finding a spot where the grade was not quite as steep. Holding on to clumps of fern, she lowered herself over the side and picked her way to the bottom of the gulch. It was so covered with ferns at the bottom that she couldn't see back up to the edge. Instead the ferns created a tunnel of green, lit with sunshine from above, as the stream chuckled over slippery dark stones.

Lei squatted beside the stream, letting her eyes drift in "see mode" over everything around her. The water followed the gentle slope of the canyon down toward the sea. Taller ferns arched over the steep dirt-and-rock banks with tender, trembling maidenhair and bright green mosses growing closer to the water.

It was an enchanted grotto—except for the straight line

of a bowstring, foreign in the natural setting. A bow, painted in camouflage colors, was caught among the rocks, almost blending with the broken branches it was mixed with. Lei stood and made her way to the weapon, which had lodged between some stones. She put gloves on to pick it up, but there were no further clues to be had from the weapon itself, at least that she could determine at that moment. She searched thoroughly for any arrows, finding none.

Back at the top of the gulch, sweaty and disheveled, Lei held up the bow. "Found what he was ditching here. Let's see if Blue can pick anything else up."

Blue didn't find anything new, and he ended up leading them back down to the body site, where Dr. Gregory and his assistant, Tanaka, were already hunched over the mound of soil.

Lei held up the bow for Pono to see. "Pretty sure this is significant."

"Good. Anything else?"

"The perp pitched it into a gulch. Nothing else down there, but I definitely got that workout."

"Do you guys need us any longer? We have to do a missing person search down the hill," Kahakauwila said.

"No, but thanks for all your help. I hope we don't need you any more on this case," Lei said. "Can I pet Blue?"

"We don't like to distract him when he's working, but since we're done, it's okay." Lee had Blue sit, and Lei squatted to rub behind Blue's long, floppy ears. The hound blinked long-lashed, soulful brown eyes and shut them in bliss.

"Good boy," she said. "Great work today."

Blue wagged his tail so hard it seemed like he might sprain it, and Lee tweaked his leash to lead him away. The dog glanced back at the shallow grave and what was being uncovered and gave another low, sorrowful howl.

Chapter 18

Lei slipped another pair of gloves on and knelt beside Dr. Gregory. He and his assistant, Tanaka, wore masks and long rubber gloves. They used trowels and wide paintbrushes to uncover the body as if it were a specimen at an archeological dig.

"Anything I can do?" Lei asked.

"Yeah. Why don't you and Pono move the dirt we take out farther away and do another check through it for any useful trace?" Gregory swiped his arm across his forehead, leaving a muddy streak. Under the rubber coveralls, he was wearing a bright aloha shirt decorated with hula dancers.

Pono turned back, his phone to his ear, holding up a finger. "I'm updating the captain," he said.

Lei moved the dirt away from the grave and sifted it through her hands, piling it a couple of feet away from the body.

Gregory glanced up and around. "Beautiful out here. What's with all the chopped-down ginger?" Lei told him what Ferreira had shared earlier. Pono rejoined them just as they got to the victim's face.

Tanaka used her paintbrush to gently dislodge the dirt from familiar features. "Six-foot white male, late twenties or early thirties," Gregory said. "Brown hair. Anyone recognize him?" Gregory turned to look at Lei and Pono.

"It's Mark Jacobsen," Lei said. She rocked back on her heels and looked at Pono. "He was our suspect, but it turns out he's a victim. I don't know what this means."

A long pause. No one else had anything to say. Lei was sickened by sorrow and anger, looking at the young ranger's gentle face, dirt filling his mouth and nostrils. Someone had murdered him and dumped him here. She wondered if he'd been the one to shoot at her—or if he'd been dead, lying in the back of his own truck, when she'd pulled up to his house.

"I already checked the pockets for ID—nothing. I'll take prints," Dr. Gregory said.

"I don't think he'll be in the system unless he has a record," Pono said. "Visual ID on the body by us should be enough, and I confirm this is Jacobsen, the ranger we'd worked with."

"Cause of death appears to be an arrow wound." Gregory pointed to the nub of black fletching protruding from the man's chest. "Looks like the killer got him right through the heart. Whoever is taking these shots is damn good with a bow."

"I know how hard it is to hit something," Lei said. "I took a shot at the tires of Jacobsen's truck and it was a total fail."

"In all these cases, the shooter hasn't removed the arrow," Pono said. "The arrow's a lead. It can be matched to others. It might carry trace. It's interesting that the killer left them."

"Be pretty messy to take them out," Lei said. "That could cause other trace, a cascade effect with wound bleed and transfer."

"Or the killer could be squeamish about what he—or she—is doing," Pono said.

"Well, since I've handled all the arrows, including the one recovered from your Chinese poacher who lived, I can tell you that these are very common, cheap arrows. Anyone could grab these down at Sports Authority in Kahului. That said, they are each a different brand," Dr. Gregory said.

"Maybe it means there is more than one shooter. Or maybe it means the perp likes variety," Pono said.

"Since this is Jacobsen, it really changes our assumptions. Maybe he wasn't the one who shot at me in his house." Lei glanced at Pono. "I'm thinking he was already bleeding and possibly dead in the back of his truck when I pulled up at his house, and the real murderer was the one to shoot at me."

"So who could it be?"

"Anyone. The biologists, another bird lover—whoever shot the poachers. We got no direction here." Lei paced back and forth a bit as Dr. Gregory and Tanaka continued to work quietly. "I can't believe I'm saying this, but I want to go back to Jacobsen's house. After we pulled the bows off the wall this afternoon, we didn't thoroughly search the place. I want to go back over it. I have a feeling we missed something there."

"Sounds like a plan," Pono said. "Dr. Gregory, if you don't mind, I'll go back down the trail to process Jacobsen's truck. Then, Lei, I'll meet you at his house if you still need me. If not, I'll see you at the conference room back at the station when we brief the captain."

"And I'll call you if anything more definitive turns up on the body," Dr. Gregory said. "With any luck at all, this young man's body will tell us something."

"Yeah, this case has been terrible that way—no trace anywhere. Okay to take your truck, Pono?" Lei asked.

In reply, Pono tossed her his keys. "I'll get a ride with the transport vehicle."

Lei rose to her feet, filled with a sudden urgency. She lifted a hand to Pono, who was helping get the body into the black plastic bag. She trotted back down the trail, carrying the bow she'd recovered from the gulch. At Pono's truck, she stowed the bow in a large paper evidence bag and labeled it, setting it on the seat beside her. Henry Ferreira, who'd been leaning on his vehicle, came to her window.

"Need me to let you out?"

"Yeah, if you don't mind."

She followed the young man's battered Haleakala Ranch Ford pickup and they drove along the one-lane dirt road through the pasturelands. Lei gazed at the rolling fields, which disappeared into a distance of lavender ocean punctuated by scoops of vanilla-ice-cream-cloud floating over the sea as sunset approached.

Everything about Maui seemed expansive and filled with light—until she came across its hidden and secret grottoes. Lei smiled at her fanciful thoughts and waved to Henry as she passed him holding the last gate and got on the steep, winding road back down the mountain toward Wailuku.

She turned on her phone with one hand, ignoring the flashing light of multiple messages. She called Stevens's speed dial, hoping to leave a message. But her heart went into overdrive when he actually picked up.

"I just needed to hear your voice," she said when he answered.

"Jesus, Lei." His voice sounded strangled. "Might have known you'd pull something like this. Got a lot of people upset with you. We're all boozing it up and eating the reception food at the vacation rental."

"It's okay. The case is so hot right now, I just had to push it back. Twenty-four hours. That's all I get, Captain says. We're on for same time tomorrow. I promise."

A long staticky silence filled her ear, then a sigh. "You better show up tomorrow," Stevens said, and Lei's breath whooshed out. It was the job. He understood that. Thank God.

"I miss you so much," Lei said. Her eyes filled with tears. "I can't wait to marry you tomorrow."

"I love you," he whispered. She could tell his hand was cupping the receiver. She heard the rumble of voices in the background.

"I love you, too." She bit her lips on all she wanted to tell him about the case: how she'd been shot at and where it had led. But it would just freak him out more. Time for all that later. "I miss you. I'm so sorry about the hassle."

"I know. You always are." He clicked off.

She set the phone on the seat and turned in to the nice Wailuku Heights neighborhood where Jacobsen lived, feeling the steel band of fear squeezing her heart loosen.

She knew Stevens wouldn't like her going to the house alone—but what could be wrong with that? No one was going to be there.

Chapter 19

Lei pulled her truck into the short concrete driveway before the closed garage door. She wasn't sure whether the house would be locked; if it was, she was going to need to get the landlord's help unlocking it, and all that could take more time—time she didn't have.

Lei checked her weapon, tightened down the Kevlar vest she still wore from hiking on the mountain, and snapped on gloves. Checking that she had plenty of evidence bags in her back pocket, she walked up to the front door. Knocked. Called out, "Police business! Open up!"

She thought she heard something inside, but it was too faint to be sure. Maybe Jacobsen had a cat or something. She knocked again, called again. No sounds this time. She tried the handle. The door was locked.

This was usually where things went wrong with her investigation process, Lei considered. Knowing Jacobsen was dead and she was fully within her rights to search it for evidence related to his murder felt reassuring—but waiting for someone to come help her unlock it was another delay. She wondered if the side window she'd kicked in was still open.

Instead of giving in to that impulse, she went back to the truck and got on the radio to Dispatch. Got who owned the address and called the landlady. While the woman was on her way to unlock the house, Lei called Dispatch again for backup in searching the house. They told her a patrol officer in her area was on his way. Lei waited, feeling impatience coil in her belly. Her eyes wandered to the window above the yard. She could see it was closed.

The landlady arrived, pulling up in a lime-green Prius. "What is this about?" the woman asked, tight-mouthed, straightening a sacklike woven dress and winding dreadlocks into a pile on top of her head. She stabbed the mound of hair with a chopstick.

"Police business." Lei held up her badge.

"Is something illegal going on in there? Mark has always been a good tenant."

"We're concerned about Jacobsen," Lei said. "Have you seen him, or anyone else around the house?"

"Come to think of it, I haven't. But rent isn't due until next week, so...I have the keys. Shall I unlock it for you?"

Lei took a breath, looking down the road. No cruiser in sight. "I'm waiting for another officer. He'll be along shortly. Why don't you just unlock the door for me and stay outside."

"I'll let you in and then go back to my car and wait. I was meditating when you called me." She sniffed.

"Well, I'd like for this driveway to stay open. Can you move your car?" Lei wanted to make sure the squad car would have room to come up close to the house.

The woman frowned but complied, getting into her Prius and backing it out onto the street. Lei found the silence of the vehicle's engine unnerving.

A few minutes later they stood in front of the door. Lei nodded, and the woman unlocked the door, turning to trot back down the steps. Lei pulled her weapon, turned the handle, and pushed it with all the weight of her hundred and twenty pounds. The door flew inward, banging the rubber stop against the wall. But before Lei had a chance to go in, a Maui Police Department squad car pulled into the driveway. A young officer got out and walked up the three cement steps to join her. He was a handsome young Filipino man she'd seen around the station.

"Lieutenant Texeira." He extended a hand and she shook it briefly, knowing hers was clammy with stress. "I'm Ben Cantorna."

"You're here for backup while I search the house," Lei said. "The occupant's body was just found. Stay behind me. Keep your weapon ready until we verify the house is empty." She crouched, weapon extended, and moved into the simple living space, rendered dim by closed drapes. Cantorna followed, imitating her, and she wondered how many times he'd ever broken into a house with possible hostiles inside.

Lei didn't have time to consider further, because she heard the clang of the gate on the outside of the house thumping shut. She realized that, with them breaching the front door, someone had taken the opportunity to run for it out the back door.

"Go through the house to the back. I'm going to try to head him off!" Lei yelled, directing Cantorna through the house to the backyard as she spun, retracing their steps. She burst out the front door and leaped down the three cement steps, chasing a man in a ball cap. The man was picking up speed through the yard and down the driveway.

"Halt! Police!" Lei cried, and was startled by the silent Prius suddenly pulling out in front of the fleeing man. The car didn't quite hit him, but the man's momentum caused him to crash into the vehicle. He bounced off the hood with a cry and landed on the asphalt.

Lei ran up and rolled the suspect onto his stomach, pulling his arms behind him to cuff him. When he was subdued and restrained with a knee to his back, she looked up with a grin and thumbs-up to the intrepid landlady getting out of the car. "Quick thinking!"

The woman raised her hand in a victory sign. Cantorna

ran around the side of the house to join them.

"It's not Mark," the landlady said, looking down at the suspect, whose face was obscured by the ball cap.

Lei tweaked the hat off. Edward Kingston glared up at them. "She hit me with her car!" he complained. "That's illegal!"

"She just blocked you from fleeing," Lei said. "And kudos to her for aiding in the capture of a foreign national in violation of his visa, at the very least. I'm taking you in for questioning."

Cantorna put the truculent Kingston in the back of the squad car. "You were supposed to get on that plane!" the young officer snapped, slamming the door on Kingston's complaints and requests for his lawyer, Shimoda. The landlady drove off, excitedly talking on her cell phone.

"So you took this man to the airport to be deported to Canada?" Lei asked Cantorna.

The young man turned red. "I saw him all the way to the waiting area at the gate," the young officer said. "It seemed like a waste of time. I thought he'd get on the plane. He'd been cooperative, said how much he was looking forward to getting home."

"Custodial duty of a deportee means making sure he gets on the plane," Lei said.

"I understand that now." Cantorna rubbed the back of his neck, stained with the flush of mortification.

Lei and Cantorna left Kingston in the locked back of the squad car, the windows down for air circulation. "You're getting a crash course in searching," Lei said. "Glove up and stick with me." She was on the phone to Pono and the captain, updating them, as she and Cantorna tore through the modest space, bagging anything that looked out of place or like Kingston might have touched it.

In the oven's bottom drawer, they found what Kingston must have returned for—a laptop. Lei held it up for Cantorna to see. "Not your typical hiding place for a personal computer, so I'm hoping this is the reason Kingston returned to the house. We didn't search thoroughly before, which is why I wanted to get back here ASAP when we found Jacobsen's body and knew there had been foul play. Don't dismiss any hiding place when you search."

"Yes, sir." Cantorna's excitement was evident in the perspiration rings under his arms as he followed her.

"I would still like to find something that clearly ties Kingston to the victim and the poacher shootings. Hopefully, we've got something. Go put up the crime scene tape, will you?"

Cantorna nodded and trotted off.

Lei did a slow turn in the living room, her gaze coming to rest on the brackets in a row down the wall showing where Jacobsen's bows had hung. There must be some connection between Jacobsen and Kingston; perhaps Jacobsen had been helping Kingston with his research all along and they'd had a parting of the ways?

They drove back to the station and put Kingston in one of the interrogation rooms as he continued to refuse to say anything without his lawyer, whom Lei had called once he was booked. Shimoda was taking his time arriving, so Pono and Lei met in the conference room with Captain Omura.

"So what's going on here?" Omura asked. "I hear you found another body in the forest."

"Yes. It was Jacobsen, shot with an arrow," Pono said. "I went over the truck while Rambo here was catching Kingston, and the blood pool there was consistent with a serious injury. Did you find any evidence he was shot at the house?" he asked Lei.

"No. I think he was shot somewhere else. I'm now wondering if it was even Jacobsen who shot at me at the house originally. It seems more likely it was Kingston, that he'd shot Jacobsen and had his body stashed in the back of his truck when I got there. Then he took him out to the Maile Trail and buried him, ditching the weapon he shot him with in the gulch," Lei said, glancing at the clock. Her twenty-four hours were melting away before her eyes—but at least she'd nailed the murderer—with the help of a lime-green Prius. She felt a smile tug her mouth at the memory of the landlady, dreadlocks aquiver, shooting a victory sign.

"So why would Kingston be back in Jacobsen's house after the fact?" Omura asked. "And why did he murder Jacobsen?"

"Those are the questions we need answers for. But I think it's because of the laptop." Lei told them about the hidden computer she'd found. "I dropped it off at Tech. I imagine it's password protected."

"Hopefully, Shimoda will get here soon and we can get this interview going," Pono said.

Just then Cantorna rapped on the door and stuck his head in. "Kingston's attorney is here."

Omura narrowed her eyes at the young man. "You were supposed to see that Kingston left us for Canada, Officer Cantorna."

"I know, sir. It won't happen again." Sweat popped out on Cantorna's forehead, and his cheeks flushed a mottled red. He dropped his eyes, suffering a long moment under Omura's stare.

Finally, Omura said, "I'm making a note in your file, Cantorna." She stood. "Texeira and Kaihale, I'm going to be observing."

"Yes, sir." They followed the young officer down the hall to the interrogation room. Lei knocked and looked through the little wire-lined port into the room. Shimoda, bent toward his client, looked up and gestured for them to enter.

Lei turned on the recording equipment and recited the date, time, and people present.

Shimoda opened. "My client would like to make a deal. Delay deportation to allow him to finish his project and immunity in return for his testimony."

"Testimony for what?" Pono led off. "We're charging him for the murder of Mark Jacobsen, whose body was recovered in conservation lands today."

Shimoda didn't bat an eye. "You do care about getting the real killer, don't you? Not only of Jacobsen, but of the Chinese poacher."

"Of course. But we have to know something of what he's going to be providing before we can authorize any sort of get-out-of-jail-free card," Pono said.

"I ditched your deportation efforts because my project is so important," Kingston said, dark eyes earnest. His beard was bushier than ever. "I'm studying blood lipids in birds who develop an immunity to malaria and factors that aid in that. I'm within months of being able to roll out a gene therapy that could save these birds—starting with our most critically endangered ones."

"That's all very nice," Lei said, with the baring of teeth she liked to employ during interviews, even as her interest piqued to hear more about his research. "But what we're here to do is catch a killer—and from where I sit, we've got one."

"Hey!" Kingston started defensively, but Shimoda cut him off with a hand gesture.

"My client knows who committed these killings and why. He's prepared to testify. But he is not a party to the crimes that have been committed, and he wants a deal."

Lei and Pono looked at each other, and Lei frowned. She'd been so sure Kingston was the killer—it all fit together so neatly. "We have to check with the district attorney," Lei said.

They went out into the hall and turned in to the observation booth, a simple space used for lineup identification and listening in on interviews. Omura was seated at the table and already on the phone. She held up a finger as they entered and said, "Yes, sir."

She hung up the phone. "DA's faxing over the immunity agreement. Good news is, we can still deport or charge him if we think it's in the state's best interest. The DA actually has no jurisdiction over Canadian visa rights, so he can agree if he wants, which he said he did, but ultimately INS will decide. We can just spell out the charges we won't charge him with and find some others. I think it's important to keep him in custody. He's a flight risk."

"His research really does sound important," Lei said, thinking of the difference it would make to be able to breed birds against malaria. Just the idea opened up interesting challenges.

"Be that as it may. This case is a double murder, and we need someone to charge. Go check the fax machine for the agreement."

A few minutes later, Lei and Pono returned to the

interview room. Lei turned the recording equipment back on, and Shimoda scanned the document before passing it to Kingston for his signature. Pulling the contract back to their side of the table, Lei eyed Kingston.

"Start talking. How did you come to be in Jacobsen's house, and what do you know about his death?" Lei asked.

"Cam told me he shot Jacobsen by accident—just saw movement from one of the blinds and nailed him before he realized what he'd hit." Kingston ran his fingers nervously through the bushy growth on his chin.

"Cam? Dr. Cameron Rinker with Hawaiian Bird Conservatory?" Lei's eyebrows rose in surprise. She resisted looking over at Pono. She tried to recall the sandy-blond scientist's innocuous face and couldn't.

"That's right."

"Well, Jacobsen's body buried in the ginger grove was no accident. What do you know about that?" Lei asked.

"After I'd dodged the deportation a second time and was back in the woods, Cam called me on the sat phone and said there was an emergency. I hiked down and met him at the Maile Trail. That's when he told me what happened with Jacobsen. He had the body in the truck bed, and we took Jacobsen out of the truck and up the trail and buried him. Cam's idea was to ditch the bow he'd shot Jacobsen with. When I got to the house and saw all Jacobsen's bows had been taken, I realized he might also be framing Jacobsen for shooting the poachers."

"So that's when you knew Rinker had shot the poachers?"

"He never said he'd done that. I just guessed. All he ever said was that I could use Jacobsen's house when I needed to get Internet and take a shower, since it was empty and it was going to look like Jacobsen had shot the poachers and fled. He had my research laptop; he took it from my lab when I was out in the field, and he put it in Jacobsen's house. Said it was to keep it from getting destroyed by the damp. I didn't believe him, but I had to go to Jacobsen's house to get it."

"So let's recap. You can basically only testify that Rinker contacted you about accidentally shooting Jacobsen. You're only speculating he shot the poachers. You suspected Rinker was setting you up when he took your laptop and left it at Jacobsen's house. Why didn't you come to us?" Lei asked.

"I just needed a little more time for my work," Kingston said pleadingly. "Just another week or two. I needed that laptop. I'm almost ready to publish this research, and I was hoping to be able to finish. I planned to call in Jacobsen's body and my suspicions as soon as my paper was done. If I did it sooner, you'd arrest or deport me and so much work would be lost. But when I heard Lieutenant Texeira pounding on the door at Jacobsen's house, I realized Cam had set me up too."

A long pause. Lei tried to picture the series of events.

It felt wrong, like a smoke screen. Shimoda gazed at her, inscrutable. Lei narrowed her eyes at the agitated scientist.

"This is all about as clear as mud. Why don't we back up a minute to the beginning? Tell us how your relationship with Dr. Cameron Rinker began."

"It all started with my work with Dr. Biswandi at University of Hawaii. I thought I was onto something, but she wouldn't let me pursue my hypothesis, so I approached the Hawaiian Bird Conservatory. Dr. Snelling also refused permission to extend my visa and continue with my project, but Dr. Cam Rinker, as the staff biologist, thought I had a good theory and signed my proposal to study the birds and stay on the conservation lands after my internship with University of Hawaii ended. He knew all about me being up there camping out, and he'd come out and help me on the weekends. He provided food and the lab supplies I needed."

"Where was this lab located?"

"It's a simple plastic structure. I'll show you. Anyway, one day when I was out there working, Cam came out to my lab with my supplies. He was really agitated, said something had upset him on the way and he wouldn't talk about it. A few days later, I smelled the body of the first poacher and saw what it was, but I was too scared to approach it or report it because I knew I was up there illegally and I worried I would be implicated."

"So why didn't you tell us all of this when we first

brought you in?" Lei asked.

"I didn't say anything because I wanted to find a way to get back up to continue my research. I was able to continue while you were investigating the shooting of the first poacher, and I didn't know Cam had shot that man for sure, or I would have been more forthcoming earlier. Time went on; then I spotted a second poacher. I told Cam about him, and then you guys captured me."

"You should have come clean about all this the first time we questioned you," Lei said. "If the accusations you've made about Dr. Rinker are true, Jacobsen might not have been killed."

"I know that now. Cam was protecting me. He hadn't told anyone about our arrangement. I know how dedicated to the birds he is—but it never occurred to me until later that he was the one shooting the poachers. The thing you have to know is, we kept our bows with us all the time in case we came across any ungulates in the forest. After the first time I almost got caught by Lieutenant Texeira here, I realized what a precarious position I was in. I buried my bow and disposed of my arrows, so when you guys did find me with the dog, I didn't have them. I didn't want to get charged—I just wanted to stay in the forest and finish my work."

"So to clarify: You suspect Rinker of shooting the poachers," Pono said.

"Yes. But he never said he did, and I never had any reason

to suspect him except that he was upset that one day. Don't even know if that was the day the first poacher was shot."

Lei and Pono glanced at each other.

"So, according to you, you've done nothing wrong but dodge getting deported and help bury a body?" Lei put some steel in her voice.

"I know it was wrong to dodge the deportation, but the research is more important than my visa. It was also wrong to help bury Jacobsen's body. But I was scared—first of being deported and charged, then of Cam and what he'd do to me if I went to the authorities."

"So you're afraid of Rinker."

"Definitely. He has a way of looking at you, like he really means what he's saying—and he's told me nothing matters but the birds. I believe he weighs a human life as less than one of the birds. Don't get me wrong—I love the birds. I've risked everything to continue this research. But I'd never kill someone over them."

"No, but you'd help drag the body of an innocent young ranger into the forest, bury him where he'd never be found, and allow him to be framed for murder," Lei said, feeling anger flash heat her cheeks and chest. She imagined how she looked: eyes glaring, skin patchy red. It didn't matter— Jacobsen hadn't deserved what happened to him. Lei saw remorse and regret in Kingston's expression for the first time as color leached out from purple hollows under his eyes, and he covered his face with his hands.

"I'm so sorry," he muttered. "This has all gotten so crazy."

"I think you have enough for now," Shimoda said.

"Yes. We still have some loose ends to tie up. But we are not releasing Kingston. He's going to be in our custody for a full twenty-four hours, and then we're going to find something to charge him with," Lei said. They stood up.

"Hold on. We just signed an agreement," Shimoda said, his brows snapping together.

"Yeah—but your client's too much of a flight and safety risk to let out of our custody, so we're going to charge him with visa violation, trespassing, and whatever else we can think of that we didn't list on your agreement, to keep him locked up," Pono said. "All we have at this point is your client's word that any of this is true, and we need to pick up Dr. Rinker to verify the story. Go ahead and take it up with the district attorney, if you don't like it."

"You can bet I will," Shimoda said, and his narrowed eyes promised a fight as Lei and Pono left him and his client alone.

Chapter 20

Lei and Pono took one of the squad cars to go pick up Rinker at his house in Haiku. Even well after dark, time was of the essence. If Rinker somehow became aware they were looking for him, he could disappear.

"He shouldn't have any idea we're coming," Lei said, unfolding the arrest warrant they'd just received for Cameron Rinker, PhD. "As long as the news hasn't released the story on the body we just found, he should be thinking we're still chasing Jacobsen and have no idea we're onto him and Kingston."

"I hope it will be that easy," Pono said, rubbing his mustache. A backup unit followed them at Captain Omura's insistence, but no one had their siren or lights on, and Lei had requested radio silence. If Rinker was monitoring the police band, he wouldn't be aware of their approach.

"A lot of people have died for these birds," Lei said. "Be a shame if Kingston's research really would have helped them."

"It should still be published. I can't see why not," Pono said.

"Well, we have no idea if he might be deported. If he is, we'll have a hassle getting him back to testify against Rinker." Lei fiddled with her medallion, frowning.

"Eh, no worries. We've got this bird freak. I'm sure once we get Rinker in custody, we can find some physical evidence tying him to Jacobsen's murder, if not the poachers," Pono said.

The cruisers swerved back and forth to stay in the narrow lanes of the back roads as they wound up into the jungled beauty of Haiku, smothering and dense in the dark. Lei kept an eye on the GPS for Rinker's address, and they turned into a narrow mud driveway, bumping up a rocky, slippery slope to pull up in front of a dingy house.

Several trucks were parked in front, and light spilled out into the darkness through a screen door. Lei jumped out with the backup officers and was right out in front as they sprinted up onto the porch and pounded on the door.

"Police! Open up!"

A worn-looking woman in her sixties, hair to her waist, came to the door. She wore a tank top and a pair of tie-dyed Lycra pants.

"What's this about?" the woman exclaimed, eyes wide.

"Cameron Rinker. Where is he?" Pono asked, pulling the

door open and marching in.

"Cam Rinker? He hasn't lived with us for months," the woman said, hand to her throat.

They searched the house and the small, surrounding illegal rental units on the property, everything from a yurt to an old school bus having been made into rental space, and finally Lei circled back to the woman who'd answered the door. "So when did you last see Cameron Rinker?" she asked.

"At least six months ago. He rented one of our units, but not for a while now," the woman said.

Lei and Pono dismissed the backup unit. "Went off the grid, I bet," Lei told them.

Pono backed perilously down the slippery driveway as Lei hung on to the sissy handle. "Drop me off at my house," she said, glancing at the dashboard clock. It was eleven p.m. She had only until four p.m. the next day, and with the case taking this turn, they'd need every minute of it. "We'll get back on this early tomorrow."

"I'll call in a 'be on lookout' for Rinker and his known vehicle," Pono said, "but I'm guessing he decided to make it harder for us to find him once he killed someone. Putting out a BOLO might alert him that we're looking for him. He could be monitoring the police band."

"We can just put it out via fax to the commanding officers. Any of our people might be able to bring him in if they come across him. Let's do the BOLO and hope someone scoops him up. Otherwise, I'm guessing the easiest way to pick him up is going to be through the Hawaiian Bird Conservatory and his job there. I bet he shows up for work tomorrow."

They called in the BOLO, and Pono drove her to her cottage nearby. Keiki barked and leaped frantically at the gate of the dark little house, and Lei realized she'd been hoping Stevens would be waiting for her, the house alight, food cooking. Her shoulders sagged. Her eyes felt gritty, her stomach hollow, and her ribs ached.

Pono patted her shoulder. "I won't remind that you could be on your honeymoon right now."

"Thanks, partner, for the support." Lei got out and slammed the door. Her heartache and disappointment made her voice hard, even as she knew her hope had been unreasonable. "See you bright and early tomorrow. Be prepared to work until the last minute."

"Tell me something I don't know," Pono said, and roared off.

Lei turned and unlocked the gate, walking up into the dark house. Her hand on Keiki's smooth head was the only good thing in the world.

Chapter 21

Morning came too early with the buzzing of Lei's cell phone beside the bed. She lifted it sleepily to her ear. "Texeira here."

"Lieutenant, good morning. This is Ben Cantorna. We picked up your person of interest, Cameron Rinker. He was trying to get on a plane."

"Glad we put out that BOLO," Lei said, sitting up and swinging her legs off the side of the bed. "Did you get ahold of my partner?"

"He's on his way in."

"See you soon. Thanks for the call." She hit Off and stood up, glancing at the clock. It was four a.m. She had twelve hours left.

Rinker blinked pale eyes and frowned. A sandy-haired man of medium height, Lei had hardly paid attention to him when he came in to be interviewed with Dr. Snelling regarding the bodies of the dead birds. Now, seated at the steel table in Interrogation with cuffs on his skinny wrists, he still looked completely unsuited to the role of criminal.

Pono sat beside Lei, holding the pad and pen they were hoping to use for a confession.

Lei decided to start off gentle. "Can I get you some coffee?"

"No, thanks. What's this about? I was pulled out of line at the airport. Quite an embarrassing scene. No one has even told me what I'm being charged with."

"Relax." Pono smiled, man-to-man. "We've had some developments in our shooting case in Waikamoi, and we just wanted to get ahold of you to talk about them, but not over the phone. Sorry for the drama; we went to your last address, and they told us you'd moved out six months ago, so we had no way to find you but to pick you up on a BOLO."

"Oh." Rinker dropped his shoulders, relaxing. This is what they wanted, to lull him into some admissions since they didn't have anything but Kingston's testimony tying him to the crimes.

"Yeah, bummer way to start the day," Lei said, sipping from her Maui Police Department coffee mug. Her eyes still felt gritty, the two Advil she'd taken for the headache she woke up with churning uneasily in her stomach. Her phone was off in her pocket. She'd listened to messages from her family and Marcella on the way into the station, and they'd just made her feel guilty. She should have deleted them. There was nothing from Stevens, and she clung to the memory of their brief conversation. "Let's get some things cleared up quickly. What can you tell us about what's been going on with research into the birds on Haleakala?"

Rinker blew out a breath and wriggled his wrists in the handcuffs. "Since you just need to ask me some questions, are these necessary?"

"Oh, sorry," Pono said, flipping through a bunch of keys for the handcuff key he carried and unlocking the cuffs. "Standard procedure."

"Okay. Well, then, there's some really promising research being done. We're racing against the clock with the malaria; the birds have to be able to develop antibodies before global warming allows mosquitoes to be able to survive at higher elevations. So I'm personally doing all I can to facilitate projects that will move us in the direction of permanent solutions."

"Would any of these solutions involve a young man named Edward Kingston?" Lei asked.

Rinker blinked rapidly. His sandy-blond eyelashes gave his light blue eyes a vulnerable, innocent look. "I thought Kingston's work showed promise, yes."

"Tell us what you know about him."

"Well, what do you want to know? Why has his name come up?"

Rinker was fishing. Lei kept her face flat. "We'd like to know everything *you* know about him."

"He has a promising theory. He pitched it to me and Dr. Snelling when he was trying to get permission to stay in Waikamoi and continue his research after his internship finished." Rinker glanced back and forth between them. "Dr. Snelling turned him down."

"And you?"

"I'm not in a position to grant such permissions."

"Really? Even if you could see the merit of his project?" Lei asked. So far Rinker wasn't volunteering anything useful. It had already occurred to her that Kingston could be playing them, and until they found hard evidence, it was all a dance of lies with these two men.

"I might have wanted to do what I could to facilitate his research, yes."

"And what was that?"

"I turned a blind eye when I suspected he dodged his visa expiration and was continuing the research project. In fact, I think he might be the mysterious camper who built the blinds for bird-watching."

"Really?" Lei said excitedly, to goad him into saying

more. This was such old news that it was hard for her to pretend. But as she'd hoped, he took the bait.

"Yes. When the rangers were concerned about who could be camping out there, I was pretty sure it was Kingston."

"What about when the poachers were shot? Didn't you also think that might be Kingston?" Pono asked.

"Well, now that you mention it, it seems likely," Rinker said. His blinking had slowed to an intermittent flutter.

"So why didn't you volunteer any of this when we conferenced with you earlier?" Lei asked.

"I wanted Kingston to complete his research. It's very important. It might save the birds."

Lei switched gears. "What can you tell us about a young ranger named Mark Jacobsen?"

"He was a fine young man." Rinker's eyes were back to rapid blinking.

Lei pounced. "Was? You refer to him in the past tense."

"I just meant—hey. Do I need an attorney?"

"Do you?"

A long beat. Lei could almost see Rinker's mind turning over his options. She decided to tip it in the direction of confession. "We picked up Kingston yesterday."

"Oh." Rinker's shoulders drew up as he blinked.

"Yeah. Said you were his inside man, keeping him

supplied so he could keep going with his research, but then you made him help bury the ranger's body and set him up to get popped for the murders."

Rinker opened and closed his mouth, and finally he spoke. "I'd like an attorney."

"So you don't deny these accusations?" Lei said.

"Yes. No." Rinker frowned. "You're trying to confuse me. Yes, I deny these accusations! I didn't do these things. Okay, I admit I knew Kingston was back in the forest. I even helped him out a little here and there, left some supplies for him and such. But I certainly didn't shoot those poachers or, God forbid, that ranger. Did you hear me ask for an attorney?"

"We did." Lei and Pono stood up. "Who would you like us to call?"

"Shawn Shimoda."

"Hmm, that could be a problem because Kingston has already retained his services. Any other names?"

"That bastard," Rinker said, his eyes narrowed and mouth tight. "He set me up and took the attorney I told him was good. Okay then, call Greg Santos."

They left the interview room, leaving Rinker to stew. Lei had Cantorna call the man's attorney. Back in the observation room with Captain Omura, Lei put her hands on her hips. "We can't let either of these guys out. They'll run."

"Agree. So we have twenty-four hours to make a case against Rinker or Kingston, or both, and charge them. Lei, you have less than twelve hours to be involved." Omura quirked an eyebrow at the clock on the wall registering six a.m.

"I'm wishing we hadn't made a deal with Kingston. I thought Rinker looked really shocked, like he didn't see it coming—that he'd been set up."

"Either or both of them could be acting. For all we know, they've done everything together," Captain Omura said. "We need to find something hard now. Something tying either of these men to the victims, and keeping Kingston in the country to testify or be tried is a big concern with how long these things take. Still, that's the DA's problem. Your job is to find something. Go search everything you can find on either of these guys and bring something in so we can charge one of them for these murders."

Lei and Pono headed back to their cubicle.

"I think things will go faster if we split up," Lei said. "I'll take Cantorna and find where Kingston's been camping, and you take Bunuelos and search Rinker's place. He'll have to give you an address. Do we have all the warrants we need?"

"Yes. Sounds good."

"Okay. Be a chance for me to help Cantorna with his searching skills."

"Trouble is, you don't know where Kingston's been living or where his lab is. I mean, he's been living rough."

"I have hopes we'll find his lab out in the forest and will find something there. He told me he'd tell me where it was and where he buried the bow and arrows he had on him before we picked him up."

Pono shook his head. "Sounds like a lot of hiking. I'll take Rinker's office at the conservation agency as well as his house."

"Okay. Keep in touch."

Pono nodded and left.

Cantorna appeared in the doorway, keen to help. "I need more field experience," he said.

Lei smiled at the young man. "I guessed. Let's go talk to Kingston."

They had Kingston pulled out of the county jail into a visiting room. The young scientist's eyes were wild, a ring of white around the iris. "Get me out of here. I'm going crazy locked up." Trembling and sweaty, he appeared very stressed. Lei frowned. "Is anyone harassing you?"

"No. I just—I just need to be outside."

"Well, I came to get the location of your buried bow and arrows and your lab."

"I can take you there," he said instantly. "But you'll never find them without me."

Lei considered this. Kingston could run like a deer, and she had no doubt he'd try—but she could keep him in cuffs, with shackles. The likelihood of finding these things without his help was slim. Even with dogs, they hadn't found his lab or the ditch site of his bow and arrows.

"I want to help." Kingston gulped. "I have nothing to hide. In fact, those weapons and my lab will clear me—and I need to get out of here. I mean I need to." He pushed his orange cotton sleeves up so she could see gouges where he'd scratched himself on the insides of his arms. "I have claustrophobia. Pain is helping me stay sane."

Lei restrained herself from looking at Cantorna and revealing her uncertainty. "Let me check with the captain," she said. She got up and called her superior.

Omura authorized her removal of the prisoner. "But keep him shackled. This guy's slippery as an eel and has no reason to stay in custody. Get him to sign a waiver that he's voluntarily waiving his Fifth Amendment rights and showing you the location of his lab and hidden weapon."

"Okay." Lei thought of Kingston, leaping like a parkour competitor down the stream when she'd fallen into the gulch. "I'll keep him on a short leash, literally."

Chapter 22

Ranger Takama, per park protocol, met Lei, Cantorna, and Kingston at the Hosmer's Grove entrance to the preserve to accompany them. His seamed face was impassive, and Lei noticed a black compound bow strapped to his back along with a nylon arrow quiver. "I see you got your bow back from our lab."

"Yes. I always carry it in the forest, just in case."

Kingston led the way down the dirt road into the cloud forest. The young scientist was cuffed, the cuffs attached to a bracelet on Cantorna's wrist by a length of light chain usually used as a leg shackle. Lei and Takama trailed a little behind the two young men.

"Been a lot happening since I saw you last," Takama said to Lei. "We're having a service for Mark on the weekend."

"I'm so sorry." Lei fell into step beside the ranger. "It's such a shame Jacobsen got caught up in this. Was at the wrong place at the wrong time, it seems." She slowed their steps so Cantorna and Kingston would pull ahead, out of hearing.

"Mark told me he was looking for the poacher's murderer on his own," Takama said, whispering to her, his eyes hard. "And he got shot for it."

"It might have been an accident," Lei said. "We're still investigating. I really can't discuss it, but what we're doing now is searching for more evidence. We needed Kingston to find the lab where he was working on his research, and his bow, which he buried."

Takama gave a brief nod and lapsed into silence.

Lei kept her eyes on Kingston up ahead. He was turning his head to look at the wilderness around him, an expression of tender wonder on his face as he gazed around. Lei could relate to his expression as the spell of nature settled over them. Nothing broke the silence but their muffled footfalls and the clink of chain. Lei wondered where the birdsong was and remembered that the native birds didn't live in the experimental conifer area, a forest desert.

"What's going to happen to my research?" Kingston asked. "I have my field journals, samples, and some other things at the lab I'd like to take back and—if I can—turn over to Dr. Snelling or Dr. Biswandi. Everything I did shouldn't be lost because of this."

"We'll see," Lei said. "Where were you with your

research?"

"It was on the laptop Cam hid at Jacobsen's," Kingston said. "I was just putting some finishing touches on my paper."

"It seems like you really went to some lengths to see it completed," Lei said carefully. Perhaps, in this natural environment, with them walking along as if they all were on the same team, he'd disclose something more.

"Well, it's not a cure or anything. But what I've discovered is that some birds are already manufacturing the antibodies for malaria. I've isolated the antibodies and made an injectable inoculation, and what's really exciting is that birds who've been inoculated then pass on their immunity to offspring. What I was going to propose was a captive breeding program to increase the malaria-resistant birds in the population. Birds with the antibodies could be released into the wild and keep breeding with the nonprotected birds—help nature along by speeding up evolution." Kingston waxed enthusiastic as they walked. "I thought we could inoculate breeding pairs of the birds with the antibodies, put them on an accelerated breeding schedule, and eventually they would outnumber the unprotected birds in the population."

Lei and Cantorna looked at each other. This was not something they could speak to intelligently, but Takama chimed in. "Do you know how expensive that would be? And all the challenges of breeding these nectar feeders in captivity?"

"Yes. That's why I thought we could just mist-net a section of forest heavy with nectar-bearing trees and concentrate the protected birds in that section to increase their population. As they had chicks, we'd release them back into the regular population. It wouldn't be that bad."

"But what about the territoriality of the *Kiwikiu* and *Akohekohe*?" Takama asked, and the two continued with discussion points too heavy with birder knowledge for Lei to keep up with. Still, the hike passed quickly until Kingston gestured to an ohia tree on the side of the road.

"This is the way to my lab."

There was no trail, but now, having become more attuned to the native forest, Lei could see Kingston had subtly marked his path with hemp strings he'd tied to branches. As they got deeper into the forest, birdsong filled the air, and Lei smiled as a red `apapane* landed near them, cocking its head, black dewdrop eyes bright, as if curious about these interlopers.

The lab appeared suddenly as they came around a large, full koa tree. Dark green camouflage netting draped the entire structure built between four tall ohia trees forming a rough square. Kingston must have looked for a grove that would lend itself to supporting a structure.

"Keeping the moisture out has been challenging," Kingston said. He and Cantorna did an awkward dance around the cuffs and chain until Kingston could open the low door, nothing more than a square of plastic Velcroed onto the plastic wall. "I'm not a carpenter, and I knew anything I built I'd have to take out. Just getting the materials up here and to this site was really challenging. I couldn't have done it without Rinker's help."

Lei squirreled this bit of intel away as they ducked to enter the crude shelter. The room inside was cool and dim as an underwater cave. Light falling through leaves above combined with the netting to throw patterns onto the dirt floor of the interior. Kingston walked straight to a plywood workbench nailed to the trees. His microscope stood upright in an extra-large Ziploc bag along with various other items swathed in plastic. "Looks watertight," Kingston said.

"Takama, can you wait outside?" Lei asked. "And, Cantorna, we'll cuff the prisoner to one of these supports while we search. I basically want to take in everything we can carry. Don't know what will have trace on it, and we need to be in the lab to test it."

"You won't find anything," Kingston said as Takama stepped out and resealed the door. Cantorna uncuffed the young man, clipping the chain onto a bracket nailed into one of the trees. Kingston moved back, standing near the bench and a box of tools.

Lei ignored his comment. She took a pile of evidence bags out of her backpack and handed them, along with a pair of gloves, to Cantorna. "Bag everything you can."

Lei flicked on her ultraviolet flashlight, looking for blood trace. The bench lit up immediately.

"That's bird blood," Kingston said. "I take blood samples from the birds, looking for antibodies."

Lei bent close with the light. The trace did look like small fingerprint smears. She took several swab samples anyway.

Kingston showed her where he kept his lab books in a sealed plastic bin, and she bagged those. It didn't take her and Cantorna long to loot the tiny space of anything that looked like it might be remotely related to their case.

"Will you send those materials on to Dr. Snelling?" Kingston asked again, his forehead scrunched anxiously as they filled their backpacks, including ones for him and Takama to carry.

"We'll see," Lei said. "Now, where did you hide the bow and arrows?"

"A ways out, maybe half a mile," Kingston said. Lei sighed. Now they had to carry everything, including the heavy microscope she'd given to Cantorna.

"Let's leave these packs here," she told them. "We'll travel lighter and come back to pick them up."

Takama was waiting when they came out. "I'll take down this structure with some volunteers," he said to Lei.

"Wait until we give the word," she said. "We have to see what we've collected first."

Kingston, reconnected to Cantorna by the chain, led them deeper into the forest. Suddenly, he stopped, turning to look around. In front of them, Lei could see one of the deep gulches that bisected the whole area, almost concealed by a stand of head-high ferns.

"I'm not sure," Kingston muttered. "I thought it was here, but I tied one of my twine markers somewhere, and I don't see it."

With a clinking of the chain, he knelt by a dense bush—and suddenly motion erupted, a crunching and crashing. A huge black boar exploded out of the vegetation.

Kingston leaped out of its way with a cry as the boar slashed curving tushes back and forth. Menacing black bristles covered a body that seemed the size of a sofa—nothing like the pink domestic pigs Lei was familiar with. She jumped behind a nearby sapling, drawing her weapon, and tried to get a bead on the boar. She couldn't with Kingston and Cantorna directly behind it and in the line of fire. The two men were scrambling backward through the ferns, tangled with each other.

Takama stood steady and even. He took a step toward the beast as it swung its huge head, tiny black eyes aglitter. His compound bow was fully drawn, an arrow nocked. The boar grunted, a deep and menacing sound, and lunged forward. The beast was amazingly fast for its size, flying past downed Cantorna, who'd tripped in the scramble. Kingston, behind him, frantically wrestled with the chain and cuffs.

Takama let fly his arrow as the animal passed him, and Lei fired her weapon after it, the report deafening.

A high, terrible sound, like a human scream, made the hairs all over Lei's body rise on end. It stumbled on, and suddenly, pitched forward onto its chest and, in slow motion, crashed onto its side. Takama's arrow protruded, deep below its shoulder, and a gunshot hole on its side welled blood. The animal's small, cloven hooves spasmed, tossing leaf litter, and the pig's screams subsided in a drowning gurgle.

"Holy crap." Lei took a deep breath.

Cantorna pulled himself to his feet, the chain clinking as it swung free. "Damn thing almost got me," he said. He turned to look behind him. "Hey! Where's Kingston?"

"Dammit!" Lei cried. The man was gone. She could hear a crashing in the underbrush down the side of the gulch. "He's getting away!" She bolted after him, followed by Takama and Cantorna.

The ground fell away in a cliff right behind where Cantorna and Kingston had been, which had prevented the boar fleeing in that direction. Lei parted the ferns and spotted Kingston at the bottom of the gulch, rock hopping away.

"Stop! Kingston, stop!" Lei yelled, pulling her weapon by force of habit—but she jerked back in horror as Kingston screamed suddenly. He pitched forward, arms outflung, into the stream. An arrow protruded from his back.

Lei spun, mouth open, to grab Takama. Cantorna yanked the bow away from the ranger.

"Takama! What the hell!" Lei exclaimed. She wrenched the ranger's unresisting arms behind his back and snapped cuffs on him, venting her shock and dismay in a series of expletives.

"He killed Jacobsen," Takama said, his voice stony. "He can't be allowed to get away."

"You don't know that!" Lei exclaimed. "No one elected you judge and jury!"

"I know he did it," Takama stated, unbowed.

"I'll deal with you later. Now I've got to see if another murder's just been committed. Cantorna, control this prisoner." Lei got the satellite phone out of one of the cargo pockets in her pants. "Dispatch, we need a medical transport." She checked that the GPS on the phone was enabled so they could be found in the wild forest as she described the situation, moving to the edge of the gulch.

Lei climbed down the precipitous cliff by hanging on to roots and bushes as handholds, wondering how the helicopter was going to land and how she'd misjudged Takama so badly. She should never have let him carry his bow along at all, but she couldn't deny he'd dealt handily with the wild pig. Lei was pretty sure his arrow had been the kill shot on the boar. Hopefully his marksmanship wouldn't have been as effective on Kingston.

"Help me," Kingston whispered as Lei squatted beside the scientist. He was facedown in the shallow water, sprawled among the rocks. The arrow protruded from just below his shoulder blade, and Lei could see bubbles forming around the hole—the man had a pierced lung. It brought back the terrible memory of when one of her partners had suffered a similar injury, also in a remote area.

"Help is on the way." Lei reached under his armpits. "This is going to hurt, but I have to get you out of the water. It's cold, and that will make your shock worse."

Carefully, painfully, she dragged the moaning Kingston out of the water and up onto a flat rock. Once she had him resting, she took out the phone and called again. "How soon is the transport? This man is bad."

"Fifteen minutes. Bird's just leaving."

Lei leaned down close to Kingston's pale face. "Fifteen minutes. Hang on."

Kingston closed his eyes and groaned. "I don't know if I have that long. Why did you let him shoot me?"

"I didn't know he was going to do that. Takama seems pretty sure you shot Jacobsen," she said. "Why don't you tell me what really happened—in case you don't make it."

Kingston's eyelashes fluttered, and she saw the whites of his eyes as they rolled back. Blood stained the corner of his mouth. She splashed some water on his face, patted his pale cheeks.

"Stay with me, Edward." His name sounded awkward in her mouth, but she wanted to ease his distress. He seemed to be suffering as much as the Chinese poacher, and if that was so, he really might not make it.

"I did it," Kingston whispered. Lei's thumping heart sped up even more. The man thought he was dying and seemed ready to confess.

"Tell me more," Lei said, leaning close to his ear. "This might be your last chance to die with a clean conscience." She thumbed the Record feature on the phone, already thinking of Shimoda and how he'd try to exclude this confession as coerced—but she'd worry about that later.

"I shot Jacobsen. It was an accident." Kingston kept his eyes shut, but his voice got a little stronger—he really wanted to tell her. "I didn't get a good look at him and he was in camo gear. I feel really bad about it. I should never have gone back to his place a second time, when you caught me. I wouldn't really have shot you at the house—I just needed to get away."

"You're talking about Jacobsen. So did Rinker have anything to do with any of this?"

"He helped me move the body and bury it. I..." Kingston coughed, and blood bubbled from the side of his mouth. His eyes opened, and Lei saw the terror in them as he struggled to breathe. Lei stroked sweaty hair off his brow and chafed one of his hands.

"Relax. You have to relax. You're making things right by telling me what happened. I understand why you did it. It was all for the birds, wasn't it?"

He nodded, the faintest movement of his head, and his eyes closed. He seemed a little calmer.

"What about the poachers?" Lei whispered in Kingston's ear.

"I don't..." Kingston's body suddenly relaxed, loosening like a puppet with cut strings, and she saw he'd lost consciousness.

The thrum of a helicopter approaching brought Lei to her feet. She took off the parka shell she wore and waved it back and forth until she was sure they'd seen her. There was nowhere to land, but a yellow metal-framed body basket was tucked close under the helicopter's runners. It trundled down out of the sky with a med-tech sitting in it.

They worked quickly to get an IV going and load Kingston, and only minutes later, Lei watched the helicopter whisk away into the deep blue Maui sky, with its innocent white clouds. She rinsed the young man's blood off her hands in the crystal-clear, cold stream and climbed back up the cliff to deal with what remained.

Chapter 23

Pono leaned forward, narrowing his eyes as he pushed a Styrofoam cup of the station's thick coffee to Lei. She munched down a granola bar to quiet her churning stomach. "I'm waiting for the full story after this afternoon's drama. How do you get all the action? My search was totally boring."

"Fill us in, Texeira." Captain Omura had left a big meeting with the Maui County Council to come back and debrief with Lei on the evidence retrieval in Waikamoi gone wrong. Her displeasure was evident as she tapped a well-shod toe on the leg of the table.

Lei picked up the coffee, took a sip, winced. "I should never have let Takama bring his bow. I know that now. But as a ranger, he's got certain privileges, and he seemed trustworthy."

"That oversight is going in your file," Omura said, olive eyes narrowed, crimson mouth a line.

Lei sighed, a deep release of breath, her shoulders rising and falling. She was bone-weary from her exertions on the mountain, covered with ground-in mud, spattered pig, and human blood. The emotional drain of the day was taking its toll, and she glanced at the clock. Two hours until her wedding. "I expect no less."

"We may also be facing a lawsuit from Kingston's family. They are on their way to his bedside from Canada."

"Well, when I called you to give an overview of the situation, I didn't include this." Lei took her phone out of her pocket and thumbed on the voice recording. She played the recording of Kingston confessing. "I'm hoping you can get him to sign a printout of this conversation before Shimoda gets wind of it, Pono."

"Good stuff, Lei, but too late. Shimoda has already sent us over a cease-and-desist from talking to his client without him," Pono said. "He was beside himself when he heard you'd used Kingston to show you to the location of the lab and the bow's burial site, so it's good you got Kingston to sign that waiver. Speaking of Kingston, how did he get out of the cuffs? I thought he was chained to Cantorna."

"He was. But in the lab, while we were occupied and searching, he picked up a pair of wire cutters. He concealed them until we were distracted with the boar, then used them to cut the chain. He was still cuffed when he escaped."

A long silence followed this. Lei remembered clambering to the top of the cliff and Cantorna, his young face downcast, holding up wire cutters he'd found on the ground behind their scuffle. Cantorna and Takama had also found the concealed bow, buried shallowly under the bush where the boar had been napping.

Lei was hopeful the bow would link somehow to the poachers. They were still short on physical evidence tying anyone to any of the murders.

"So how's Kingston doing?" Lei asked.

"Hanging on," Pono said.

"If he dies, Takama will be charged with homicide. I worry the DA may want to bring charges against Texeira, too," Omura said. "As it is, we've got Takama booked on attempted murder."

"It should be assault with a deadly weapon," Lei said. "And if he dies, manslaughter. Takama was grieving for his dead protégée, Jacobsen."

"Well, it's not up to you, is it?" Omura snapped. "I'm in talks with the DA, believe me. In the meantime, you might have that religious father of yours pray that Kingston survives."

"Speaking of Kingston's confession, can we bring in Rinker to corroborate what Kingston admitted? Even if we have to exclude the confession, if we can get Rinker to talk, we won't need it," Lei said. "Maybe Rinker knows something about the poachers, too."

"I was already working on that," Pono said, looking up

from his phone. "An officer is bringing him in."

"And on that note, Lei, you're on administrative leave pending an investigation into the shooting of a prisoner in your custody," Captain Omura said. "Your gun and badge, please."

Lei felt her stomach plummet. It seemed like she was always doing something wrong, always under investigation, even when she solved her cases. She took her weapon out of the shoulder holster and unclipped her badge, slid them, crunching grittily, across the table to the captain. Both were still speckled with forest mud.

"Now go get ready for your wedding. We'll be in touch," Omura said, picking up the items and standing.

"Can I just watch your interview with Rinker?" Lei begged.

The captain shook her head. Lei stood, gave Pono a little half wave, and walked out ahead of the others. Her feet dragged, and she'd never felt so tired and discouraged. She'd solved the case—but as often happened, it hadn't been by the book.

Her phone dinged with a text as she got into her truck. She slid it out of her pocket to check. It was Pono. *I'll forward you the recording of the interview on e-mail if you still want to see it after the wedding.*

Thanks, partner, Lei texted back. Pono knew how much she hated missing the denouement of the case.

Lei got on the road, her heart a little lighter. If only Kingston's research was worth all the blood that had been shed for it—and if it was, would it be tainted by its author's record? Would it ever be published?

She had no answers for any of those questions.

Lei drove up to the vacation rental mansion at three p.m. Marcella met her at the dented truck, dramatic brows knit in worry and anger. "I can't believe you! Seriously, you need your priorities adjusted!"

Lei, hot, exhausted, and irritable, snapped at her friend.

"What I shouldn't have done is have a big wedding. Me and Stevens at the courthouse would have made a lot more sense." She whisked the dress, pristine in its plastic drapery from a day ago, off the seat and handed it to Marcella. "I need a shower, just to start."

Lei made her way through the accusatory gauntlet of her aunt and father toward the bathroom. "I'm here on time to get ready, and I got the killer!" she exclaimed. "Can we just have a wedding already? Please!" Her voice filled with tears as she slammed the giant teak bathroom door.

In the large glass-block shower enclosure, under a foot-wide metal showerhead raining soft water over her, she began to relax a little—but she still hadn't heard from Stevens, and she wondered where he was. Probably at his apartment getting dressed with his brother. She pictured submitting to all the upcoming hair pulling, makeup patting, dressing, and walking down an aisle of flowers at the lush park—only to end up alone at the altar.

Lei felt queasy thinking about it. She was drying off, looking at her pale face and wet head in the mirror hopelessly, when someone knocked at the door. "Who is it?"

"Marcella."

Lei let her friend in. "Come to lecture me some more?"

"No. I'm just worried about you. Your aunty fixed you a sandwich—said she doubted you had eaten today." Marcella, already wearing the formfitting red sheath she'd chosen as her maid-of-honor dress, set a glass plate with a purple poi roll loaded with kalua pork on the granite counter.

Lei pressed her hand against her stomach. "I don't think I can eat that. That dress is tight, and I'm so nervous I feel sick."

Marcella put hands on her hips and gave Lei her best FBI stare. "Are you pregnant?"

"Maybe." Lei sat on the toilet and put her head in her hands. "I might be. I got a test, and I've been too scared to look at it. I decided to look at it with Stevens on the honeymoon."

"Oh my God. Typical Lei—stick your head in the sand and hope for the best." Marcella's warm voice took the sting out of the words. "Here, I'll eat the pork. You just have the roll." She separated the sandwich and handed Lei the roll, scooping the pork into her mouth with her perfectly manicured fingertips. "*Mmm.* This is so good. Your aunty is a really good cook."

"I know." Lei ate the roll, swallowing the dry bread with difficulty. When she stood up, tightening the towel around her body, she felt a little better. "The worst is, I told Stevens I wanted some space a few days ago. I was feeling anxious; you know how I get. And then I postponed the wedding. Do you think he's going to show up?"

"He's going to show up, because there's a whole FBI and police department who'll kick his ass if he doesn't— just like they'd hunt you down if you tried to run off. But seriously, Lei, did you have to make the poor guy stress out like that? He's wondering if *you're* going to show up."

"So I guess I just have to get the dress on, go, and hope for the best."

"I can have Pono track him down if you want."

"No. I was the one asking for space and creating this drama. I deserve whatever happens next."

"Lei." Marcella shook her head, pulling Lei's stiff body into her arms in a hug. "It's not about deserving anything. This is about *love*. Don't you trust that he loves you?"

Lei shut her eyes, leaned on her friend. "Yes. I know he loves me. I guess I need to prove I love him too."

"He'll show up. Now, stop procrastinating, and let's get you into that gorgeous dress."

Chapter 24

Wayne Texeira wore a short-sleeved black aloha shirt in a subtle print and black pants, his version of a minister's outfit. A slack-key and ukulele band played mellow music as they stepped out down an "aisle" of plumeria blossoms, heading toward an arbor of palm branches. They followed Tiare's sturdy figure, clad in a red fitted muumuu, leading Keiki. The Rottweiler kept her head up and ears perked, enjoying being the center of attention, the ring pillow tied to her collar. Marcella was already at the end of the aisle in front of the palm frond arch, and she encouraged Lei with a smile.

Michael Stevens stood directly in front of the palm frond arch.

A wave of relief made Lei's knees go weak.

His piercing blue eyes were on her, alight with passion. She needn't have worried he wouldn't show up.

She knew how different she must look from her normal casual style. Her hair had been coiled onto the top of her head, a *haku* lei of maidenhair fern and pikake circling her forehead. Ringlets framed her face and trailed down the back of her neck. Lei's shoulders were bare and her olive-tan skin glowed with gardenia-scented coconut oil. Her mouth was colored a deep rose, her tilted brown eyes set off by silvery plum shadow. Nothing hid the freckles sprinkled across her nose. Stevens had said he loved them.

The dress began with an ivory silk kimono-style collar, hinting at her Japanese heritage, attached to simple open netting that merged into a slender silk column. The graceful, modest shape hugged Lei's torso all the way down to her hips, from which the skirt flowed in a double layer of tulle and silk to the grass. "You'll look like a lily in this design," Estelle had said. And glimpses in the mirror at the house had showed Lei that she did.

Lei set her fingertips lightly over the tattoo of the Hawaiian Islands that twined around her father's brown forearm. Her father's strong, calm presence grounded her as they walked forward across the grass. Folding chairs in rows held seated guests who'd risen at the sight of her, their faces turned toward her in a sea of smiles.

Lei could feel her heart fluttering, a trapped butterfly in the cage of the dress, as she forced her feet to move. Her father closed his warm, work-hardened hand over hers on his arm, and his wordless support helped her move forward.

Stevens stood tall and splendid in a crisp subtly-patterned dress shirt tucked into black pants, a masculine maile lei's glossy, deep green leaves draped regally over his shoulders. His usually tousled dark hair was cut short, showing the clean, solid lines of his head. His tanned throat worked as she drew close enough to see him swallow, his eyes a blue flame as they gazed at her.

No, she needn't have worried that he wouldn't show.

Her father took her hand and put it in Stevens's large, long-fingered one. She turned partway and looked out at the crowd, her eyes picking out special friends: Ken Yamada, her partner from her days in the FBI, dapper in his familiar gray suit. Sophie Ang, gorgeous in a scarlet pantsuit, her smile wide and luminous. Jack Jenkins, Lei's partner from Kaua`i, aloha-wear casual with his arm around his new wife, Anuhea. Pono and Tiare, resplendent in their wedding apparel, stood on either side of them at the front. Captain Ohale from the Big Island sat in the second row back beside a smiling Dr. Wilson, Captain Omura and her date beside them. Aunty Rosario, in a sumptuous velvet-trimmed formal muumuu, was seated in the front row with Tiare and Pono's children on either side of her. Her grandfather Soga, his stern face suspiciously shiny, sat next to them with Lei's smiling young protégée, Consuelo Aguilar. Stevens's handsome brother, Jared, sat on the other side of them. The chair reserved for Stevens's mother was empty.

Way at the back, Lei spotted another familiar face, shaded by a dramatic hat—Stevens's first wife, Anchara, stunning as ever. Lei felt her own eyes widen, but Anchara only smiled as they made eye contact. Stevens had said she was okay with the wedding, and her presence must mean she was. Lei felt a tiny weight she hadn't even known she was carrying drop away.

A host of dear friends and family, missing only a few, were all here for her and Stevens. Lei turned back and made the mistake of looking into Stevens's eyes. They were so icy-bright she knew they were filled with tears.

"I love you," he whispered, and she felt her own eyes fill. She blinked to keep them from spilling over.

"Dearly beloved," Wayne Texeira began. Lei handed her simple orchid bouquet to Marcella and took Stevens's other hand. Their voices at first halting and whispered, but gaining volume, they took turns speaking timeless promises.

"I, Lei, take you, Michael, to be my husband, to have and to hold. For better or for worse, for richer, for poorer, in sickness and in health, to love and to cherish; from this day forward, until death do us part." Lei managed to get through the traditional words she'd chosen in some long-ago conference with Tiare. Her head felt like a balloon, way too far from her feet, but her body was suffused with an incredible feeling that pushed all the exhaustion of the last few days somewhere far away.

"I, Michael, take you, Lei, to be my beloved wife, to have and to hold you, to honor you, to treasure you, to be at your side in sorrow and in joy, in the good times and in bad. To love and cherish you always and defend your life with mine. I promise you this from my heart, for all the days of my life."

She hadn't known what he would say. He spoke boldly with no hesitation or prompting, and when Stevens took her in his arms for the first time as his wife, Lei let her eyes overflow. She sank into the possessive kiss, her arms twining around Stevens's neck as his arms wrapped her body close.

Lei didn't hear the clapping, or the band, or the good-natured hooting and teasing. *"Hana hou! Hana hou!"*

Marcella finally tapped her shoulder with the bouquet and brought them back to earth, and Lei shrieked as Stevens scooped her into his arms and carried her down the aisle to a roar of joyful applause.

Chapter 25

Lei turned away from the circular portal window that looked out across the water and twinkling lights of Kahului Harbor. "Whatever I expected for a honeymoon, it wasn't this! I love it." The limo had taken them from the reception party straight to the dock, where they'd drawn congratulations getting on board the ship still in their wedding clothes.

"Duchess Cruises sent us a discount," Stevens said, draping his maile lei over the lamp. "I just tucked the letter away for our hoped-for honeymoon. Got all kinds of touristy things planned, like diving with the manta rays. But this is only the first week. We're going back to California to hike Yosemite next. We'll visit your aunty and dad on the way back to Hawaii."

"You are so amazing." She walked back to him and pulled his head down for a kiss. "I'm so tired from the last few days—but I can't wait!"

Stevens hadn't let her change after the wedding and reception in the park, saying, "I want to take this dress off you myself."

"Let's see how tired you really are," he whispered against the curls that had further escaped from her hairdo. "Alone at last."

Stevens turned her away from him, and she smiled at him puzzling at the row of tiny pearl buttons. The dress's only embellishment began at the top of the prim collar and followed the line of Lei's spine all the way to low on her hips, where the froth of skirt began.

"How am I going to get through all these buttons without ripping this right off you?"

"There's a zipper hiding in there," Lei said, her voice gone husky. "But before you find it, I need to know something."

She turned, setting her hands on his arms and looking up into his eyes. "Why didn't you call or text me in the last few days? I was so scared."

"I was scared too." He took both her hands in his, stroking his thumbs across her skin. "I needed to know you'd come anyway. I needed to know you loved me—enough to take a chance on me."

Lei gazed into his blue, blue eyes for a long moment, reading the pain there, the longing, the love. She blinked, looked down. "There's one more thing."

She walked over to her suitcase, took out the brown-paper-wrapped package. "I don't know if there's ever a good time for this, but I figure whatever it tells us, it might be better to start our honeymoon knowing."

They sat side by side on the bed, Stevens's dark brows knit in puzzlement as she unwrapped the package. He sucked in a quick hard breath at the sight of the pregnancy test box. "Whoa."

"Yeah. I was too scared to look at it alone."

He slid a long arm around her and drew her close. "Whatever it tells us, we're in it together."

She leaned her head on his shoulder and took the little wand out of the box. She pulled the plastic sections apart so the stripe of color showed. If it was blue, she was pregnant. If it was white, she wasn't.

The little strip was white.

They both blew out a held breath at the same time.

"Not pregnant," Lei said aloud, feeling an unexpected sorrow steal her breath.

"Not pregnant," Stevens echoed, and she heard the same sorrow in his voice. "Well, that's good, right?"

"Right, of course," Lei said, but tears obscured her vision as she slid the wand back into the box, got up, and walked it to the trash can, dropped it in.

"We can work on reversing that result right now, you know," he said, following her to brush a curl off her face.

"I'm game if you are."

"No. Not ready," Lei said. "I guess I'm more ready than I thought I was, because I never expected to feel even a little sad about it. But no, I'm on the pill and going to be more careful until we really are ready."

"In that case, champagne is in order, and lots of it." Stevens went to the wet bar, already stocked with a sweating metal bucket of ice and a bottle of Dom Pérignon, accompanied by a card offering *Congratulations from Duchess Cruises!* "I was wondering why you didn't drink at the reception. Chalked it up to nerves."

He filled her flute, careful to keep the bubbles from welling over the side.

"Well, it's bottoms up now," she said. "Can't believe I made it through the whole wedding ordeal without drinking."

"Ordeal? Just all the people we know from everywhere, cooped up for a day and dying to party," Stevens said. "Even Jared." His brother had come, bearing their mother's transparent excuses. "Hope he enjoys Maui. He's been saying he'd like to transfer over here." Jared was a firefighter in Los Angeles and had complained of the severity of the fires and stress in his area.

They wandered the two large adjoining rooms, sipping champagne and commenting on the size of the honeymoon suite with the opulent satin-covered bed and mirrored ceiling.

Two glasses of champagne later, Lei was ready to resume where they'd left off, turning to offer her back. She'd considered telling him about the case and decided later was soon enough. "Unzip me, please."

Stevens sat on the edge of the king-sized bed, pulling her between his legs. He fumbled under the collar until he found the long zipper concealed under the placket of buttons. Lei turned her head to look up at the mirrored ceiling, watching him slide the zipper down by degrees, kissing his way down her spine and sucking in a breath as he came to the scrap of ivory G-string and garter belt she wore.

"Lei! Oh my God," he whispered, cupping her buttocks in his hands, nibbling the dimples at the base of her spine. "You know I really married you for this ass, don't you?"

She laughed, and turned in the puddle of silk at her feet, feeling glorious in the white demi bra, G-string, and ivory silk garter set that had been Sophie Ang's bridal gift to her when she heard Marcella had bought Lei's dress.

"My friends know how to take care of us." She pushed him in the chest so he fell backward onto the bed. "Look up and watch me take your clothes off in the mirror."

Even as she undid each mother-of-pearl button of his dress shirt, her head buzzing with champagne and hunger, another part of her was imagining his view of her astride him in her erotic underwear, undressing him.

The thought was so arousing she could hardly stand it, could hardly make herself slow down. She tried to be as torturous as she could, stroking him through his clothes, taking her time on him with tiny bites and kisses. She slid back and forth over his chest, circling her tongue over his rock-solid abs, bending and posing her body so he could see and appreciate every sensuous movement and the contrast of their bodies: his large and hard, hers slender and toned.

His inarticulate exclamations goaded her on, leaving no doubt she was having an effect.

Her own desire rose with spiking urgency, heat humming along her nerve endings, every movement increasing the craving that pooled in her lower abdomen.

When she had him down to his black silk boxers, whimpering with desire, she stood back, reaching up to undo the pins anchoring the ladylike hairstyle she'd worn for the ceremony. Lei shook her hair free, a wild, curling mane around her shoulders. Turning and doing a little striptease, she slid the G-string off with a sexy shimmy, leaving on the ivory stockings and bra. She turned and slid his boxers down.

More teasing and torturing ensued.

Only when he finally begged, "Just kill me now and be done with it," did she climb back onto the bed, and into his arms.

Lei sat at the table on the tiny balcony that looked over the ocean as the cruise ship sliced through the water toward their next stop, Kaua`i. They ate fruit from a basket that had appeared in the morning outside their room. Up near the top of the ship, the equivalent of four or five stories above the water, Lei felt a little breathless at the beauty and luxury around her. She could see a whale blow off in the distance. At the bow, a pod of dolphins leaped through the water alongside them. Clouds paraded in snowy splendor alongside, and she spotted yet another whale.

She could see the appeal of traveling this way, especially cocooned as they were in their room. The breeze was cool, tugging at her hair and ruffling the apricot silk of her robe. Stevens reached across the table holding a strawberry from the fruit basket. Lei leaned over and bit into it, brushing his fingers with her lips. "Mmm."

"Mmm, is right." Stevens finished the strawberry and reached out to trace the line of her throat as it disappeared into the robe. He lifted the battered, matte silver medallion around her neck. "I think you might be due for an upgrade on this."

"I have the upgrade on my finger." She wriggled her left hand, and the shiny platinum wedding band sparkled next to the simple channel-set engagement ring. "I'll never give this necklace up—it's a symbol for our relationship."

He laughed. "What—my grandma's wedding ring? Lost, burnt in a fire, and hammered into shape? I guess you could say so."

Lei smiled. "I told you. It's been through a lot, and so have we."

"And now's the time to relax and enjoy life a little bit."

"Any more enjoying and I won't be able to walk."

"You can take a break from enjoying and tell me about the case that was so important we had to postpone our wedding."

"Not sure it's entirely over, but at least we have someone in custody." Lei filled him in, with pauses for exclamations. Stevens narrowed his eyes at her when she finished her story.

"So I think we can safely say a precedent was established here."

"What's that?" Lei ate another strawberry, licking her fingertips provocatively, hoping to distract him from a lecture.

"Nothing gets between Lei Texeira and solving her case. Not even her wedding. I hope you're okay that I'm okay with that, since next time it might be one of my cases."

"I look forward to a life of mutual workaholism." She leaned over and kissed him.

He winked. "Up for opening some presents? Pono filled

a suitcase with smaller gifts for us to bring along."

"Perfect!" She stood up, but when she tried to pass him, he caught her around the waist and pulled her into his lap.

"I haven't told you I love you yet today. I'm going to try to do it every day, for the rest of our lives."

"I like the sound of that." She kissed him, a little peck on the lips. "That will begin to make up for you not calling me before the wedding."

"Still mad about that?"

"I was really worried. Thought something happened to you. Thought you might not show up. I just needed to hear your voice. Now to find out you were testing me—I don't know." She shook her head. "I don't like it that you did that."

"Maybe it was wrong of me. But yes, I was testing you, and the good news is, you passed." He growled and snarled, nibbling on her neck. "Don't think just because I'm crazy about you that you get to boss me around."

Lei narrowed her eyes, stiffening in his arms. "So this is some sort of pissing contest about who's in charge?"

"Oh God." Stevens stood up abruptly, dumping her back onto her feet. "It was going too well. You had to pick a fight."

She followed him in, suddenly sick of the whole conversation. She aimed a gentle kick at his butt. "There. We're even. I don't want to fight either."

He spun, caught her in his arms. "Ever see *The Taming of the Shrew*?"

"The what?"

"Shakespeare. A spanking is involved."

"No!" She kicked and wriggled, but he carried her under his arm to the bed and put her over his lap, smoothing the bright silk of her robe over her bare bottom, squeezing it like sampling fruit in the supermarket.

"This is going to hurt me more than it does you." He smacked her butt with his open hand, immediately massaging the stinging spot.

She squeaked, "Ow!" and wiggled some more. Tipping her head to the side, she could see in the mirror above that their little tableau was ridiculously sexy. She leaned over to bite his leg, not hard but just enough to let him know she had teeth.

He gasped and smacked her again, and this time she put some moan in her voice. "Ohhh." And then she laughed. "That all you got? Seriously, I want a turn. I'll show you how it's done."

"Shrew," he said, and brought his hand down again.

It was a good deal later and both of them were sweaty, laughing, and flushed when they finally sat down with the suitcase of presents.

"We should make a list," Lei said. "Thank-you notes and all that."

"How very bridal of you," Stevens said, tossing the pen and notepad from beside the bed to her.

She caught them and faced the pile of presents. "I'm going in."

Two salad tong sets, three kinds of mixers, and a cookbook later, Lei looked up at Stevens propped on an elbow on the carpet beside her. His eyes were sleepy, his tanned chest an inviting contrast to the white terry ship's robe he wore. "I'm detecting a kitchen trend. When do I get a present?"

"Ha-ha. I think these are tools for you to build some kitchen skills," Stevens said.

"Good luck with that." Lei took a small, square box out of the stack. "This one looks promising."

She shredded off the silver paper, tossing it aside, and opened the top of a lightweight cardboard box.

Inside was a brochure and a receipt. Lei frowned at the simple graphic of a wooden coffin on the brochure, with a list of prices. "The DeathStore," she read aloud. "Hawaii's first 'green' funeral home, offering a full range of goods, services, and burial options."

Stevens snatched the brochure out of her hand, leaving her holding the receipt that had been stapled onto the back.

"This is a receipt for 'two pure linen shrouds' as a green burial option. They were purchased for three hundred dollars each." Lei's lips felt numb and tingly at the same time, making forming words difficult. She pressed her fingers against them. "Whose gift is this? Talk about bad taste."

Stevens scrambled up onto his hands and knees, gathering the bits of silver paper. They reconstructed the paper like a puzzle, working silently together, and finally Lei sat back on her heels. "There's no name. No note. No card. No identifying information. Let's call the DeathStore and find out who bought this."

"You go take a shower. I'll do it," Stevens said, picking up his phone. "I hope we still have cell service."

"I'm not going anywhere," Lei said. Stevens couldn't get a signal, and Lei couldn't either, so Stevens used the phone beside the bed for the internal intercom and had the concierge place the call via satellite phone.

"We were given a wedding gift," Stevens said to the salesperson at the DeathStore, holding the receipt by one corner. Lei had already bagged the brochure in a plastic bag from the bar. They'd touched the items, but it couldn't hurt to reduce how much they handled them—maybe there was still a usable print. "Two linen shrouds. We don't know who gave them to us, and we need any information you can give us. Who bought them, how they were paid for. We're police officers."

A long pause as the funeral home employee digested this. "Well, we believe in an open dialogue about death, but I've never heard of giving burial wear as a wedding gift," the clerk said. "What's the date on the receipt? I'll see what I can find out."

Stevens read off the date, two weeks before their wedding. "Wondering if you're still holding the shrouds. We just received the brochure and receipt."

"Can I get back to you on this?"

"Unfortunately, no. I'll hold." Stevens's brisk, authoritative tone left no room for argument. New Age Muzak came through the speaker as the clerk put him on hold.

"I think I will pop into the shower after all," Lei said. "I'll be out by the time the guy gets back on the line." The teasing, sensual spell they'd cast had been broken, and Lei felt a chill wind blowing through the sliding door.

The bathroom was small but beautifully appointed, and Lei got into the shower, soaping up quickly, wondering about the receipt. Could this be some tasteless but well-intended gift? But if so, wouldn't the giver have identified themselves? Maybe made a joke of it?

"Until death do us part," Lei whispered. "It's a threat. It's definitely a threat." She didn't want to take the time to shave and wash her hair in case she missed the rest of the phone call, but then Stevens joined her in the narrow stall.

"They don't have the shrouds. They were paid for with cash. Because they don't sell too many of them, the clerk remembered the purchase once he had the record pulled up.

Described the purchaser as a 'white male, wearing a ball cap, not old' and I quote."

"Dammit," Lei said, looking up into his eyes. Water from the shower trailed off his dark brows, and she brushed them clear. "Do you think it could just be a creepy gift?"

"No." He was in full cop mode, taking the soap from her and washing briskly. "I want to get ahold of the station next. With all the people the two of us have pissed off over the years, it could be anyone threatening us. I want to make sure our houses are secure and our friends are on alert."

"Let me." She ran the soap bar down his chest, playing, sliding it around in all his nooks and crannies. "We can't let this wreck our honeymoon."

"It won't. But I need to focus right now." He took the soap gently out of her hand and put it back in the dish. "We need a break to recharge anyway. I'd like to go talk to the captain of the ship, explain what's going on. This could have some connection to the Duchess Cruises bust, even."

They got out and dressed in silence, and Lei said, "I'm pissed now. This asshole knew just what he was doing, putting that in our presents. Trying to wreck our honeymoon."

"Spent some money doing it, too. A six-hundred-dollar prank? I don't think so. Let's just take some steps, make some calls—and then get back to where we were." Stevens drew her into his arms, tucking her head under his chin.

She could hear his rapid heartbeat and smell adrenaline on his skin. She knew in that moment he would defend her to his death, and she him. She shut her eyes and rested in the security of that knowledge.

"I love you," he said.

"I love you too." It was still not something she said easily, and she wanted that to change. "I like the 'say I love you once a day' plan so far."

"Gotta get some things right from the start." He grinned, a quick flash of teeth, but his eyes had already looked away, at the room safe. "Getting our weapons and my creds out. Never leave home without 'em, right?"

"I'm sorry every time I do," Lei said. She had brought her backup Glock though her department-issue weapon and badge were still with Omura. "I need to talk to Pono about the case anyway."

"Why don't you get the concierge to call Pono, and I'll go see the captain about our security," Stevens said. She nodded. "Put the chain on the door," he added as he slipped out into the hall.

She put the chain on. It gave her no sense of security, because one thing she knew from law enforcement was that no chain ever stopped someone who really wanted to get in.

Chapter 26

"What'chu calling me for, Sweets? You're supposed to be at sea and away from cell phones!" Pono's voice boomed in her ear, reassuringly cheerful and close. She let out a breath.

"Yeah, I don't want to be talking to you either. Here's what happened." She told him about the strange gift from the DeathStore. "Stevens is talking to the captain of our ship about security here. I just wanted to make sure Keiki was okay and that you knew what's going on. We were hoping you could keep an eye on my house and Stevens's apartment while we're gone."

"Of course. In fact, my nephew from the Big Island is visiting, and our house is kind of small for him too. He's nineteen, a good kid—why don't we have him and Keiki go back to your house, and he can keep an eye on the place?"

Lei thought this over for a moment. "I'm not sure I think it's a good idea for anyone to be alone out there. Why don't you put him in Stevens's apartment? It's closer to your house in Paia and there are more people around in the building."

"Sounds good." She told him where the keys were stashed, and they firmed up the details. "So, while I've got you on the line, what's going on with the case? Our cell phones don't work. We're on the ship's sat phone."

"I was able to verify Kingston had an alibi for the most recent poacher shooting, which sucks because we wanted to nail those on him as well as Jacobsen. Also, we've been contacted by the Chinese embassy. They want the victim released into their custody. I've got a call in to the attorney general on what to do."

"I wish I wasn't gone right now," Lei said, playing with the medallion at her throat. "I hate leaving all this on you."

"If it wasn't this case, it'd be another one," Pono said. "So don't worry, okay? Let that husband of yours distract you from all this, including the DeathStore thing. I bet it's just some weird hippie gift."

"I think if it was, they would have left their name, don't you? The fact that the box was unmarked shows they didn't want us to know who gave it, which puts it in the threat category as far as we're concerned."

A pause as Pono considered this. "I guess you're right. Do you think it's anything to do with the Changs?" Pono brought up Lei's oldest enemy.

"I don't know. There hasn't been anything from them since Terence Chang was put on probation—though that would be ending about now," Lei said. "Can you put out some feelers? See if our contacts know anything about activity on their end?"

"I'd think if he was moving against you he'd be quiet about it. Buying linen shrouds is pretty big drama."

"The man who purchased the shroud was white and he wore a ball cap—but it could have been anyone buying it for Terence Chang. Sophie Ang got to know him a little through his online persona, and this kind of gesture seems like it might be his style, actually."

"Well, I won't be calling you and updating you on the case—you're on your honeymoon. Don't forget it. Just know we're monitoring Kingston, the Chinese poacher is still in custody for now and not going to die, as far as anyone can tell. Put it all out of your mind and have some fun with your husband."

"It still sounds strange to hear him called that," Lei said, pressing her hand against the medallion at her throat, a feeling rising in her chest—she was pretty sure it was happiness. "Just make sure my dog is safe, okay?"

"You can count on me, partner."

She hung up the phone. Stevens still wasn't back, so she got into exercise clothes and left him a note saying she was going to the gym.

He eventually joined her on the treadmill facing a giant picture window. "Captain's got the hallway surveillance cameras redirected at our suite and the shipboard security team on alert. We have permission to carry our weapons, but I don't want to."

"Me neither." Lei had been running for fifteen minutes or so, and she swiped sweat off her brow and playfully flicked it at him. "This is our vacation and I feel safe. I won't let this jerk steal one more minute of our fun."

"Good." Side by side, their bodies in sync, they ran, watching the ocean slide by—but Lei knew that, no matter how far they went, if Terence Chang was making his move, with the Internet as his playground, there was nowhere he couldn't reach them.

Lei and Stevens had routed their return through Oakland Airport to spend a couple of days in San Rafael with her aunt and father. They pulled their rental car up at Aunty's restaurant, the Hawaiian Food Place. Aunty's business partner, Momi, enfolded Lei in a big hug, dropping a couple of shell leis over her and Stevens's heads. "Congratulations!"

Lei inhaled the delicious smells coming from the unpretentious fifties-era restaurant with its plastic-lined booths and bar stools. "So good to see you, Aunty Momi,"

Lei said, glancing around at the restaurant, fairly full for a Tuesday evening. "Where are my dad and Aunty?"

"They're at home. Your aunty, she not feeling so well." Momi's broad face was immobile with suppressed emotion. "She wants to see you right away."

"Oh no. Is she sick?"

"Well, she wants to talk to you herself."

Lei felt her stomach tightening up. She wasn't feeling so well herself. Her period had started a few days ago with bad cramps, and they'd already been traveling all day. The case and the DeathStore threat were also never far from her mind. "Okay. We'll go straight to her house, but I really need something to eat. That airplane food was terrible."

"Of course!" Momi led them to a booth. "Don't worry about menus. I know what you like." She bustled off in her bright plumeria-print apron.

Stevens reached across the table to take Lei's hands. "I'm sure she's okay."

"I don't think so. She told me in a phone call she was having tests; she wouldn't tell me what was wrong before the wedding. Said it was news that could wait. But too sick to come to work? I've never seen that before." Lei frowned. "She's the closest thing I have to a mother. She better be okay."

He lifted her hands and kissed them. "You can have my mom," he said with a quirk to his mouth. "I'll share."

"I'll take a rain check on that," Lei said, with a reluctant smile. His mother, a chronic alcoholic, had been on a bender and missed her flight to Hawaii for their wedding. Stevens had shrugged when his brother, Jared, told him, but Lei could see it hurt him by the cord of muscle in his clenched jaw.

Momi returned with big bowls of beef stew and purple poi rolls. "Eat up. I called the house and let them know you'll be there in a half hour or so."

"Thanks." They dug into the stew.

Half an hour later, as they pulled up at her aunt's modest bungalow on D Street, Lei felt better, stronger, ready to face whatever they needed to. She was fortified by Stevens's warm bulk beside her and a tummy full of savory comfort food.

Her father opened the door, smiling and welcoming them with hugs. "How was the honeymoon? You sure picked up some color."

"The cruise, then the Yosemite sun." Lei noticed more gray in his mop of curly salt-and-pepper hair and deeply chiseled lines beside his mouth. "We stayed in the park at the Ahwahnee Hotel. Did a lot of hiking. Saw so much wildlife. It was amazing."

"Well, good. I'm so glad you two made the stop here."

"Yes, I hear Aunty Rosario isn't feeling well," Stevens said, lifting his brows, inquiring.

"No, she's not. But she wants to talk with you about it herself."

Lei dropped her bag and purse and hurried through the untidy and dimly lit house. Her aunt was in bed, propped up against pillows, the television muted on the wall as she opened her arms to Lei. "My girl! You look wonderful."

Lei embraced her aunt and patted the bed beside her. "Move over. I'm getting in."

When Rosario took Lei in at nine, after her mother's death, Lei had slept in the same bed as her aunt for two years. Only when she'd been physically close to Rosario could she relax enough for sleep. Now Lei climbed onto the bed with her aunt, putting her arms around the older woman. She was alarmed by Rosario's gray color, weight her aunt had lost leaving wrinkles in its wake.

Stevens came in and Wayne followed, bringing a chair for him to sit on. "I'll go make some coffee," her father said, heading back to the kitchen.

"Aunty. You wouldn't tell me what's wrong when we were on Maui. What did those tests say?"

"I have cancer. Pancreatic cancer."

Lei gasped, and her arms tightened around her aunt. She didn't know much about cancer, but even she knew pancreatic cancer was inoperable and often a rapid killer. "No, Aunty! No!"

"I'm sorry, sweet girl." Rosario stroked Lei's tumbled

hair. "I don't want to go any more than you want me to."

"What are they saying about your treatment?" Stevens asked, hunched forward, his hands resting on his knees and his eyes shadowy.

Rosario just shook her head, but Wayne had reappeared in the doorway. "She's decided not to have treatment."

"I don't want to spend my last few months on this earth sick and miserable just for the possibility of a few more days. I'd rather feel okay more of the time and keep my hair all the way until the end."

Lei had been bracing herself as best she could for something like this, but there was no buffering this news— her beloved aunt was dying.

"Oh, Aunty," Lei choked, and tears overflowed.

"Michael, why don't we give them a minute. I'll show you where your room is," Wayne said, and the two men left, pulling the door shut behind them.

Lei sobbed, and her aunt held her, weeping into Lei's curly hair. Finally, Lei lifted her streaming face out of Rosario's bosom. "Where are the tissues?"

Rosario handed her the box, and Lei sat up, blotting her face. "This sucks," she said, wads of tissues against her eyes.

"You don't have to tell me," Rosario said. "I feel really sick some days, can't keep anything down, can't work much. Having Momi and your dad put their lives on hold makes me feel terrible."

"How long has this been going on?"

"I got the diagnosis two months ago."

"Aunty! You should have told me!"

"And ruined your wedding? No way."

Lei subsided, blowing her nose. "I have to stay with you longer. Take some leave."

"No. I have plenty of support right now, and usually I'm at the restaurant in the afternoons, just was feeling crappy today. I still have a lot of tread on these tires. Maybe later… closer to the end."

"Dammit!" Lei exclaimed. "There has to be something we can do! I can't stand hearing 'the end' like there's no hope."

"There's always hope."

"I take it Dad's got his church praying."

"There are many documented miracles from prayer," Aunty said. "And the doctors aren't offering any solutions I can live with, pardon the pun."

Lei lowered her aching head onto Aunty's shoulder. "I'm so sorry, Aunty. Now I'm wishing I was pregnant after all so I could share that with you."

"You were?" There was no mistaking the excitement in Rosario's voice.

"No. Just a scare."

"Well, having a baby when you're married to a loving husband and making good money is nothing to be 'scared' of."

"I don't want to raise a child without you, Aunty! I need your help, your advice!" Fresh tears welled.

"Don't." Aunty gave Lei a shake. "The Lord will bring people into your life to help—your friends are terrific. I'm sure that Tiare is full of all the advice you'll need."

Lei snuffled a laugh. "She definitely has a lot of opinions."

"And I'm not so perfect. I've made my share of questionable decisions—keeping you and your father apart, for one. But that's not the only one."

"What do you mean?" Lei sat up, blew her nose again.

"Never mind. We have enough to deal with now. Come here." Her aunt drew Lei's head down on her shoulder, and they eventually fell asleep that way.

Chapter 27

Lei and Stevens lay facing each other in bed in the guest room of her aunt's house hours later. She'd snuck out of bed with her aunt to join him. Lei's head thumped with a terrible headache, the aftermath of heavy crying. She felt her whole body tighten and contract with pain as once again she remembered the bad news. "I still can't believe it. My aunty. It's so unfair!"

"I know." Stevens folded her even closer, so her head was tucked under his chin. "I'm so sorry, Sweets."

She closed her eyes and breathed in his scent, warm and a little salty. She felt it becoming embedded in her own DNA—they'd begun to share a smell, too.

"This is so wrong," Lei whispered. "It's not like I have a lot of family to lose."

"Maybe we should get started on expanding your family, after all."

She stiffened. "I don't know. We've just had a threat we still have to run down. All my personal issues aside, is it really fair to bring another person into this dark world, where we have real enemies?"

"We've always had enemies. We'll always have enemies. We fight them. It's what we do. We're the thin blue line."

They were law enforcement: that thin blue line between good and evil, anarchy and peace. That line was flawed, broken, and stressed, but Lei, Stevens, and their brothers and sisters in arms, in all their humanity and courage—they were all there was.

Lei turned her head to kiss the hollow of Stevens's throat, feeling his heartbeat under her lips. "All right."

"All right." His voice was a rumble of satisfaction. He kissed the top of her head. "Not tonight, though. I feel too weird with your dad on the other side of the wall and those sounds you make…"

She tugged his chest hair. "You mean those sounds *you* make! Let's get home and see what happens, but I think that's the least of our worries right now."

Much later the next day, Lei tucked Aunty Rosario into bed, pulling the antique Hawaiian quilt up under her aunt's chin and patting it into place. "I'll be in the next room, Aunty."

"I know," Rosario mumbled, eyes already shut. Stevens

was out, doing some shopping for the family. They'd spent a couple of hours in the morning catching up on pictures and stories from the honeymoon. Then, suddenly as a light switching off, her aunt had wilted and declared she was going to bed. Lei shut the curtains and went out into the hall, closing the door. She met her father in the tiny living room.

"She's really going downhill," Lei said, and her eyes filled. "Oh, Dad, I'm not ready for this."

He was settled deep in his La-Z-Boy, angled toward the big-screen TV on the wall. He flicked it off, making a welcoming arm gesture. "Come here."

Lei had found her father only four years ago, after his lengthy incarceration had separated them, so she wasn't used to being physically close—but snuggling in her father's arms to grieve felt like a necessity. She bent down, hugging him in the chair, and let him draw her onto his lap, her head on his shoulder, his arms around her.

Lei had a good cry, soaking her father's soft sweatshirt, wondering even as the tears flowed at how far her little family had come—only to be separated by a barrier that couldn't be crossed in this life. Wayne patted her back, and she felt five years old again. It was as if all that had come between them, all the years they'd lost, had folded like a ribbon to connect them in this moment. The feeling she had, lifting her streaming face, was gratitude.

"Thanks, Dad. I needed that."

His dark eyes were shiny too. "You wouldn't believe how much I've been crying. Every day."

Lei hauled herself out of the La-Z-Boy and stood up. "Once you're in this chair, it really gets ahold of you." She sat down on the nearby couch, pulled some tissues out of a box, and dried her face, blew her nose. "I'm going to stay as long as the job will let me."

"What about your husband?"

It still surprised her to hear Stevens called that. "He understands. He has to go home tomorrow, though. Work."

"You're newlyweds. I'll be worried if he understands for too long." Her father winked.

Lei laughed, a damp chuckle. "You're right. It will be hard to be away from him, but this is about as important as it gets."

"Speaking of important. There's something I want to get your opinion on." Wayne hoisted himself out of the recliner with the aid of a lever on the side of it. He rummaged in a nearby closet and came back carrying a plain brown cardboard box, the top opened. "This came in the mail. Fortunately, I intercepted it before your aunt saw it."

He set the box on the coffee table in front of Lei, opened the flaps. As soon as Lei saw the white linen fabric inside, she gave a cry—and wished she had her crime kit. "*Auwe*! Don't take it out! There might be explosives or something!"

"Too late," Wayne said. "I opened it without realizing

and took out these big pieces of material. There's nothing else in the box but a note." He took the fabric out and set two folded, fat squares of the linen on the coffee table.

"Here's the note. It was at the bottom. I'd already taken the fabric out by then, shaken it out to see what it was. I still wasn't sure until I went and Googled 'long white linen fabric' and it came back with 'shroud' as the most likely answer." He handed Lei the note. She took it, holding it by the edge with a piece of tissue.

It was a creamy white card stock square, hand lettered with black block lettering: PLENTY OF THESE TO GO AROUND.

Lei suppressed a shudder of revulsion and anxiety as she held the card by the edge. "I know where these shrouds came from—a place on Maui. We got a brochure and the receipt for them boxed and given to us with our wedding presents. I was wondering what happened to the actual shrouds. We'll take this package home and have everything checked out."

"What do you think this is about?" Her dad's craggy features were chiseled with worry, his brows drawn together.

"Someone's threatening our family. Packaged the receipt, gift wrapped it, and gave it to Michael and me in an attempt to ruin our honeymoon, which we didn't allow it to—and then the bastard mailed the shrouds to you guys to scare you. It's kind of a sick twofer."

"Twofer?"

"Two for the price of one."

"Who do you think is doing this?"

"Most likely our new enemy, Terence Chang the Third." She filled her dad in on the case last year that had ended Healani Chang's life.

Stevens returned, arms loaded with groceries, and his eyes went straight to the box on the coffee table between Lei and her father. His gaze sharpened and brows drew down. "The shrouds?"

"You got it."

He dropped the bags of groceries on the table and rummaged under the sink, returning with a large plastic garbage bag. "Dad's fingerprints are all over the box and he handled the shrouds," Lei said.

"Not a problem. We have your prints, right, Wayne?" And Lei couldn't believe it when Stevens winked, man-to-man, at her father.

Wayne laughed. "You sure as hell do. Not everyone gets to add a convicted felon to the family cop tree."

"We'll just eliminate your prints." Using the edge of the bag, he guided the box inside and tied it shut. "Not a problem."

"Don't you want to see the shrouds?" Lei asked.

"No," Stevens said, and carried the bag into the back

bedroom. Lei knew he was compartmentalizing the threat, like he was so good at doing with his police work. He returned. "Time I got home. Lei's staying a little longer."

Chapter 28

Lei had spent the morning with Rosario at the restaurant. Her aunt's best hours seemed to be in the morning, and when she felt good, she insisted on going in to work. In the kitchen, swathed in her plumeria-print apron, working alongside Momi, Rosario seemed almost her old self. Lei saw the affectionate gestures that passed between the women and the one time that Momi actually kissed her aunt on the top of her head.

That day as they drove home at lunch, Lei tackled a situation she'd suspected for a long time.

"Aunty. You and Momi—you love each other, don't you?"

Her aunt turned from gazing out the window to frown at Lei. "Of course I do. She's my best friend in the world and my business partner."

"I mean love, love. Romantic love."

"There are all kinds of love." Rosario looked away. "We don't need to put words on what we have."

"Don't you think, now, with your health the way it is… you might want to come out of the closet?"

"Stay out of my business, girl!" Rosario snapped. "You don't know a thing about it."

Lei felt her cheeks flush. Her aunt barked at her so seldom it hurt as if she'd been physically slapped. "Okay. I'm sorry."

"Your father would never understand, and she's married," Rosario finally said, her voice a whisper. "Not that we have ever been like that, you know. Physical. But I would like to have her by my side at the end."

"And you will," Lei said. "I'll make sure of it."

Her aunt's hand stole over and clasped Lei's. "Thank you. I just don't want you to get the wrong idea."

"I just love you and want you to be happy. I'm sorry if I had the wrong idea." They were both in tears as they pulled into the driveway, and Lei supported her aunt into the house and back to bed for a nap.

Lei took her phone and went outside. The street was deserted during the middle of a workday, and she had a lot of calls to make. First she called Stevens. He'd just landed on Maui.

"It's windy here," he said. "I wish you were with me."

"I know. I'll be home when the captain says I'll be cleared to come back on the job, but I need to be with Aunty as much as I can."

"I love you. There. You've had your daily dose of love."

"I wish I'd had my other kind of daily dose of love," Lei said, smiling at the sidewalk. In all the turmoil, they hadn't made love since Yosemite.

"God, I know. I won't wish you'd come home sooner. That wouldn't be right. Just know I'll be missing you."

"Love you too." Lei cut the connection, hardly able to speak. She walked rapidly back and forth on the sidewalk, breathing and getting her emotions under control. She called Pono and asked him about the interview with Rinker.

"I can send you the recording if you want," Pono offered again.

"I don't want you to get in trouble. Just gimme the lowdown."

"Well, he basically corroborated the confession. He agreed to testify against Kingston in return for reduced charges for his role in covering up the body. The DA's on board with that, and so was Rinker's lawyer. Captain was pleased."

"But why did he agree to cover up Jacobsen's murder? And what about the poachers?"

"He claims he doesn't know anything about the poachers, and he agreed to help dispose of Jacobsen's body since, quote: 'He was already dead, and Kingston's research needed to go forward,' unquote. Both these guys say they planned to anonymously call in the body dump after the research was published."

"Man, they seem to think the research justifies anything! So how's Kingston doing with his injury?"

"Slowly improving. Takama's been charged with attempted murder, you know. Captain told me she was dickering with the DA over charges against you too; they've decided on criminal negligence in the care of prisoner, which is a misdemeanor. Captain's working on a disciplinary plan for you to come home to."

"Great," Lei muttered, rubbing bloodshot eyes. "Thanks, Pono." A car swished by, putting her back in her body. Well, at least she wasn't going to jail. She had to focus on the positive.

"How's your aunty?"

"Hanging in there. But something bad has happened." She told Pono about the package.

"So that's where the actual shrouds ended up. Someone's playing games with your whole family! Pretty theatrical gesture."

"I think it's in keeping with Terence Chang's personality. In fact, I've got to call Sophie Ang about the poaching order on the birds, and I'll check with her about her impressions of Chang."

The next morning, Lei borrowed Aunty's car while she and Wayne were at work and drove to the Marin Headlands. She set out on a sandy trail through the park, letting a good run sweat out all the worries she was struggling with.

The rolling hills, carpeted in golden dried grasses and punctuated by the dark green of live oaks, surrounded her with a different beauty than the lush green of Hawaii. San Francisco Bay's muted, steely blue water glittered far below her, and the sky smoldered with sunshine banked by fog forming on the coast.

Her heart thudded as her feet pounded, and eventually, that metronome drowned out the buzz of her thoughts, circling endlessly around questions she didn't have answers for. Finally, she sat on one of the rough wooden benches poised in front of the view, did some stretches, drank some water, and took out her phone.

"Hey, Lei." Sophie Ang's slightly husky voice with its lilt of an accent conjured her riveting friend, almost as if the agent were seated on the bench beside Lei. "How's married life?"

"It would be great if we were together, but I'm in California. My aunty Rosario's got late-stage pancreatic cancer."

"Oh no! She seemed so healthy at the wedding!"

"She puts a good face on." Lei sighed. "But she's not getting treatment, and I'm trying to spend as much time as possible with her. Anyway, I called about a couple of things. I wondered if you found out anything about the native bird poaching online."

"Oh yes. I didn't want to bother you on your honeymoon, but I found an order for them, live if possible, from someone in China. Probably a collector or an aviary of some sort. I took the ad down, reported it to Interpol. But it's always possible they'll just put up another one, so I've got multiple alerts out looking for it."

"Oh thanks. Good. The case is wrapping up." Lei filled Sophie in on Kingston's confession and apprehension. "Unfortunately, it's a mess with him getting away and getting shot while in my custody."

"I'm so sorry, Lei. For that and for your aunt's health."

"Well, speaking of, there's this other thing." Lei told her about the shrouds mailed to her aunt and father and the receipt they'd received in their wedding gifts. "The only person I can imagine who hates me and my family enough for this kind of gesture is Terence Chang. You interacted with him online a lot in our last FBI case together; does this shroud thing seem like something he might do?"

A long pause as Sophie considered this. "I don't know. He had a dramatic side, that's for sure, liked the whole online world of smoke and mirrors. I'd see some sort of Internet-related harassment as more his style—there's a kind of childish drama about this threat that bothers me. Have you talked to Dr. Wilson about it?"

"No, but that's a good idea. Well, at least you found the posting for the birds. Hopefully, we can keep that shut down." She bid her friend goodbye and got back on the trail. After her cool down at the car, she turned on her aunt's elderly Honda's AC, blasting it in her face as she called Dr. Wilson.

"Lei!" The psychologist's voice was upbeat. "How was the honeymoon?"

"You were right when you told me I just needed to follow my head, not my heart this time. It was all amazing. I feel like I passed through a gauntlet."

Caprice Wilson laughed, her warm voice a familiar comfort to Lei—though just as often the psychologist had pushed Lei outside her comfort zone and provoked anger and defensiveness. "That's a wedding, in a nutshell. Only the brave and committed make it through—especially weddings that are postponed a day."

"I'm calling you with a question, though. From California." Lei filled Dr. Wilson in on the honeymoon, her aunt's illness, and the threats they'd had in the form of the shrouds and their purchase on Maui. "I suspect Terence Chang, the new head of the Chang crime family. Young, creative, and hates me just as much as the rest of his family did. He blames me for his grandmother's death in that last big case I had with the FBI. So I'm thinking it's him. What do you think?"

"I need a lot more information. Can you get me anything

from that old case where you discovered each other?"

"Unfortunately, no. The case where we crossed paths was when I was with the FBI, and I don't have access to their records anymore. I can write up what I know, though, and you can think about it."

"Yes. Happy to help with that under the umbrella of my role as police resource psychologist. Now, you never told me—are you pregnant?"

Lei realized she'd forgotten all about the question that had seemed so pressing just before the wedding.

"No. No, I'm not." Lei sighed, tilting the vent so the air-conditioning blew the curls off her forehead. "We looked at the test together on the honeymoon, and I got my period eventually. I've always been irregular, so I shouldn't have been so nervous about it—but I had those other symptoms too. I think I was just freaked out by the whole thing."

"I'm proud of you. You didn't run away this time."

"No, I didn't, and whatever anybody else thinks, I'm glad I postponed the wedding. Kingston and Rinker would have been long gone when I got back. Not only that, Stevens and I are considering letting nature take its course, if you know what I mean."

"That's a big step—but for what it's worth, I think you'll be excellent parents. Send me what you have on Chang, and I'll venture an opinion."

"Will do. That will give me something to focus on in

the next few days. It's so hard being here with Aunty the way she is." Lei told the psychologist about the constant tearfulness, about crying on her dad's shoulder. "I can't believe we've come all this way and I'm losing her."

"It's terrible." Dr. Wilson said. "Life just isn't fair, is it?"

"I think I said that first," Lei said. "But I'm trying to make the best of what we have left."

"That's all you can do. I'm proud of you, my dear."

Lei hung up with that small warming comfort, held close against all that was wrong and couldn't be changed.

Chapter 29

The phone buzzing beside her little twin bed roused Lei from a sleeping-pill-induced grogginess. She fumbled over to lift the phone, still plugged into the charger, to her ear.

"Hello?"

"Did I wake you, Texeira?" Captain Omura's crisp voice brought her awake and upright. "It's late to be in bed back there." Lei squinted over at the small old-fashioned clock on the nightstand.

"It's ten a.m. here, Captain. Yes, I should be up, but I had to take a sleeping pill last night."

The captain's voice softened. "I was sorry to hear about your aunt from Pono. Listen, I won't keep you—but I need you to come home. We've run into some issues with the Bowhunter case. Shimoda wants to depose you, and we're trying to keep Kingston's prosecution out of a full trial, settle it by plea bargaining. He seems to be pulling through, you'll be happy to hear."

"Yes, very much so," Lei said, getting out of bed and unplugging the phone. She turned and began stripping the bed, her heart accelerating in anticipation at the thought of returning to Stevens and work. "I'll call you as soon as I land. I will need some more time off for family leave—in the coming months."

Rosario seemed to have rallied in the last five days with Lei there, and the doctors had cautiously pronounced her stable for the moment.

"Of course. Call me when you land." Omura hung up.

Lei took her bundled laundry into the laundry room and started the load, going to check on her aunt. She was surprised to see the bed empty and neatly made and a note by the coffeemaker: *You seemed to need the extra sleep. Your aunty and I are at the restaurant. Love, Dad.*

Lei helped herself to a mug of dark brew and began making calls for her departure.

She took a cab to the restaurant, hugging and kissing her aunt and Momi goodbye.

"I'll be back in a few weeks. Stay healthy," Lei ordered her aunt in stern tones, hands on her hips.

"I'll do my best," Rosario said, smiling as she wiped her hands on a dishcloth. This morning she looked bright and healthy, her hair glossy and curling out of its braid, the weight she'd lost complementing her petite figure and bringing out the strong bone structure she shared with Wayne—which he'd passed on to Lei. "I'm going to miss you, but I know you need to get home to that husband of yours. I'll be fine."

"And I'll let you know if she isn't," Wayne rumbled, hugging Lei hard. "Come back soon," he whispered in her ear. "And thanks for handling that shroud thing."

"We're working on it," Lei whispered back, and gave him a kiss on the cheek. "Aloha to all." She waved to the whole noisy roomful of customers and got into a shuttle to the airport.

Getting off the plane in Maui was always a relief because the wind made landings bumpy flying into the island. Outside the terminal, on the sidewalk, that same wind tossed her already disordered curls into a frizz, and she was irritably bundling them into a rubber band when Stevens pulled up in his Bronco.

"Don't," he said, jumping out and coming around the SUV. He plucked the rubber band out of her hand. "I like your hair wild."

He pulled her into his arms. His kiss was hard and hungry.

"I missed you," he said, and she just nodded as they kissed again. "Let's get home. Now."

"The captain wanted me to call as soon as I touched down," Lei said.

"This won't take long," Stevens said, and Lei's knees buckled at the promise behind his words and how instantly she responded to him. She had to grab the door handle for support to get into the Bronco.

That first time really didn't take long, and it was nowhere near enough. The next time did, though.

It was a good long while before Lei finally called the captain.

Late evening on a Tuesday wasn't the busiest time at Kahului Station. Going into the familiar urban-ugly building had begun to feel like home, and Lei grinned at Torufu, who was looming over a sudoku pad, taking a shift behind the watch desk.

"Bet you scare everybody straight who walks through that door," she said.

"I do my best," Torufu said with a flash of his giant teeth. "Hey, what ever happened with that metal box you found, the non-bomb?"

"Case is wrapping up. Someone was trying to poach our rare birds, but I think it's shut down," Lei said. "Thanks for your help that day."

"I hardly ever get a real bomb," Torufu said wistfully. "One of these days I'll get lucky."

"We have different ideas of what luck is, obviously," Lei said, heading to the cubicle where Pono was waiting.

She hugged her partner briefly.

"Had a quick stop at the house, I see, and a shower." Pono winked, tugging on one of her wet curls. "Newlyweds will be newlyweds."

"My hair was a mess from the plane," Lei said, blushing. "Where does the Steel Butterfly want us? And what's going on?"

"I'm not sure. I just know she said she was bringing you home ASAP." They walked down the hall to Omura's office with a quick stop for Lei to grab a cup of coffee. Omura swiveled away from her computer. As usual, her desk was a pristine expanse and her manicure fresh.

"You finally got here," she greeted Lei, sharp eyes taking in Lei's freshly groomed appearance. Lei decided not to answer, instead sitting on one of the hard plastic supplicant chairs in front of the desk.

"I got here as soon as I could. What's going on with the case?"

"Well, there have been some developments." Omura aimed a red-tipped nail at Pono. "Close the door, please."

Pono obeyed, and he and Lei glanced at each other—the captain seldom shut the door.

"I was talking with the DA and we were on our way to a deal with Kingston through his attorney, Shimoda.

We were going to prosecute him for two second-degree murders and one attempted murder, reducing charges for his cooperation. It seemed like things were moving forward, and then suddenly Shimoda pulled the plug. Petitioned to get the confession excluded, changed Kingston's plea to not guilty."

Lei frowned. "Why change his tune? We still have Rinker."

"But we don't." Omura steepled her fingertips. "District Attorney Hiromo called. Rinker was out on bail and he's disappeared. Hiromo tried to bring him in for another deposition, and he can't be located. I wanted to bring you two in to inform you and brainstorm next steps. We never did pin the poachers onto Kingston—or Rinker, for that matter."

"Yeah," Pono corroborated, looking at Lei. "The bow we recovered had Kingston's prints on it, but when Gerry and I field-tested it and the other bows we'd collected, it didn't have the power to penetrate a body as deeply as the poacher was, from the blind's position."

"Well, dammit," Lei said. "Could Rinker be the one who shot the poachers? Could that be why he cooperated with burying Jacobsen's body? Or why he fled now? Maybe those two were in bed together on all these murders and were hoping to get away with them, pointing fingers at each other to confuse us. Does Rinker have a bow?"

"Already checked and searched his house while you were

in the Mainland." Pono rubbed his lips. "And we haven't found any weapons of any kind at his place."

"Not that that means anything," Omura injected. "He'd have a good incentive to conceal any weapons."

"Murders aside, I wonder if he left the island trying to get Kingston's research published," Lei said. "Whatever else he and Kingston did, they both believed that project was worth any human cost."

"I agree," Omura said. "I'd already authorized a watch at the airport and a statewide BOLO for Rinker, but it might have come too late."

"I'm sorry, Captain," Pono said. "I didn't think he was a flight risk. I thought having Kingston's laptop, which we found in Jacobsen's house, and lab books locked up, kept that research under control—but maybe Kingston had already given Rinker another copy somewhere, somehow."

"Another concern. Shimoda's subpoenaed Lei's deposition for his case. He's going to try to discredit you," Omura told Lei, her brows furrowed. "Get you to admit you coerced that confession and mishandled the search. If he gets that confession excluded, we won't have anything but circumstantial on Kingston, and Rinker's taped interview— which should be allowed, but is just hearsay with nothing to back it up. Don't go to that deposition without our union attorney. I'm concerned. Both these men could walk, and

Shimoda could be trying to pull something on you, Lei."

Lei felt her stomach curdling with anxiety and apprehension as they were dismissed.

Chapter 30

Shimoda's conference room, with its long mango-wood table topped in glass, framed print, and whiteboard on one wall, was unpretentious. Shimoda, dapper in a lightweight tan suit, stated the date and time after he activated a black recording unit. Present were Shimoda himself, Lei, and Lei's union attorney, Gordon Kelly, a pale man in the button-down pinstripes of a recent Mainland transplant.

Lei kept her hands in her lap, where she could employ one of her old stress-management techniques, squeezing the web of flesh between her thumb and forefinger. Shimoda smiled. His mouth moved, but his cold eyes never changed.

"Thanks for joining us, Detective."

"Lieutenant. Lieutenant Texeira." Lei felt irritation prickle along her jangled nerves. He knew her rank perfectly well, was just trying to put her down.

"Lieutenant, then." He inclined his head, patronizing. "So tell us what led to the decision to take Edward Kingston out of custody in the correctional facility and use him to find items you would then use in his own prosecution, a clear violation of his Fifth Amendment rights?"

"Is there a question in that accusation?" Kelly said. "Rephrase." Kelly looked like a skinny prep school kid, but he had the gravelly voice of a much older and more jaded man. Lei relaxed marginally—Kelly appeared to have some skills and wasn't afraid to use them.

"Tell us about the decision to have Kingston show you the location of his lab and the weapon he'd buried." Shimoda bared his teeth again, and Lei realized it was his version of her own "evil grin." She relaxed a little further—he wasn't going to intimidate her with tricks she already knew.

"Kingston volunteered to show us the location of his lab and hidden weapon. I went with my partner to talk with him in the county lockup, and he offered to take us up to where his lab was. Seemed confident we wouldn't find anything incriminating there—in fact, at one point inside the lab, he said definitely, 'You won't find anything.' Not only that, he signed a waiver."

"Were you aware it was against Kingston's Fifth Amendment rights to use him to procure items that might then be used against him in a court of law?"

"Kingston volunteering to guide the detectives was an implicit waiver of those rights," Kelly said. "And as the lieutenant said, he signed a waiver."

"But he was never informed of his rights and that he was waiving them," Shimoda said. "He didn't know what he was agreeing to."

"I wish I had thought of reading him Miranda again and getting the whole thing on tape," Lei said. "If I knew what a sticking point it would be, I certainly would have. As it was, I took his volunteering as an implied waiver, as Mr. Kelly here has said, and he signed further documentation, informal as it was. And, as you know, we never did find anything in the lab that tied him to any of the murders."

"So you admit you endangered a prisoner, still wearing restraints, by taking him out to the wilderness."

"Kingston begged me to take him out of the jail, even for a day. He didn't care. And he was the one who tried to escape." Kelly caught Lei's eye and gave a quick head shake, and Lei shut her mouth.

"So. To rewind back to the events of that day: You and a young, unseasoned officer took Kingston, in restraints, up to a wild area in the company of an armed civilian."

Lei felt sweat prickle under her armpits. She glanced at Kelly, but he gave no sign. She looked back at Shimoda and nodded.

"Please speak up for the recording," Shimoda said. "Use 'yes' or 'no' for the record."

"Yes," Lei said.

"Would you call this decision a reckless one? Perhaps a bad idea?"

"Objection. Leading," Kelly said.

"I can lead all I want. This is a deposition under oath, not a courtroom," Shimoda shot back. "Answer the question, Lieutenant Texeira."

"In hindsight, I should have tried harder to find another way to locate the items in question," Lei said carefully.

"So you admit it was a mistake."

"No."

"How was it not a mistake?"

"We found the items." Lei set her jaw and stared Shimoda down as best she could.

"You have a history of reckless police work, do you not?" Shimoda flipped open a file Lei hadn't noticed until now. "I've subpoenaed your personnel files, and there are numerous irregular instances documented here. Shall I go on?"

"I'd rather you didn't," Lei said, looking desperately at Kelly. He gave a slight shrug, indicating Shimoda was able to proceed.

"Let's see. First note is way back when you were a patrol officer. Corrective action for letting your personal attack dog off leash to find an intruder endangering civilians— and we go on from there."

"No one was hurt," Lei said, through numb lips.

"That's a matter of opinion. Insubordination, failing to inform your superior officer, improper evidence collection. Oh—and here's an interesting one from your stint in the FBI: reckless endangerment in jumping out of a helicopter to capture an escaping perpetrator."

"I was trying to save the suspect's life," Lei said, but Kelly made a cutting-off hand gesture. He addressed Shimoda.

"Make your point."

"My point is that Lieutenant Texeira here has a long history of going off half-cocked. I even see a very fresh note in here, signed by Captain Omura last week, that she's going to be docked three days' pay and has a mandatory workshop to attend on rights and responsibilities of law enforcement toward those in their custody. It appears her superior officer also had some concerns about her actions in this situation."

Lei looked down at her hands in her lap, squeezed the web of her hand as hard as she could. It didn't seem to be helping.

"Let's move along," Kelly said. "If you have any actual questions for my client."

"Why didn't you remove the weapon from Ranger Takama?"

"He seemed trustworthy. He stated that he used the

weapon for ungulates in the forest and that he always carried it. As a ranger, I assumed he had a degree of authority to do so. Later, when a boar came at us out of nowhere, he effectively dispatched it."

"And one could say he'd just proved both mettle and marksmanship. Why didn't you remove the bow from him at that point?"

"It was a very stressful situation. We had just escaped injury from the boar and were distracted. Then we discovered Kingston had escaped. There was no time."

"What did you do at that point?"

Lei glanced at Kelly. He had no guidance for her, so she said, "I exclaimed and went after Kingston. I called out to him to stop. I drew my weapon. Kingston had already made it to the bottom of the gulch and was getting away by hopping rocks down the stream. I'd chased him before and knew how fast he was."

"Was he still restrained?"

"He was still in cuffs, yes, but they were in front and didn't slow him down a bit that I could see."

"Tell us how he got out of the other restraint you had on him, and what it was."

"We'd clipped a length of light chain from his cuffs to a bracelet on Officer Cantorna's wrist."

"Were you aware Kingston sustained bruising and injuries to both wrists and soft tissue damage to his neck from the restraints?"

"No, I was not aware." Lei felt her voice rising. "I was too busy trying to save his life. If the defendant had not tried to run, none of this would have happened."

"Were you aware Kingston has stated, under oath, that he fled because he was in fear for his life?"

"Bu—baloney," Lei said, amending her language. "The fact that he found a way to take, conceal, and use the wire cutters shows premeditation."

"He says he always felt in danger from Ranger Takama because of the ranger's friendship with Jacobsen. He was afraid from the moment he saw the ranger and decided to get away."

"Disagree," Lei said. She took her hands out of her lap and spread them on the table, gave Shimoda her own evil grin. "Cantorna can verify that Kingston was thrilled to be back in the forest and never batted an eye over Takama's inclusion in our hike. Never addressed him directly, true, but certainly didn't exhibit any fear. Also, your statement supports an admission of guilt in Jacobsen's shooting. Because not only did I record that confession, but I heard it with my own ears. I'm prepared to testify under oath: Kingston admitted to killing Jacobsen."

"We'll come back to that," Shimoda barked. He clearly didn't like her going on the offensive. "Explain how he escaped."

"Kingston found a pair of wire cutters in the lab while we were searching it. I remember him standing up near a box of supplies set on the wooden shelf he used as a workbench. We attached his chain to a bracket on one of the trees while we were searching. He must have concealed the cutters on his body. Later, during the distraction with the boar, he cut the chain and ran off."

"Is there some reason you didn't search Kingston after you'd gone through the lab?"

"I didn't have reason to." Lei bit the inside of her cheek, suppressing her own second-guessing. "I moved the box very shortly after he was chained into place. I didn't suspect his actions. Until then, the day had been very cordial."

"So take us back to his escape, just after both you and Takama shot the wild boar."

Lei paused a moment to recall the action-packed moments. "I verbalized a command to stop. I had my weapon out as a matter of habit, when I saw him fall. The arrow he'd been shot with was visible, protruding from his back. Cantorna disarmed Takama, and I restrained the ranger with handcuffs. I called for help on the sat phone. I climbed down the cliff into the gulch, moved Kingston out of the water to help deal with his shock. He asked for help, and I said it was on its way."

"Then you coerced him to confess. You told him he looked bad off, and this was his last chance to talk."

"No. I made a second call for help from the transport, and I said, 'This man is bad off' to Dispatch, which was true. I could see he had a pierced lung. I was concerned for his life."

"And then you encouraged him to confess."

"I asked him what really happened, yes."

"And you were right there recording what he said. Then you prompted him further, after he'd admitted accidentally shooting Jacobsen, to tell you about the poachers."

Lei stayed silent. Shimoda prompted, "Lieutenant?"

"Yes. I asked him if he shot the poachers too."

"And what did he respond?"

"He did not respond. He'd lapsed into unconsciousness."

"I will submit that your recorded confession is inadmissible. It was coerced from a man who thought he was dying, manipulated out of him by an officer who planted fear for my client's life in his mind and played on his emotions. Texeira, you even tried to get him to admit to murders he had nothing to do with. The whole expedition was unconscionable."

"Was there a question for my client in your diatribe, Counselor?" Kelly said. "If not, we'll be on our way." He took Lei's elbow, and she stood with alacrity. Shimoda's mouth was still ajar as Kelly hustled Lei out and down the hall.

"That was all foreplay. He just shot his load, and I don't think we need to hang around for the pillow talk," Kelly told her.

Lei snorted at his unexpected crudity. She couldn't resist stretching her arms overhead and filling her lungs as full as they would go with fresh air the minute they stepped into the sunshine outside.

"Whew. Thank God that's over. Thanks for your help."

"I kind of think you're lucky he hasn't brought any charges against you," Kelly said as they walked toward the parking lot. "Shimoda wants to obscure his client's guilt by getting the focus on you and perceived mishandling of the case."

"Believe me, I know," Lei said. "And I hear Kingston's family might still be working on a civil suit against the county, naming me. I'm just worried because now we're worse off than ever with this case. Rinker's in the wind with his corroborating testimony, the confession might be excluded, and Pono says we don't have any physical evidence connecting Kingston to any of the murders. We're back at square one."

Kelly gave her shoulder a reassuring whack. "Sometimes it's darkest before the dawn."

"Cliché, Counselor," Lei said, grinning. She liked him. "How long have you been on Maui?"

"Just a couple of weeks. Relocated from Minnesota."

They'd arrived at her truck, parked next to his red Mustang. "Former rental car," Kelly said. "Got it for a song."

"Looks fun." Lei's chest tightened for a moment, remembering another friend who'd loved a red Mustang. "Well, you've come to the right place to get away from the cold. Here's a local cliché about solving this case: 'If can, can. If no can, no can.'"

Kelly looked blank, and Lei laughed. "It's pidgin English, our dialect here in the islands. It means '*If you can, you can. If you can't, you can't.*'"

Now Kelly laughed, a big, barrel-chested rumble. "How do you say that?"

"If can, can. If no can, no can." Lei shook her head. "I guess that's really where we are."

"I hope that's not where you are for long. But try coloring inside the lines from here on out, why don't you?"

"I'll do my best," Lei said. "But then, believe it or not, I always try to."

Chapter 31

I want to take you up on the mountain," Lei told Stevens. She'd arrived home before him, for once, and after updating the captain and Pono on her deposition, felt a great need to get back outside into nature. She packed a picnic she'd put together into a Foodland cooler bag. "We haven't gone up the crater once together to watch the sunset. It's past time."

"Excellent. I like the domestic goddess moment," Stevens said, kissing the back of her neck. "Can I take a shower first? Had a nasty traffic accident investigation and got sweaty."

"Long as I can join you," she said. "I got sweated too— under the hot lights with Shimoda."

It wasn't long before they were on the road to the top of the mountain, leaving a mournful-looking Keiki behind— dogs weren't allowed in the national park. Stevens rolled his window down, taking in the views. "Can't believe I haven't been up here."

"Yeah. That's criminal." Lei glanced away from the road to grin at him. "Maybe I ought to spank you."

"Ohh, I'm trembling with—anticipation."

"You should be." She reached over to squeeze his leg, then had to swerve to avoid a tourist drifting across the centerline, trying to get a picture of the view. "Guess I better pay attention to the road."

"So what brought this idea on?"

"I don't know. I'm just so frustrated with the whole case, so worried about the birds. I want to show them to you." Lei's holster dug into her arm. She didn't know why she'd put it back on after the shower—maybe because it felt good to have it back after the mandatory leave. "I've heard the sunset off the top of the crater is amazing. Why should the tourists have all the fun?"

"Yeah, it's so weird how when you live somewhere, no matter how amazing a place it is, you do the same things. Go to work, run errands, come home. It's a rut."

"So how about one of our new ruts is that we have to take a picnic or eat out somewhere on our beautiful island once a week."

"I like it." He reached over to play with the curls tossing in the wind of her open window. "We did it, Lei. We got married."

"Yeah. I'm pretty proud of us. Wasn't without hurting

someone, though." Their eyes met for a moment, and reflected in them was the haunting memory of Stevens's first wife. Lei would never forget the moment she spotted Anchara in the audience of their wedding—and the sweet smile the other woman had given her.

"She's okay," Stevens said. "She sent me an e-mail not long ago. Got into the culinary arts program at UH Maui. Really happy with it."

"Good." Lei preferred to forget his disastrous first marriage had ever happened, but she knew she was at least partly responsible for it—both that it had occurred and that it hadn't worked out. "Speaking of old business—Consuelo graduates from her group home next month. She's in college full-time and fielding offers for her memoir." Consuelo, Lei's young protégée, had a story well worth telling.

"Now, that's good news."

They reached the booth entrance to the park and, since it was after hours, no personnel were there. "Just a quick stop at Hosmer's Grove before we go to the summit," Lei said. "I want you to get to know the birds."

"I like to see you this passionate about something."

"I can't help it. I seem to have fallen in love with them. I've got the bird bug."

"Lotta bird lovers in the world. You're in good company."

They parked the truck, and Lei took Stevens's hand. "We have to hurry. I just want to show you the canyon; then we have to get to the top before the sunset."

They broke into a jog on the short, well-worn trail that wound through the grove of nonnative trees to the edge of the deep canyon where Lei had taken Marcella and Sophie.

"Here." Lei took his big hand in both of hers, and they sat on the bench, looking out at the multilayered green tapestry of native forest. Beside her at the end of the bench, tiny purple-and-white blossoms of a rare live sandalwood tree tickled her nostrils with a subtle citrusy scent. Lei closed her eyes. She felt the pure, sweet notes of native birdsong through her body, vibrating to the sound like a plucked string.

She felt Stevens draw her into his arms, pulling her across his lap and tucking her under his chin, and when she peeked up she saw his eyes were closed too.

There was nothing but the whisper of wind in the trees, the liquid grace of the birds' song. Near enough to touch, a cloud rolled down from the summit like an angel in full flight and covered the canyon with soft gray mist.

"This place is magical," Stevens whispered. "I see a red bird. What is that?"

Lei pointed out the various species they could see, scanning the forest to pick them out and show him.

Deep in the gulch, she spotted movement.

Lei sat upright, leaping quick and quiet off Stevens's lap and dropping down low behind the handmade stone parapet that bordered the view area. She turned back, held a finger to her lips, and made a "get down" gesture. He slid down off the bench and hurried over to her. Together they peeked down into the dim at the bottom of the canyon.

"I don't see anything," Stevens whispered. Lei didn't respond. She'd learned to sit quiet and let her eyes roam, searching for the odd angle or glint that signaled something out of place in a totally natural environment.

There it was—Lei spotted a tiny glint, though in the wavery light of evening, with cloud cover, it was hard to tell. She spotted a dark shape, too—and it started moving.

"Someone's down there," Lei whispered. Her gut was telling her something again. "We're looking for Rinker. It might be him." Lei scrunched down low and moved to the edge of the viewing area, climbing through the low steel barrier. She could see a faint wear pattern in the brush leading down into the canyon, an extremely steep descent. She grabbed a handhold and lowered herself over the edge, feeling for a foothold, and did it again.

"Lei!" Stevens's whisper was harsh from above her. "We're off the clock. You don't even know if this has anything to do with your case!"

"I have a feeling, and I brought my weapon," Lei whispered, looking up at his distressed face, blue eyes almost black in the shadows. "It's okay. Call for backup."

And she kept climbing, down and down, into the murk at the bottom of the canyon.

Chapter 32

Lei crouched behind a boulder in the dry creek bed, engulfed in the shadows of approaching evening and underbrush. She moved forward, heading as quick and quiet in her athletic shoes, keeping behind cover as she was able.

Up ahead, she saw movement again—this time spotting the outline of a man moving away down the creek bed.

Could it be the missing Rinker? Perhaps he'd come back up to stash something incriminating in the canyon, or finish something with the research—or perhaps he was just hiding, camping in the forest until he could get off the island.

He was probably armed.

Lei drew her weapon and realized in that moment that something in her had been waiting, hunting her prey even as she outwardly packed a picnic.

On the other hand, it was also quite possible she'd just ruined her evening with Stevens to chase a tourist who'd gone off the beaten path sightseeing. It reminded her of her early days, chasing black Toyota trucks for no good reason but her gut telling her to.

Didn't matter.

She was committed. Instinct was telling her to follow this guy.

She scrambled as fast as she could, worrying she was going to be spotted, worrying she was going to lose the figure so far ahead she could barely glimpse him.

And then he disappeared.

Time to go faster. Lei stopped trying to hide and simply ran down the streambed as fast as she could. She remembered Kingston's speed hopping from rock to rock, energy like a hurdler as he flew over the uneven terrain— but she wasn't the wiry grad student with his months of practice. She hit a loose rock and tripped, going down hard on a knee. She stifled a cry of pain.

Lei decided to stay down for a minute. After checking her knee was only bruised, she hunched in the shadow of the rocks and lifted her head to look around.

Nothing was moving. The sky, encroached upon by trees, was streaked with gold and red high above, reminding her she was missing the sunset on this fool's errand. Her breathing slowed, and she continued to lie and wait and watch.

Her patience was rewarded.

Movement behind a tree on the edge of the streambed. A male figure, height around five foot ten, coalesced from the shadows and moved toward her, light and careful, silent as the whisper of wind in the leaves above.

She realized he was coming to investigate where she'd gone down. He'd watched her go by, and now her fall had caught his curiosity.

She scooted backward, further behind the shelter of a large rock, and gathered her body into a crouch, drawing her weapon. Pulled back, she could no longer watch his approach—so she listened and finally heard the faintest rustle of movement. She rose just high enough to set her weapon on top of the rock and yell with the volume and command of a cannon: "Police! Stop right there! Drop your weapon and put your hands on your head!"

An arrow buzzed by in answer, so close it nicked the top of the rock, sending slivers of rock dust flying into her eyes. Lei brought her weapon back up and fired without looking—and, rubbing her eyes, peeked up over the rock.

Ranger Takama stood before her, hands raised. He was only about six feet away, wearing camo gear from head to toe. He dropped his bow with a clatter onto the rocks. "Don't shoot."

"Did I hit you?" Lei was so surprised it was Takama that

she knew her voice came out high and squeaky.

"You missed." Takama's voice was calm as ever.

"Well, I won't miss a second time," she said. "Get on your knees and put your hands on your head."

He obeyed, and she got up out of her niche and came around. She didn't have her cuffs with her, so she patted down his pockets and slid his backpack off his arms. Keeping her gun on him, she rifled the pockets until she found a length of rope and then used it to bind his hands behind his back.

"What are you doing down here?" Lei asked. Takama stared straight ahead and stayed silent. Only when he was secured did she sit down facing him, gun in hand, and call Stevens.

"Got Takama down here. Any backup coming?"

"They're on their way. Goddamn it, Lei!"

She hung up on his expletives and slid the phone back into her pocket. "Get up. Let's move."

Takama stood, turning. She hoisted his backpack herself and they moved back up the creek, much slower this time. The backpack was heavy, and her knee had begun to throb.

"What are you doing out of jail? I thought they had you in lockup."

"They let me out on bail," Takama said. "Yesterday."

Lei mentally cursed the gap in communication that had

led to this surprise even as she recited the Miranda warning to him.

"You shot the poachers, didn't you?" Lei said.

Takama didn't answer.

"Tell you what. It's just you and me here. I think I know what happened. Just nod your head yes or shake it no. I won't capture you on tape or anything. I just want to know for my own—closure."

Takama nodded, his buzz-cut, salt-and-pepper hair blending with the darkness forming around them. He stumbled in that darkness. Lei hid her jubilation. She might not be taping him, but she'd Mirandized him, and she could testify to any nonverbal admissions he made.

"Okay. Here's what I think you're doing here. You got out, packed up, and decided to live out here for a while and keep any poachers away from the birds."

Takama gave a single brusque nod.

"You shot the two poachers. You pretended to find the first body after it had been there awhile and the stink would have brought attention."

Takama gave a single nod, and she continued, encouraged. "After you found out birds died on the first poacher, you called in the second one to get us up here quicker and save them, which we did. You didn't want to approach the body yourself and leave any trace—you've been very good at avoiding any trace."

Takama gave his taciturn nod.

"You didn't know your buddy Jacobsen would take it on himself to find the bow hunter, as we've been calling him, and get himself shot by Kingston," Lei continued.

A single nod from Takama.

"You must also have been worried that Kingston saw something more, that he might trade that information when he was captured. It made you look for an opportunity to get rid of him and point the finger at him for all the murders."

A head shake from Takama, and he glared over his shoulder. She pushed him lightly so that he stumbled forward.

"Keep moving. Okay, you don't like that as your motivation. You shot Kingston because he shot your friend. For revenge."

The brusque head nod again.

"Well, I'm sure it also would have been nice for Kingston to die and take the fall for all the murders."

Nothing from Takama. The dark was getting so thick, Lei took out her phone and thumbed on the flashlight app, shining it at their feet as they made their way along. She spotted another light, bouncing toward them—probably Stevens.

"What about Rinker and Kingston's arrangement? Did you know about that?"

Head shake.

Stevens reached them. He took one of Takama's arms, but his eyes had gone straight to Lei. "You okay?"

"Bruised knee is all. This backpack's heavy and I've got this bow—it's bulky. Can you help?" She handed him the backpack, and they hiked on through the dark lit by their phone flashlights.

"Time to face the music, Takama," Lei said as they reached the ascension area. The man's proud shoulders sagged. Lei realized she'd never heard his first name. He was so completely identified with his identity as a ranger that he didn't seem to have one.

But that identity was over now, and Lei felt a pang of something like regret as she handed him over to the officers who'd descended the cliff.

Chapter 33

Stevens took the wheel of her truck for the drive down the mountain, his jaw set. The sunset was long gone, and the headlights of the truck cut through velvet darkness, following the narrow winding ribbon of road leading down the volcano. The adrenaline from Takama's capture had drained away, leaving Lei shaky and exhausted. She hauled the cooler bag out of the backseat, unwrapped a sandwich, but the movement of the truck had begun to make her queasy.

"I'm feeling carsick—I kind of get that way on this road. Can we pull over and eat? There's no hurry now."

"Shouldn't you follow them to the station? Help book him?"

"Nah. I told the responding officers to take care of that."

"Okay, then. We need to talk, anyway." Stevens drove until they reached a pullout. He parked the truck.

"I need some fresh air," she said, opening the door. "There's a towel or two behind the seat." Lei made her way through the steel barrier of the overlook and onto the rolling grassy hillside that made up most of Haleakala. With the lights from the truck off, the stars blazed overhead, tossed like glitter into the vast black void. Way to the north, the moon was just beginning to come up. Distorted by the horizon's atmosphere, it was cartoonishly gigantic, casting a silver path on the surface of the ocean.

"I think I see the man in the moon, and he's fishing into the sea," Lei said, pointing. Her attempt at whimsy didn't appear to move Stevens. He spread the towels on the tussocky grass. It was cool, almost cold enough for a sweater, and Lei was glad she'd packed her parka shell as she sat down with the cooler bag. Her knee had begun to throb, and she retrieved the reusable ice pack she'd stowed in the cooler bag and put it on her straightened leg.

"You should probably get that looked at," Stevens said.

"You can kiss it and make it better." She handed him a sandwich, unwrapped hers, and bit into it. She'd made sliced teriyaki chicken on Hawaiian sweet bread, and it was delicious.

"Stop trying to be cute," Stevens said, but his mouth was full.

"I'm too hungry to fight with you," Lei said, and bit into her sandwich.

A few minutes went by as they devoured the meal and sucked down the bottles of root beer she'd included. Finally, biting into sweetly sour starfruit, Stevens said, "You pull a stunt like that, it won't only be your knee that's hurting."

"Gonna spank me?" Lei teased.

"No. I'm going to put you in restraints and call for backup to deal with whatever the situation is, and we're both going to be embarrassed as hell. But I'm not going to lose my wife in some damn-fool situation that could have been prevented!" By the end of his sentence, his voice was raised. She couldn't see his eyes but knew the flat steely look they'd have.

Lei felt something a lot like shame hollow out her stomach. She'd known he was going to be mad, but when she was honest with herself, she realized she hadn't really slowed down to consider his feelings at all. Capturing the suspect was all she'd had in her mind when she spotted Takama down in the gulch—not the first time something like this had happened.

In fact, this was an argument they'd had before. Lei's impulsiveness and lack of a sense of personal safety frustrated Stevens. She knew it was because he was afraid for her, and wouldn't let him protect her. She hadn't told him how close Takama's bow shot had come to her head, and she didn't plan to.

A chain of cars, pairs of golden eyes, wound down the mountain and passed them on the road.

"This is an old argument," Lei said. "I'm sorry I freaked you out, running off like that, not waiting. But he'd have gotten away."

"You could have called in a suspicious sighting. Checked on Takama and Rinker's locations again tomorrow. Taken dogs and done a manhunt, run this thing safely and with the same good results, and we could have enjoyed the sunset and our picnic on the summit. But no, you always have to do it now, do it your way, and you know what? I'm the one who suffers when you get hurt. I need to find a way to stop caring; that's what I need to do." He stood, an abrupt uncoiling, and walked off into the darkness.

Lei bundled the leftovers back into the cooler bag and carried it up to the barrier. She wrapped herself in one of the towels and stood waiting, looking into the darkness, but he didn't return.

Maybe he was giving her a taste of her own medicine. He'd done that before, too.

She could just drive off and leave him up here, but he'd be angrier than a cornered mongoose when he finally got off the mountain. She remembered he had the keys, so it was a moot point. Sitting, waiting, looking out into the picturesque blackness, Lei was reminded of the shrouds. Just like now, there was nothing to do about them but wait.

Stevens had found no useful trace in the box he'd bagged and brought home. The lengths of white linen remained, a spooky threat, in the evidence room in a box labeled

Texeira-Stevens Harassment Case # 45336.

Texeira-Stevens. Is that what they'd name a child, if they had one? Or did it sound better the other way around? Lei muttered both names out loud, decided either way was too much of a mouthful. She spread one towel on the grass below the raised turnout and lay down on it, covering herself with the other towel and looking up at the stars. She tried to spot some constellations, and felt her eyes grow heavy.

It had been a very long day.

Someone shook Lei awake, and she sat up so abruptly her head cracked into Stevens's forehead.

"Ow!" they both exclaimed, and then Lei laughed and heard Stevens give a rusty chuckle.

"Are you still mad?" she asked him, rubbing her head. "Or did you cool off?"

"Cooled off so bad I've got hypothermia," he said, his teeth chattering. "Let's go home."

"I'm sorry," Lei said.

"You always are. And I'm sorry I lost my temper." He slung an arm around her and kissed the top of her head as they stumbled through the bunchy grass toward the truck.

They blasted the heater, but Lei had to keep the window down because of her churning stomach. The cool night air raced by her face, a lacy net of tiny colored lights filling the valley and marking Kahului far below. She could see the black negative space of ocean on either side of the "waist" of the island, and she noticed a feeling she'd never felt before: contentment, a love for the land that felt connected.

"I don't know why, but I feel like Maui is home." Lei tilted her face in Stevens's direction. "It's so beautiful here. This island is the perfect size—more action going on than Kaua`i, fewer people than Oahu, spacious but not sprawling like the Big Island, big compared to Lanai and Molokai. Room to explore and have adventures but not so big you get lost. I love it here."

"I'm glad, because we should have moved to Oahu last year if we were going to. Oahu's where you go to get ahead in law enforcement in Hawaii. But I've had the big city. I'm ready to settle here, see if we can stay married now that we made it to the altar."

"And past our first fight," Lei said. "That same ugly fight we've had before."

"Well, I made you a promise. You will be embarrassed if you run off without me again. It's for your own safety. You've been warned."

"And I take that seriously. I just have a hard time remembering in the moment. Let's hope this situation never happens again, because if you were the one going after a perp and I put cuffs on you, you'd be pissed as hell. At least some of this is because I'm a woman."

"I don't think so. It's because I love you and don't want

you dead," Stevens said. "If the shoe's ever on the other foot, you have permission to take me down."

"Good. I will."

Silence prevailed until they pulled up at the cottage. They got out, and Lei rolled the gate shut behind the truck.

"I love you," she said. He didn't answer, just turned around and swept her up, throwing her over his shoulder. Lei shrieked and laughed, pounding on his back, and Keiki jumped and barked at this new game, cavorting beside Stevens as he climbed the steps, punched the alarm, and opened the door. The door banged shut behind them, and the lights went out.

Lei yawned repeatedly at the staff meeting the next morning. She had a brace on her knee and a pair of crutches she'd borrowed from the supply closet.

"You should get that looked at, Lone Ranger," Pono said. "Thanks for busting Takama. No thanks for doing it without me."

"Did you find anything at Takama's house?" Lei had called Pono and had him search Takama's place with a warrant last night.

"Yeah. Got some promising trace on his boots, and he had pictures of the poachers in his phone—pictures of them before and after they were shot. Not definitive, but close. With your testimony, we ought to be able to make that case."

"Texeira and Kaihale! My office," Omura snapped, sweeping by them on a waft of sophisticated scent. Lei hobbled into the captain's office behind Pono, and Omura closed the door herself and went back behind her desk.

The captain steepled her fingers. "What the hell is going on? First I get a call that Takama's been captured and charged with murder when I didn't even know he was out of jail; then I get a call that Rinker's in Canada, resisting extradition, and has published Kingston's bird research in *Avian Journal of Science*."

Lei and Pono looked at each other. "It's better than where we were yesterday," Lei said. "After my deposition, I felt like we were back at square one, and I for one am happy if that research can help the native birds, even a little bit."

"Texeira." Captain Omura steepled her fingers and leveled hard, dark eyes on Lei. "I'm busting you down a rank. You're a sergeant as soon as this trial is over—I don't want to give the defense any more ammo by putting it in your file before that. I'm taking too much heat about you, and I'm afraid a workshop isn't going to be enough to satisfy Mayor Costales. I'm sorry, but you're clearly not ready for the responsible behavior called for by the rank of lieutenant. Also, your reports are consistently behind. I need someone in the lieutenant position who wants to train and develop others."

Lei's mouth opened and shut. She thought of Consuelo, whom she was mentoring, and Officer Cantorna whom she'd wanted to train. She did like to train and develop others, but as usual, her difficulty with protocol was getting in the way.

"Yes, sir." Lei's whole face felt numb and tingly. She wished she could disappear.

"In addition, you're both also being reassigned to new partners and different duties. I feel this particular pairing isn't helping either of you grow professionally."

Lei was already frozen in her seat, but Pono spoke up. "Sir, I disagree. Lei and I have the highest closure rate of any team."

"Yes, but at what cost? I want both of you alive to pull down a pension in twenty years," Omura said. "I'll let you know when I have your new partners figured out. Dismissed."

Lei crutched her way back to the cubicle in stunned silence. She didn't respond to any of the cheerful razzing about Takama's capture and her knee from colleagues through the office.

"I think I'll go get my knee checked out," she said to Pono, her eyes on the ground, when they arrived at their cubicle.

"It's going to be okay," Pono said. "You didn't like all the lieutenant paperwork anyway. It's not the end of the world."

"I don't care about that, really. Demotion's embarrassing, but I'll survive, and we'll be okay for money. I really don't want a new partner, though." She looked up at her oldest friend, pulled a sad face. "I might have to…you know. Be nice and get to know someone new."

"Heaven forbid," Pono said, and picked up the phone. He punched a few intercom buttons. "Stevens, come take your wife to the hospital. Her knee is really acting up."

He hung up the phone. "You should be able to do workman's comp even though you were off the clock. I'm guessing your kneecap's busted."

"Just what I need," Lei muttered. Pono fetched some boxes and they both began packing their possessions, since they didn't know whose cubicle they'd be sharing. Pono carefully detached the last of his daughter's drawings from the corkboard and set them on top of his boxful of personal items as Lei did what she could to pack, sitting down with her leg straight out on a chair in front of her.

Stevens walked up, jingling his keys, with Torufu following. The giant Tongan carried a big box with one hand and dragged his special jumbo-sized office chair with the other.

"Texeira!" Torufu grinned, and Lei couldn't help smiling back. "You're my new partner, and we're the bomb squad of two on Maui. Captain told me to tell you. We leave for special partner training on the Mainland next week."

Pono shook his head. Stevens's brows drew together in a thunderous scowl. And Lei put her head back and laughed.

Watch for these titles:

Lei Crime Series:

Blood Orchids (book 1)

Torch Ginger (book 2)

Black Jasmine (book 3)

Broken Ferns (book 4)

Twisted Vine (book 5)

Shattered Palms (book 6)

Dark Lava (book 7)

Companion Series:

Stolen in Paradise:

a Lei Crime Companion Novel (Marcella Scott)

Unsound: a novel (Dr. Caprice Wilson)

Wired in Paradise:

a Lei Crime Companion Novel (Sophie Ang)

Middle Grade/Young Adult

Island Fire

Contemporary Fiction/Romance:

Somewhere on Maui,

an Accidental Matchmaker Novel

Somewhere on Kaua`i,

an Accidental Matchmaker Novel

Nonfiction:

Under an Open Sky

Children of Paradise:

a Memoir of Growing Up in Hawaii

Sign up for Book Lovers Club or news of

upcoming books at http://www.tobyneal.net/

Acknowledgments

Dear Readers:

I am SO GLAD the Lei Crime Series didn't end with Twisted Vine like I'd planned. Turns out I've got a lot more books in this series to write!

I want to begin by saying that there have been no bird poachers that I know of on Maui, and the loss of even one of these precious birds would be too many. In the last five years, through my photographer husband Mike Neal's conservation work with the Nature Conservancy in Waikamoi Preserve, I've come to fall in love with the native birds much like Lei did. I was excited to come up with a plot idea that would take readers to the top of Haleakala and into some of the most pristine cloud forest in the whole state of Hawaii. I hope this book teaches the public a little about these "jewels of the forest" through the story.

I went my whole life, most of it in Hawaii, with nothing more than a vague knowledge of these birds because of their scarcity and habitat restriction to the highest elevations, and I am now a passionate supporter of the biologists working hard to keep them from extinction. My thanks go out sincerely to Hanna Mounce, Ph.D. candidate, Program Director of the Maui Forest Bird Recovery Project, an agency that focuses mainly on the preservation of the critically endangered Maui Parrotbill. Hanna took the time to read my manuscript and made corrections, and made my day by pronouncing the scientific solution Kingston comes up with "plausible." I can't thank you enough, Hanna, for taking the time in your very busy life, to make sure I wasn't too far afield.

Agencies working on Maui in conservation include:

Maui Forest Bird Recovery Project:

National Park Service, Haleakala National Park

The Nature Conservancy

East Maui Watershed Partnership:

Maui Bird Conservation Center

Check in and support any and all of these worthy groups to find out more about the native Hawaiian birds.

I also want to thank retired Captain David Spicer for his early read of the manuscript and procedural corrections. He helps me keep Lei from bending too many rules and messing up the prosecution of her cases beyond help, and with David's input I've learned about witness interviewing, evidence retrieval, shooting a fleeing suspect (not done) and all sorts of procedural arcana. Thank you, David!

Extra kudos go to my faithful beta readers, Bonny Ponting and fellow writer Noelle Pierce, who had the courage to tell me the unwelcome news that I'd lost the "emotional tension" of the book by having the wedding right in the middle and solving the case after. So, credit goes to Noelle for Lei's last minute deferment of the wedding, (something Lei would definitely do!) ratcheting up the stakes of the book to a satisfying conclusion. I was so darned eager to get to the wedding, I forgot I was writing a mystery. Shoot. It happens.

Last but never least, thanks to my great book development team. Mike Neal and Julie Metz did an amazing cover, Kristen Weber kept me honest with her editing, and Penina Lopez, my copyeditor, pulled out all the stops to fit my manuscript into her queue, knowing readers were bugging us for it. I couldn't do these books without you!

A special thanks to my extraordinary husband, Mike Neal, whose photography and conservation/docent efforts for the Nature Conservancy have drawn me into the magical world of Waikamoi. It's amazing to walk in that cathedral of pristine wilderness and hear the music of our native birdsong, and I hope this book inspires readers to stop in at Hosmer's Grove on Haleakala and experience the birds just a little bit.

Don't miss the teaser Chapter for Dark Lava, Lei Crime Series #7, included at the end of this volume! Releasing summer of 2014.

With much aloha,

Toby Neal

Sign up for the Book Lovers Club or new title notifications at http://www.tobyneal.net/

Dark Lava

A Lei Crime Novel

By Toby Neal

Chapter 1

The worst things always seem to happen at night, even in Hawaii. Lieutenant Michael Stevens stood in front of the defaced rock wall, hands on lean hips, brows drawn together. A chipped hole gaped raw as a torn-out tooth where the petroglyph, a rare rock art carving, should have been.

"I keep watch on the heiau," the witness, sturdy as a fireplug, glared up at Stevens from under the ledge of an overhanging brow. "I live across da street. I come, check 'em every day, pick up trash, li'dat. Last night I hear something, like—one motor. I was sleeping but I wake up cuz it goes on. Then I see a light ovah here." He spoke in agitated pidgin English, hands waving.

"What's your name, sir?" Stevens dug a spiral notebook out of his back jeans pocket, along with a stub of pencil tied to it with twine. He knew it was "old school." Many officers were using PDAs and tablets these days—but he liked the ease and confidentiality of his personal notes.

"Manuel Okapa. Our family, we guard the heiau. This—so shame this!" Okapa spat beside their feet in disgust. "I like kill whoever did this!"

Stevens waited a beat. He caught Okapa's eye, shiny and hard as a polished kukui nut. "Sure you want to say that to a cop?" Stevens asked.

Okapa spat again in answer, unfazed. "I wish I brought my hunting rifle over here and blow 'em away. But the light go out, and the noise stop. I thought someone was maybe dropping off something. Sometimes, the poor families that no can afford the dumps, they drop their broken-kine rubbish here. They know I take 'em away."

Stevens noted Okapa's threats and disclosure of a gun in his notebook for future reference. He turned a bit to take in the scene. The heiau, a site sacred to Hawaiian culture, was situated on a promontory overlooking the ocean, separated from Okapa's dilapidated cottage by busy two-lane Hana Highway. Even this early, a steady stream of rental cars swished by them, on their way to experience the lush, waterfall-marked Road to Hana.

"What kind of trash do they leave? Appliances?"

"Yeah, li'dat." Okapa squatted down in front of the wound in the rock. His stubby brown fingers traced the hole, tender and reverent. "I heard this kine thing was happening on Oahu but nevah thought we get 'em over here."

"Looks like it was taken out with some sort of handheld jackhammer," Stevens said, squatting beside the man. Okapa's touching of the rock's surface would have disrupted any fingerprints, but it was too late now. He took out his camera phone and shot several pictures of the defaced stone, inadvertently catching one of Okapa's hands, gentle on the rock's wound. "Did you see anything else missing? Disturbed?"

"Come. We go look." Okapa stood up, and Stevens glanced back at the blue-and-white Maui Police Department cruiser parked close to them, his Bronco just behind it off the busy highway. One of his new trainees, Brandon Kealoha, had responded to the defacement call and immediately contacted Stevens as his superior to come investigate. Kealoha was a Maui boy born and raised, and immediately appreciated that the stealing of a petroglyph was more than ordinary property damage. The young man, hands on his duty belt, looked questioningly at Stevens.

"Stay here and don't let anyone pull over," Stevens said. "Find something to cover the damage for now—some branches or something. We don't want to attract attention to this yet."

Stevens' mind was already racing ahead to the press coverage this would draw, potentially connecting this crime with a string of looted heiaus on Oahu. He knew the pressure would be on MPD as soon as the community caught wind of this outrage.

He followed Okapa's squat form, feeling overly tall as he towered over the shorter man. He'd found his height sometimes provoked defensive reactions in smaller local people and his wife's partner and friend, Pono Kaihale, had given him a frank talk on how to interact with the locals more effectively. "Don't stand too close and loom over them unless you like scrap. Not a lot of eye contact, because that's seen as challenging. Be prepared to disclose some personal information about who you are, where you're from, and try to find some common connecting place, family or history. Tell 'em you married to a Hawaii girl if they give you hard time."

As if reading these thoughts, Okapa tossed over his shoulder, "How long you been here?"

"Two years, Maui. Big Island and Kauai before that," Stevens replied. "Maui no ka oi."

Okapa's gapped teeth showed in a brief smile. "As how."

Apparently he'd hit the right note, because Okapa's shoulders relaxed a bit. Every island had its pride and special uniqueness, Stevens had discovered.

They followed a tiny path through waist-high vegetation. Thick bunchy grass, ti leaf and several hala trees, their umbrella-like structures providing pools of shade, created a uniquely Hawaii landscape.

"I used to cut da plants back, keep it nice here. But then

I see the tourists always pulling over to the side, trampling in here with their cameras. So I let 'em grow, and less come here. Only the hula halaus come out for dance. This is one dance heiau."

"Oh. I didn't know there were different kinds. Anything you can tell me would be helpful."

"Yeah. Get some for worship da gods, like the big one in Wailuku. This one for dance. Halau is one small-kine school with a kumu, teacher. That kumu leads and trains dancers in the group. This place was used to teach and worship with hula by the halaus."

They reached a wide area, ringed by red, green and striped varieties of ti leaf growing taller than Stevens had ever seen. The layout was an open area of flat stones ringed by a wall of stacked ones. He'd noticed Hawaii's monuments were simple, made of materials naturally occurring, and without the oral traditions of the people and the movement to reclaim the culture, much history would have been lost and the heiaus themselves swallowed back into the land.

Beyond the large, rough circle of stones the cobalt ocean glittered in the distance. Hala trees surrounded the edge of the cliff, bracketing the view with Dr. Seuss-like silhouettes. Stevens thought the hala and ti plants must have been planted there deliberately because he knew Hawaiians wove the long, fibrous hala leaves into basketry and matting and made dance costumes with ti.

"Auwe!" Okapa cried, pointing. On the far side of the

heiau were three large stone slabs, and the one in the middle had a raw, chipped-out crater. "They took the other one!"

Stevens followed the distraught guardian, thumbing on the camera phone. He held up a hand to stop Okapa as the man bent to touch the stone.

"Let me dust this one for prints." Stevens unhooked his radio off his belt. "Kealoha, bring my kit from the Bronco. Over."

"Ten-four," Kealoha said.

"Tell me who knows about this place," Stevens said, hanging the radio back on his belt and taking pictures of the stones and the surrounding area.

Okapa's rage was evident. He muttered under his breath as he stomped across the stones, ripping out weeds in the dance area. He looked up with a fierce frown.

"Everyone. Because of that damn book."

"What book?"

"Maui's Secrets. One stupid haole wen' collect all our sacred places and put 'em in that book, now everybody can buy it and find whatever. I like beef that guy myself."

Stevens narrowed his eyes. "Where can I find a copy?"

Okapa spat. "ABC Store. Anywhere get 'em. I like burn all those books."

Stevens wrote down the title just as Kealoha burst into view at a trot, carrying Stevens' crime kit. The young man's square, earnest face blanched at the sight of the second desecration. "Auwe!" he cried.

Stevens looked down from Kealoha's dismay, mentally filing that expression away. Maybe his wife Lei could help him learn how to say it right. The exclamation seemed to capture a wealth of grief and outrage.

"I need to dust for prints and photograph this area," he told Kealoha. "You can watch me work the first rock, then I'll have you do the other two. Who knows, maybe whoever it was didn't wear gloves. Mr. Okapa, why don't you investigate the entire site and see if you can see anything else out of place, since you know it so well." Searching over the rocks would occupy the man. Okapa walked off, still muttering as he pulled the occasional weed.

Stevens flipped the clasps of his metal crime kit and opened it, exposing several canisters of dusting powder, a soft long-bristled brush, various other tools and supplies. He snapped on gloves and handed a pair to Kealoha.

"This is probably just a review for you from training, but remember when choosing your powder that you want to pick a color that will contrast with whatever you're dusting. These stones are a dark gray. Which one do you think I should use?" he asked Kealoha, testing.

"White."

"Good." He took the soft-bristled brush, dipped it in the powder and twisted it to load the brush, then spun the powder in gentle twirling motions over the rock face.

This was not the porous black lava stone that much of the heiau was made of; these three stones were the much harder 'bluestone' often harvested for decorative rock walls. The surface held the powder well, the face of the rock gently sloping and weathered by the elements.

"Mr. Okapa, what did the petroglyph here depict?" Stevens called as the heiau's guardian returned, still glowering.

"Was a dancer with one rainbow on top." Okapa gestured, demonstrating the way the stick figure stone carving would have been drawn. "That one at the front marked the heiau. It had three dancers."

"Why do you think someone would steal these?" Stevens asked, still spreading the powder until it covered the entire rock face.

"I've been watching the news about the other defacements on Oahu." Kealoha was the one to answer. "They think some underground collector is hiring people to take them."

"How much would something like this be worth?" Stevens took out his bulb blower, squeezing gently to blow the powder off the rough surface now that it was covered.

"There are not that many early Hawaiian artifacts, period," Kealoha said. "Every petroglyph is priceless and can't be replaced."

"As why it so bad this wen' happen," Okapa said. "Cuz

this heiau only had two. And these were good ones. We were so proud of them."

Stevens blew more air on the rock, and white powder drifted down onto the red dirt soil beneath like misplaced snow.

"I think I see something. A partial," Stevens pointed out to Kealoha. "It's over on the side. Maybe there were two people digging out the carving, or one of them rested his hand on the side of the rock for leverage."

Already they could see there was nothing on the face of the rock. Stevens handed the brush and powder to Kealoha and let the young man dust the sides and top of the stone, and the ones on either side of it.

Several prints picked up, all around the edges of the defaced rock. Stevens squinted at the prints, held his hand up. "I think whoever was using the drill or tool grabbed onto the rock for support. These prints look smeared because of the pressure, but I'll try the gel tape and see if we can lift some and get a good impression."

He unrolled gel tape and pressed it lightly over the print, pulling away carefully. He did several and then set the tape in a plastic case to photograph with a scanner back at the station.

"Let's see you do one." He handed the roll of tape to Kealoha.

"Eh, Lieutenant!"

Stevens looked up at Okapa's shout, toward the gesturing man on the other side of the heiau. Okapa was pointing at a hole in the ground on the other side of a lantana bush.

"They took a stone from here. Was one oval stone brought up from the ocean."

"How do you know what stone it was?" Stevens joined him.

Okapa just fixed him with a belligerent stare. "I know every rock in this place."

Stevens took out his camera phone and shot a picture of the hole. "How big was it?"

"Big enough to need two people to carry it."

Stevens made a note on his spiral pad. His eyes roamed the area and he spotted a gleam of something in the grass. He squatted, found a beer can. Using the tips of his gloved hands, he picked it up by the rim and put it in an evidence bag.

"You think they wen' drink em?" Okapa said, his bushy brows drawing together. "Drinking beer while they taking our sacred carvings! I like kill em! Prolly was one stupid haole with no respect, no Hawaiian would do this!"

Stevens looked up at Okapa. He could feel the other man's rage, and he stood deliberately, uncoiling to his own full height, without breaking eye contact. "You want to be careful about what you say, Mr. Okapa. It's just a beer can. We don't know anything about it."

Okapa whirled and stomped off through the underbrush toward the road.

Kealoha rejoined Stevens. "I took off everything I could find." The young man had packed up the crime kit too. Stevens glanced at the carefully stowed evidence collected. "Good job. What can you tell me about our volatile friend here?"

A flush stained Kealoha's neck. "He one kupuna—an elder. He…" Stevens could see the struggle the young man had in disclosing anything negative about a respected man in his culture. Stevens remembered something from Pono's cultural tips and looked away from Kealoha, turning to align his body with the officer's, standing side by side. He addressed his remarks out over the heiau. "I'm worried about Mr. Okapa. I don't think some half-cocked vigilante justice is going to help the situation. I don't like the idea of Okapa having a gun."

"I know." Kealoha blew out a breath and Stevens could sense his relief that a superior officer wasn't suspecting the respected kupuna. "I'm worried about him too. He has a reputation for anger, that's why his wife left—but this heiau is his life. I think he'll cool down. I'll talk to him."

"Good." Stevens moved out toward the narrow, overgrown path. "As terrible as this is, the last thing we need is some kind of violent racially-motivated outburst when we haven't even identified a suspect." He paused. "Speaking of—what is this scene telling you? I want to hear what you've been able to assess from it."

Kealoha swiveled, hands on hips, imitating Stevens's stance. "I think there were at least two in the crew. They had proper tools, came prepared. They knew exactly what they wanted from what I can tell, and they worked fast according to Mr. Okapa, which means they probably came ahead of time during the day to case where the artifacts were."

"Very good." Stevens clapped the young man on the shoulder, and set off down the narrow, overgrown path with Kealoha following. "Further, I think they were professionals in removal technique. I could see very little waste or fracture on the rock faces, and believe it or not, those hand jacks are hard to operate. So, my sense is that these are pros procuring something for a buyer, which means they're probably connected with the Oahu desecrations."

"We have to stop this," Kealoha muttered. "Whatever it takes."

They emerged beside the cruiser and the Bronco. Okapa had already crossed the now-busy highway, and Stevens could see him glowering at them from a chair on the front porch of his battered, tin-roofed cottage.

"Why don't you go take his official statement?" Stevens said. "Give him a chance to tell the tale and cool down."

"Yes, sir." Kealoha looked both ways and trotted across the road, already taking out his notebook.

Stevens beeped open the Bronco and stowed the crime kit and evidence bags in the back. Getting into the SUV, he looked over at the tableau across the street. Kealoha was seated beside Okapa, one hand on the older man's shoulder, head down listening as the older man gesticulated.

Turning the key, Stevens hoped this was the last he was going to see of Okapa, but he had a bad feeling about it.

Haiku Station was a small former dry-goods store across a potholed parking lot from a large Quonset-style former pineapple-packing plant that had been converted into a shopping center. He had a small crew under his command—one other detective, four patrol officers and Kealoha, a new recruit.

Stevens felt good about how Kealoha was coming along. The benefits of nurturing talent had been drummed into him by his first commanding officer in Los Angeles, along with the fact that all the training in the world couldn't make up for a recruit without the "gut instinct" for police work.

Stevens lifted a hand briefly to the watch officer on duty as he passed through the open room where his team's desks were situated, heading for the back room where his office was located. He hadn't seen Lei since yesterday—his wife was at a one-day training in a wilderness area learning ordinance retrieval, and he missed her.

He supposed that was the word to apply to a feeling like a limb had been amputated, like something vital was missing. He wondered how he was going to deal with it when she left for a two-week multi-agency intensive training on IEDs in California.

Sitting at his desk, he phoned her on speed dial even as he twirled the dial of the lock on the evidence locker in the corner of his office.

"Hey." Her slightly husky voice conjured her instantly before him—tilted brown eyes sleepy, curls disordered, that slender body he was always hungry for, warm in their bed. "You woke me up—I just got home and we were up most of the night."

"Wish I was there waking you up some other way." He stacked the bag with the beer can and the labeled plastic boxes holding the gel tape on the shelf and picked the clipboard dangling from a string to log in the items.

"Me too." He heard her yawn, pictured her olive-skinned, toned arms stretching, her small round breasts distending the thin tank top she liked to wear to bed as her body arched. He felt himself respond to the rustle of her tiny movements in a way that wasn't appropriate for work, and he gritted his teeth. "So, when are you going to be home?" she asked.

"Usual time. Got called out early—a heiau desecration." He sketched a few details—as a fellow officer, she often helped with his cases, and he hers.

"That sucks so bad." Lei yawned again. "I'm too fuzzy to make sense. I'm going to turn the phone off and try to get some sleep."

"I'll see you later. I love you," he said. He'd said it to her every day since their marriage a month ago.

"I love you too. Come home soon. I'll keep the bed warm." She clicked off.

Lei Texeira. Scary brave. Smart, intuitive, neurotic as hell. As necessary to him as breathing.

Stevens set the phone down, trying not to think of her under the silky sheets in that skimpy tank top, and that he was doing his best to get her pregnant. Trying not to think about the spooky threat that had come against them on their honeymoon, always somewhere on his mind. Well, she'd have the alarm on, and their dog, Keiki, on the bed with her.

A knock at the doorjamb. He looked up, irritated. "Yes?"

Kealoha came in and shut the door. "I gotta tell you something, sir."

....To Be Continued.